PRAISE FOR THE FALL BEFORE FLIGHT

My favorite book of the year! The Fall Before Flight is sexy, dark, and unexpected. The characters are unique and brilliantly written into a story filled with emotion, humor, and jaw-dropping moments that stick with you long after you've finished the final page.

NEW YORK TIMES BESTSELLING AUTHOR JB SALSBURY

Leo and Amelia's story consumed me. I could not put this book down. This was a novel that will be on my top 2018 reads for sure.

THE HOPELESS ROMANTICS BOOK BLOG

This book...well this book pretty much blew me away. This author has quickly found herself a top spot on my *MUST READ* list.

BETWEEN THE BOOKENDS

THE FALL BEFORE FLIGHT

L.M. HALLORAN

COPYRIGHT

Copyright © 2018 by L.M. Halloran

ISBN: 979-8-8692-6431-2

Editing by Emily A. Lawrence, *Lawrence Editing*

Proofreading by *Judy's Proofreading*

lmhalloran.com

For Cece and Marika

&

anyone who has felt
the limitations of gravity

This is love: to fly toward a secret sky, to cause a hundred veils to fall each moment. First to let go of life. Finally, to take a step without feet."

RUMI

PART 1

THE FALL

PREFACE
DAY 0

I DIDN'T TRY to kill myself. It was an accident. No—more than an accident. A natural disaster, unanticipated and sudden. Fate's fickle lightning strike. Unseen forces joining in cataclysm. No stopping it. No way to prepare.

Et cetera.

No one believes me, of course. Try explaining to your binary-minded father that it wasn't intent, but bad luck, that propelled the car off the cliff. It wasn't even a cliff, really. I've seen cliffs. I've flung my body from them more times than I can count, lips in a rictus of glee, arms arrowed with cutting purpose toward roiling waters.

Not a cliff. Just a little hill. Grassy and rocky, with a mellow incline beyond a short, dinged guardrail. There's no guardrail anymore, at least not where the impact of my car tore a section free, where pressure pushed sparks of defiance from rusted bolts that were no match for a luxury coup going forty-six miles per hour.

"It's for the best, Mia."

Blinking away residual thoughts of sparks and smoke, I look at my twin brother. Jameson's haggard face bespeaks his sleepless worry, his eyes rimmed with red and underscored with shadow. The stress of my accident has triggered his insomnia.

Our demons exact different prices.

"I'm sorry," my voice whispers between us, a vibration divorced from meaning. I don't feel remorse, and he knows it.

Cold fingers descend onto mine, which clamp harder on the padded armrest.

"This place comes highly recommended. Secure and private. You'll be well cared for."

His voice, unlike mine, holds some semblance of emotion. Pleading, perhaps. A thin veil of grief. Or is it relief?

I don't know why I bother, but I try again. "It was an accident. My shoe—"

"It's all right."

I swallow the words on my tongue. Choke on the spike of disgruntlement. No one believes me. And I have no one to blame but myself—I've been courting danger with increasing brazenness since I was seven years old, when I broke my arm jumping off the roof.

But the memory of the pain, even the initial searing jolt, has always placed a distant second to the transcendent feeling of weightlessness. For mere moments, I'd been free.

There's a soft knock on the door. An empty platitude, for it swings inward without delay. Jameson straightens from his crouch beside my chair, running fingers through his disheveled brown locks.

"Time for a trim, J," I murmur.

He glances at me, eyes reproachful and amused at once, before facing our visitor. "Car's here?"

My father nods, gaze darting to me and away. His evasiveness doesn't bother me—it isn't anything new. He clears his throat, and I watch his Adam's apple bob beneath his square chin.

"Are you sure this place is better than… than a…" He doesn't finish, but the words hang heavily in the air.

Psychiatric hospital.

Funny farm. Looney bin. Nuthouse.

I almost laugh.

Almost.

"Yes," answers my brother. His fingers twitch toward his head, but he stills the urge by tucking his hands into his pockets. "Their program has a ninety-four percent success rate."

I snort.

Jameson scowls at me. He, at least, isn't afraid of my stare. "It was a fucking nightmare getting you into this place, Mia. You have no idea the convincing I had to—"

"Jameson," snaps our father.

My brother's lips compress to a white line. At length, he expels a heavy sigh, tension unraveling from his shoulders. His eyes, though, remain fixed on mine, the blue depths clouded gray with emotion. Fear. Resentment. Hope.

I look away first.

Gripping both armrests, I propel myself to my feet. Dull

pain radiates from my bruised shoulder down my spine, and my muscles blare a sharper reminder of my infirmities. The limitations of my flesh and bones.

The constraints of gravity.

Jameson reaches for my arm, but I jerk away, wincing as my shoulder protests.

"Don't be such a brat," he says, but his lips are twitching.

Fighting the familiar lure of our shared, twisted humor, I smirk. "At least tell me this place has good drugs."

He laughs, but it has an edge. "If by drugs you mean therapy, then yes. The best drugs on the West Coast."

I open my mouth for a waspish retort, but what comes out instead is a broken plea. "I swear, J, on Mom and Phillip, it was an accident."

My father makes a small noise. From the corner of my eye, I see him lumber from the room. Jameson stiffens beneath my words as if each one is a blow. His jaw clenches and unclenches as he struggles. He wants to believe me. It's something.

Just not enough.

His shoulders sag. His eyes—so tired, the left eyelid twitching—find mine. "Do this for me, Meerkat," he says softly.

He has me.

My molars grinding, I nod. "For you, Jaybird."

My gaze swings around the sterile guest bedroom a final time. My meager wardrobe is already packed, the single suitcase outside. The only remaining evidence of my stay is my cell phone sitting on the nightstand. The small fissures of its cracked, lifeless screen momentarily hypnotize me. A memory of the spiderwebbed cracks of a car windshield drift through my mind.

Jameson takes two steps and snatches the phone, tucking it into the breast pocket of his blazer. My trance broken, I sigh. Now there truly is no trace of me left in my father's Malibu house. Not that there's ever been; his home isn't mine.

"Let's go, Mia."

I wordlessly follow my brother from the room, down an airy hallway, across a tiled foyer, and into the golden, afternoon sunlight. Lifting a hand to shade my eyes, I pause on a terracotta step to stare at the heavily tinted town car. My suitcase is already in the trunk. The back door is open, held by the gloved fingers of a suited man. He's nondescript in every way, his individuality no match for the crushing gears of wealth.

I wonder if he knows I'm a fellow prisoner, or if he cares.

Smiling tightly, I ask my brother, "Will the padded walls be fur-lined, too? Caviar and champagne before my daily shock treatment?"

Jameson snorts, snaking forward to drop a kiss on the top of my head. I bat him away with my good arm, then walk toward the shadowed portal of the car's back seat. I'm not scared, my steps even and steady. Just another day, another disaster.

Nothing scares me anymore. Very seldom does something move me. Not beauty. Not death. Not pain. Not joy.

I'm fairly positive my father thinks I'm a sociopath. The

first diagnosis came from a psychiatrist who treated me at thirteen, after an incident wherein I nearly drowned. The second was screamed by a terrified maid after she found me juggling knives in the kitchen. The third and final judgement came from my ex-fiancé after I made a bonfire of his priceless record collection.

Maybe I am a sociopath, but I don't think so. I have feelings aplenty, just not fear. I love my twin, robust red wines, blueberry pancakes, and eighties flicks. And I even love my father.

I loathe my ex and the dumb cow he screwed in our bed. I abhor the smell, texture, and taste of pickles. Baby animals make me cry, and there's nothing funnier than crass jokes.

See? Feelings.

And I have a conscience. I don't willfully hurt or manipulate others, unless they deserve it. I'm not crazy.

Then again, crazy people rarely think they are.

Sliding onto the smooth leather back seat, I duck to see my brother one last time. Shadows blanket me while sunlight highlights his handsome, weary face.

Apropos.

"Catch ya later, Alligator," I taunt.

His lips curve in a small smile. "In a while, Crocodile."

The door slams closed.

2

THE STORIES WE TELL
DAY 6

THERE ISN'T much to the story. My story.

My mother and younger brother died in a car accident when Jameson and I were seven. Their deaths broke something fundamental in my father and he hasn't been the same since. It's nothing external. If anything, his career as a defense attorney took off in the years following the accident. But we lost both parents that day.

Jameson and I are fraternal twins. It's not as bad for him —he resembles my father. But I'm a spitting image of my mother, which is why my father can't stand to look at me.

Yeah, it's fucked up that my father checked out emotionally from his remaining children after the death of his wife and son. It hurt as a kid, and occasionally still does. But as an adult, at least I understand where he's coming from. He's only human.

My teenage years were tumultuous. I didn't have an outlet for channeling my frustration and grief, not like my father did with work and Jameson with sports. So I ended up in a lot of trouble. Misdemeanor stuff and reckless stunts.

My record, though, is squeaky clean. Special thanks go to Harrison T. Sloan, dad-of-the-year, and one of the state's top defense attorneys.

"And that's it in a nutshell." I end my spiel with a sigh. "Just a misspent youth that's finally caught up with me. Sorry to waste your time."

I'm not actually sorry—I'm annoyed.

This is the sixth day, my sixth private therapy session in which I've repeated the same damn story. Thank God there's no therapy on Sundays; I might lose my shit.

This time, there's a ten-second pause, then the figure sitting in a leather armchair opposite me says, "Tell me more about your mother."

I uncross my legs, then recross them. The voice, dark and deep, ripples through the following silence. It's not a voice easily ignored; neither is the attached body. I've always had a thing for men who wear glasses.

I blow out a breath, wisps of hair riding the draft and tickling my cheek. "Look," I begin, staring at my knees, "I already told you, I barely remember her. She sang a lot. Braided my hair. Read me bedtime stories. She died. It's sad. There's no drama there."

"Amelia—"

"Mia," I correct.

Dr. Chastain is a consummate professional. His voice lacks any trace of irritation as he asks, "And what about your father's second wife? Can we talk about her?"

My startled eyes snap to his face. "How the hell do you know about Jill? What did that bitch say?"

He's unaffected by my outburst. An ocean of unflappability. "Ms. Richmond declined to speak with me, but their marriage and subsequent divorce is public record."

Pale blue eyes lower briefly to the notepad in his lap. I breathe a little easier without their attention.

"I did find a picture of her just prior to the divorce."

Uh-oh.

Long, elegant fingers lift a single sheet of paper, angling the printed image in my direction. It's Jill, all right—with no eyebrows, her visible skin a mottled orange.

I bite my lips.

Dr. Chastain's eyes narrow, flaring with something I can't identify. If he wasn't a robot, I might think it's amusement. The image descends back to his lap. Rolling my eyes to the ceiling, I wait for the urge to cackle to recede.

"You don't deny you're responsible for her transformation?"

I shrug, lowering my gaze to his chest. Even under the disguise of suit and tie, I can tell he's extremely fit. Promiscuity has never been my drug of choice, but I'm still a red-blooded, twenty-eight-year-old female. And Dr. Chastain is a visual treat.

Allowing my gaze to dip lower, I entertain the fantasy of riding him right in his weathered leather armchair.

"Amelia."

"Hmm?"

"Stop."

The command cracks like a whip. Heat sizzles up my

neck and face. I turn quickly to look out the nearest window.

"Sorry," I mumble.

He sighs, leather creaking as he shifts in his seat. "Let's stop for today."

I leap to my feet and am halfway across the office before he even stands. "Thanks, Doc. See you tomorrow."

The door closes on his reply.

Releasing a full-body shudder of nerves, I pace down the elegant hallway toward the Fish Tank, the central hub of the U-shaped facility. The moniker derives from the floor-to-ceiling windows that dominate the northern and southern walls, as well as the multitude of discreet-ish cameras mounted across the beamed ceiling.

Aesthetically, the space looks much like the lobby of a swank mountain resort, all rustic wood, low tables, and squat, understated furniture. But instead of trees and mountains outside the windows, there's desert.

Lots and lots of nothing.

I'm not sure exactly where I am—I fell asleep halfway into the drive here. I know we'd been headed east from Los Angeles, and when we'd arrived, the sky had still held the barest touch of sunset. Somewhere past Palm Springs, maybe? Or the Mojave?

Wherever we are, it's secluded and fortified. With the sun now shining heavily on the bleached land, I can see the high fence I missed under the cover of darkness.

"What are you doing, Goldie?" asks an amused voice.

I glance behind me at the owner, a tall man with mussed auburn hair and a teasing grin.

I match his ironic smile. "Whatever I want."

He laughs and walks forward until we stand side by side. "Think it's an electric fence?" he asks, squinting.

"Nah. It's probably just to keep the paparazzi off your ass."

The man beside me, Callum Rivers, happens to be one of the highest paid models in the world.

He huffs. "This place is like Area 51. No way they'd find me. I'm on an Indonesian retreat, anyway. Soaking up spiritual vibes."

I laugh, but it feels forced. Born with the gene for aggressive curiosity—read: nosiness—it's growing increasingly difficult not to ask why he's here. But digging into each other's pasts is a big no-no. It was drilled into me during my orientation six days ago, and is reinforced constantly by the facilitators of our group therapy sessions.

No questions or specific comments about the past. If we veer toward any topic other than the *right here, right now*, they interrupt or call on someone else.

Only Dr. Chastain knows our secrets.

"How was your session?"

"Transformational," I answer flatly.

He smiles knowingly. "I'm telling you, just dump all your baggage. It's all he wants, and you'll feel better. He's a magician. The shit he picks up on... It's worth it, trust me."

I give him the side-eye. "You've been drinking the Kool-Aid."

He bumps my shoulder with his. "Better than vodka."

My head turns sharply, but he dismisses my interest with a wave of his hand.

"Just messing with you. It was cocaine." His head tilts. "Or was it porn?"

I shake my head chidingly. "Tease."

He smirks, hazel eyes glittering with magnetism. I recognize it as the trademark, panty-melting expression that made him famous. When I roll my eyes instead of swooning, Callum finally smiles like he means it, wide enough for me to see his slightly crooked bottom teeth.

"I like you, Mia."

"Yeah, yeah," I say dismissively. "You only like me because I'm the only one here who hasn't tried to get in your pants."

He says nothing, but I can tell he wants to ask why. Not because he's interested in me sexually—though I know he finds me attractive—but out of simple curiosity.

To a man used to having women of all ages and walks of life fawning over him, I'm an anomaly.

In another life, I'd probably be first in line to tackle him naked. Callum is physically breathtaking, smart and charming, and has a great sense of humor. But this isn't another life, and the crude fact of it is I don't fuck men I like. Not for years. Not since Kevin.

Callum, responding to the prickly mojo I'm giving off, asks, "Wanna go for a swim before lunch? Nix and Kinsey are already out there."

"Sure." I don't actually want to be around anyone else. Callum is the only resident here who doesn't get on my nerves.

"Great. I'll get my trunks and meet you there."

His footsteps fade, but I stay at the window a few

moments longer, staring across the dystopian landscape. In the bright afternoon sun, the distant fence looks like a mirage, blinking in and out of existence.

A weird sense of disassociation tingles through me—I'm that fence, visible one second and invisible the next. Impossible to pin down. Impossible to reach.

The muted sound of footsteps breaks my trance. I turn, thinking Callum is back already and I've been staring at the fence for minutes instead of seconds. But it isn't Callum.

Dr. Chastain strides across the Fish Tank toward the opposite wing housing the kitchen, dining room, gym, and various rooms for meditation, group therapy, and art. He walks with his chin down, glasses hanging from his fingers while his other hand rubs a spot on his forehead.

Still resonating with the feeling of invisibility, I watch him, appreciating his smooth stride, the cut of his suit, his perfectly combed dark hair, and the way his starched white shirt sets off his strong, tanned neck. His last name, Chastain, is French, but besides the blue eyes the man is all Italian. His mother, maybe?

He's steps away from disappearing into the adjoining hallway when he comes to an abrupt stop.

I'm invisible.

He speaks to the empty room. "Did your mother call you Mia or Amelia?"

I blink back into existence but can't open my mouth. My legs are solid wood, rooted to the floor, my heart a trapped and pounding presence in my chest.

"Amelia," he says softly, nodding to himself.

Then he's gone.

3

THE MYSTERY OF GLACIERS
DAY 6

WE AREN'T ALLOWED to share with other residents why our loved ones shipped us to this place, but I still have a brain.

Callum isn't the only famous person here, and while his presence is a mystery, neither Kinsey Kemper nor Jason Nixon have the luxury of even a sliver of anonymity.

Kinsey is a former teen pop star turned cokehead and viral sex-tape victim. If my limited recollection of trash culture is correct, she's twenty-six or seven, on her third round of treatment for drug addiction *and/or* plastic surgery addiction *and/or* sex addiction.

Reports vary, but align in one respect: Kinsey is a train wreck. A living, breathing stereotype of a good girl gone wrong, with dark roots beneath long platinum hair, perfect fake breasts, unnaturally plump lips, and jaded eyes. If she hadn't consistently been a bitch to me since I arrived, I might feel sorry for her.

Jason Nixon—who only answers to Nix—is Kinsey's rehab boy-toy. He's an indie movie star known for his off-the-wall antics, drug use, and run-ins with the law. His angsty persona is almost as canned as Kinsey's sex-vixen one. I'm convinced neither one can find their own consciences, much less authentic personalities.

I'm a bit of a hypocrite, but at least I can admit it.

The final two members of our motley crew are Preston Williams and Tiffany Beauchamp. Preston is a wisp of a man, thin in every way from his face to fingers to lips. He has the most incredible eyes I've ever seen—an undiluted emerald that catches ambient light as well if not better than the actual gemstone.

My guess is he's in his early thirties. By his soft, concise voice and inability to maintain eye contact with anyone for more than a second or two, I figure he makes the big bucks from behind a computer screen. When he shares in group sessions, the predominant themes are isolation and depression. That, coupled with his penchant for long sleeves, have led me to the conclusion that he either practices self-harm or tried to commit suicide.

Unlike Kinsey and Nix, Preston plucks a chord of sympathy inside me. I want to bundle him up and carry him around in my armpit to keep him safe.

"You're heartless."

The snarled words come from Tiffany Beauchamp, our final misfit. She's speaking to me, as I've just told Preston of my impulse to shelter him.

We're working on interpersonal relationships today—our moderator, Frank C., asked us to say something nice to another member of the group. It was the only thing I could come up with.

"How is that heartless?" I ask, mystified.

She rolls her eyes and sniffs, her pert, freckled nose upturned in disdain. "If you don't know, I'm not going to tell you."

Ugh. Such a sanctimonious pain in my ass.

I'm half-convinced Tiffany has multiple personalities; she changes moods more than she changes clothes—which is at least four times a day. No more than eighteen or nineteen, she's petite and cute, with a smile that lights up a room. Right before she sets it on fire.

I imagine her as the daughter of a senator or a billionaire CEO. A debutante drowning in designer duds and fancy cars. Maybe she got a DUI or wrapped her car around a tree. Or maybe she slept with one of her father's friends, or stole her mother's Norcos and accidentally OD'd.

Whatever landed her in this prison for broken people, she's seriously messed up.

I don't feel sorry for her—I feel sorry for Dr. Chastain.

"It's okay," whispers Preston, those beautiful eyes darting to me and away. "Thanks."

I nod, shifting. My skin must be itchy from the chlorine I didn't have time to wash off before group. His gratitude doesn't bother me. It doesn't.

Our moderator Frank, who looks like a tenderhearted biker in his sixties, nods approvingly. "Good sharing, Mia. I like how you really owned your emotion."

I barely stop my eyes from rolling.

"How about you, Kinsey? Can you share something about Mia that you appreciate?"

Here we go.

Kinsey's dark blue eyes latch onto me. Her mouth moves around for a minute, as if dealing with a bad taste. Finally, she grumbles, "She has long legs."

"Oh, Jesus," mutters Callum.

Frank clears his throat. "What about her as a person? Something you appreciate about her personality, or anything else that comes to mind." After a pause, he adds, "Something complimentary."

Kinsey picks at the split ends of her bleached hair. "I guess she, um, seems pretty normal. Like, well adjusted." She looks at me, eyes narrowed and burning. "You're fucking normal. You don't belong here."

I blink, floored.

Seated in the folding chair beside Kinsey, Nix stirs. "Yeah," he seconds.

For a minute, no one speaks. Even Frank looks flummoxed. Finally, he offers, "We all belong here. We are all exactly where we should be."

The itch on my skin is now in my bones. I think of Jameson and his twitching eyelid, and then about our sixteenth birthday party—I gave his best friend of five years a blow job in the garage while everyone ate cake. Jameson blamed his friend, not me. It ruined their relationship.

"I'm a horrible person," I say flatly. "I use people. I eat them up and spit them out. I don't care about anyone. I love my brother, but that's it. Everyone else can burn."

"Tell us how you really feel," murmurs Callum.

I glance at him, an eyebrow raised. "Did you think we were friends? I'm sorry. The only reason I talk to you is because you won't leave me alone."

Hurt flashes across his face before he turns to look out a window. I don't feel regret.

I don't feel anything.

The door opens. Everyone looks except me. I already know who it is. Some sixth sense warned me of his approach, like an aching joint before a storm.

"Amelia. Come with me."

Someone being pulled from group isn't uncommon. It happens almost every day. We all know Dr. Chastain watches and listens to the afternoon sessions from the sanctuary of his office.

This is the first time I've been summoned, though. I'm kind of proud it's taken almost a full week.

"You got it, boss," I chirp, jumping to my feet.

By the time I reach the doorway, it's empty, Chastain's suited frame dwindling down the hall.

Lengthening shadows creep along the walls as I cross the Fish Tank, vacant but for a staff member watering plants. Outside, the sun hangs low to the west. Atop the smokey blue canvas of the sky are angry streaks of orange and magenta, broken in intervals by gleaming white clouds.

I turn from the sight and walk into the hallway that houses offices, medical exam rooms, and presumably, a security monitoring station. The only room I've been in is the one I now approach, its open doorway a portal of light against a backdrop of shadowed walls.

Pausing on the threshold, I allow myself to feel the hammering of my pulse. I don't want to be here.

4

———————————

PUZZLE PIECES
DAY 6

Across the room, Dr. Chastain stands with his back to me. He removes his suit jacket and hangs it on his desk chair. His movements, as always, are elegant and precise.

Standing just outside the glow from several lamps, I watch him loosen his tie, then unbutton his cuffs and roll the fabric up his forearms. The skin revealed is muscled and bronze, dusted lightly with dark hair.

With the long fingers of one hand resting on the desk, he lifts his head and turns until his profile is visible. Stern mouth that, in brief moments of repose, softens to sinful fullness. A nose almost too long for his face, but that perfectly complements the sharp lines of his jaw.

The muscles of his back bunch as he shifts again, just enough to glance in my direction. "If you're done with your examination, I'd like to speak with you."

That he knows I was ogling him doesn't embarrass me. He's fully aware I think he's hot; I told him so in our first

21

session. His only response was a scowl and a stern command to sit.

Dr. Chastain sighs. "Amelia."

Pleased to have elicited a response—a sigh from him is the equivalent of another man's scream—I smile and flop into his usual seat during our private sessions. Throwing my bare, tanned legs over the arm of the oversized leather chair, I examine my fingernails.

"Was it the comment about being a horrible person?" I ask idly. "I was just trying to dig up some sympathy from my fellow inmates."

The rustle of his pants brings my eyes up. Chastain leans against his desk, arms crossed over his chest. Perfect black hair gleams in the light from a nearby lamp.

I really, really want to scratch my fingers through those thick strands and pull them into disarray. I also want to shave him bald. Maybe get rid of his eyebrows, too, which are currently drawn together in a frown.

"Why do you think you're here, Amelia?"

I groan. "Must you call me that? It's so predictable, trying to make me think about my mother by using that name. I expect more from you."

He shifts again, hips lifting slightly before settling back against the desk. I manage to stop myself before my eyes veer to his crotch.

It's disturbing, the effect he has on me. The last man who flooded me with need by merely existing was... Shit, it's been a long time. Maybe Kyle, the hockey player from Canada.

"What are you thinking about?"

Angry for a reason I can't digest, I tell him the truth, "The hottest fuck of my life."

Dr. Chastain's expression doesn't change. Calm. Contained. "Did you have a relationship with him beyond sex?"

"Nope." And because I'm annoyed, I add, "And we didn't have sex. We *fucked*."

There.

Finally, a physical response. His lips have thinned. Behind his glasses, his blue eyes remain sparkling ice. "Have you ever fucked someone you love, Amelia?"

I widen my eyes dramatically. "You just said a dirty word, Dr. Chastain! Shame on you."

No smile. Nothing.

I concede defeat, admitting, "My high school boyfriend, maybe."

"Donovan Vicks?"

I squeeze my eyes closed. "Jameson is getting castrated when I get out of here."

Chastain ignores my muttered vow. "You were together during your junior and senior years, correct?"

My skin starts to itch again. "Yes," I grind out.

I listen to his footsteps coming closer but don't open my eyes. My nose catches a subtle waft of his light, expensive cologne and the muskier scent beneath. Desire dances from my breasts to my belly.

"Why do you think you're a horrible person? A user of others?"

I open my eyes, finding him where I expected—in the chair across from me. His tie is gone, and the patch of golden skin at the base of his throat teases me. Begs me to lick it.

"I'm sick," I whisper, trying to make him understand something I don't really understand myself. "When I see people, I don't see... *people.* I see puzzles to solve. Weaknesses to exploit. Answers to find. I like watching people break." I shake my head. "No, I *love* watching people break."

"What you love is making them feel," he says, that deep voice fluttering between my legs.

I tense. "What? No."

His head tilts, pale eyes floating over my features, leaving frostbite behind. "You shock and hurt people because their responses tell you they care. More than anything, you want people to care."

My eyes burn. My throat aches like I just smoked a cigarette to the filter. I laugh—it's more of a croak. "Whatever you say, Doc. You've got me all figured out."

Chastain pulls off his glasses, rubbing his eyes with two fingers. "What you do—the pranks, the manipulating, the lying—you're in search of human experience. And believe me, you would thrive just as easily on happiness and gratitude as you do on hurt and surprise."

I have no pithy response. His words scratch and rip into my gut, tossing soul debris left and right.

I want to curl into a ball and sob. I want to leap off my chair and scream, *You don't know me!* and throw a lamp at his head. Or slap him, then kiss him.

But I do nothing, fighting impulse tooth and nail. I

breathe through the itch in my bones, the maelstrom inside me. And I stare at him.

He finally blinks, younger looking without his glasses, the blue of his eyes more stunning against thick, inky lashes and olive skin.

"Tell me what you want to do to me, Amelia. What punishment have I earned for making *you* feel?"

I can't. Won't. And I don't know why. Maybe because although I don't like him, I respect him. Envy him a little— his control and maturity. Or I don't want to disappoint Jameson by getting kicked out of here.

Or maybe, some part of me realizes this is the last house on the block. This is either where I end, or where I begin.

"No."

"Why not?" he asks, more curious than I've ever heard him.

I look out a window and try to appreciate the sunset's daily artwork. "Because I don't want to hurt you."

"Lie," he says, so calmly that I bristle. "Do you think telling me would give me power over you? That I would then abuse that power?"

I blink, stunned at his admission—his mistaken impression that he has any power over me at all. My heels drop to the floor and laughter bubbles in my throat.

"Are you serious right now? You think that because you have a bunch of facts about my life you have *power* over me? That you can jerk me around like a puppet? I don't dance for anyone, Doc!"

One dark eyebrow cocks upward. "I was speaking in

terms of doctor/patient confidentiality, Amelia. What kind of power were you referring to?"

Dear God, get me out of this nightmare.

I rub my face roughly with my hands, then drag my fingers through my hair to the crown of my head. Whatever expression I'm wearing must be alarming because for the first time in our more than six hours of conversation, Chastain reacts.

With swift grace, he kneels on the floor before my chair. The heat of his chest radiates onto my legs. For a pregnant moment, his hands hover over my knees, then fall to his sides.

"Are you all right?" he asks, eyes scanning my features.

Unnerved by his proximity, I sneer. "If I were all right, do you think I'd be in a treatment facility for fucked-up adult children?"

He lowers back onto his heels, the fabric of his slacks pulling tight against the muscles of his thighs. "What I think is you're an intelligent, capable woman, and I have faith that our work will be... what did you call it earlier? Ah, yes. *Transformational.*"

It's the gleam of humor in his eyes that undoes me. I laugh. The itch in my bones subsides.

Blue eyes still dancing, he rises smoothly to his feet. "That's all for this evening, Amelia. I'll see you tomorrow."

He turns away, and I'm dismissed.

5

NUTS FOR THE FARM
DAY 8

THE FACILITY DOESN'T HAVE a name. No website or media presence. No official purpose statement.

Callum first found out about it when another male model, a close friend, disappeared for six months before reappearing a changed man. Prior to his vanishing act, he suffered from debilitating panic attacks and agoraphobia, both of which had brought his career to a standstill. The astounding success of his treatment stayed in the back of Callum's mind for a year, until the day he hit his personal rock bottom and asked his friend for details.

"He called it Oasis." Callum's words are punctuated by puffs as we jog side by side. The circular trail around the facility is two miles. We're on our second go-around.

I wipe sweat from my forehead with the back of my hand. "And gave you a phone number or something?" I pant.

He nods. "Yeah. I felt like I was in a spy movie. It was a

voicemail service with no message. Just a beep. I must have dialed a hundred times before I finally left a message."

"Huh."

He glances at me. "Can I ask a question? A kind of personal one?"

We're approaching the doors of the Fish Tank. I slow to a walk and Callum matches my pace, swigging water before handing me the bottle. I take several swallows, then wipe my mouth.

"Yeah, sure. But I might not answer."

He grins, gorgeous in the bright morning light, his skin glistening with sweat. "Fair enough." His gaze drops to the dusty trail beneath us. "Why did you say what you did in group yesterday?"

I stare at his bowed head. "I already apologized. Do you want me to do it again?"

Callum looks up, his eyes searching mine. "You know what I mean."

Eye contact is suddenly too much, so I drop my head back to gaze at the endless, empty sky. "What do you want me to say?"

"The truth."

"Truth, truth, truth," I whisper, then find my backbone and meet his earnest eyes. "When I was seven years old, I took my mother's lipsticks and smeared them all over the walls in my parents' bedroom. I was angry because she wouldn't let me come to my little brother's swim lesson. She told me how disappointed she was. Then she left with my brother Phillip. I never saw her again."

Callum goes still. "She died?"

I nod. "Both of them. Car accident on the way home. Even when I heard my father screaming downstairs and Jameson crying, I kept scrubbing the walls. When I was finished, I climbed out the attic window and jumped off the roof."

As expected, Callum is speechless.

I drain the water bottle and hand it back to him. "I didn't want to die. Still don't. I just wanted to be free." I meet his searching gaze. "There's something wrong with me. A flaw in my makeup. I might be a sociopath. I'm also a compulsive liar."

He shakes his head slowly. "You shouldn't be telling me this."

I shrug. "Manmade rules are just words. False boundaries put into place by people trying to make sense of things. To establish order where there isn't any." I gauge his expression but can't tell if it's one of intrigue or revulsion. "Told you I'm fucked up."

"Was that story true? About your mom?" he asks softly.

It's partly true. There hadn't been a lipstick incident. But I had jumped off the roof that night.

"Maybe," I tell him.

After a moment of stunned silence, Callum laughs. "You're the most intense person I've ever met."

I wink. "Thanks, sweetcheeks."

Shaking his head, he asks, "Breakfast?"

I glance at my watch. "Nah. I need to shower before my session with Doc."

"Want company?"

I know what he means, but ask mildly, "Couples therapy already?"

He smirks. "The offer's open. I think we'd have a good time."

"No doubt, but you're not my type."

His jaw drops. "Why the hell not?" he asks, stupefied.

I shove his chest lightly and tell him the truth. "Because I like you."

IF THE MAIN facility is the bottom half of an oval, the resident cabins comprise the top curve. There are ten in total—spacious studios with a queen bed, bathroom including full-sized tub, quaint sitting area, and a small kitchen. The furnishings are plain, the cream walls bare, but the bed is comfortable and water pressure decent.

I walk past the pool, turquoise and glistening in the sunlight, and follow a gravel path that winds through a succulent garden, rock garden, and a huge labyrinth for meditation I have yet to see used. When the path widens, branching into separate trails for each of the cabins, I take the rightmost one.

I'd left the door unlocked, figuring the only person who might snoop is Tiffany. She has that shifty, kleptomaniac vibe to her. There isn't anything of personal or monetary value inside, anyway, so I don't care if she pokes around.

Kicking off my sneakers, I leave them on the doormat and step inside. The cabin is stuffy, but at least ten degrees cooler than outside thanks to the pulled curtains. I shut the door with my hip and yank off my sports bra, then flip on the recessed lights.

"Nice rack."

My arms fly to my naked chest as I spin toward the bed, where Nix is sprawled in all his pasty, heroin-chicness.

"Get the hell out, Nix."

His thin eyebrows rise. "I want to talk to you."

I cross the room to my dresser and open a drawer. Pulling out a tank top, I tug it on, then face the bed with a scowl.

"Serious invasion of privacy, asshole."

Nix sits up and swings his legs to the floor. "We don't have privacy and you know it." His brown eyes roll toward the ceiling. "The cabins are probably wired for sound, if not video. High-tech nano shit. In the lights or something."

The thought brings equal parts disgust and curiosity. If he's right, does it mean Dr. Chastain watches the feeds? I sleep naked and rarely with a sheet.

Nix laughs, an oddly lighthearted sound. I've never heard him laugh before.

"What?" I frown.

He points at me. "You *like* the thought of being under surveillance."

I force my shoulders to relax as I walk into the tiny kitchen for a glass of water. "I don't really care. We're already lab rats. What's another breach of our so-called rights?" Turning with my water in hand, I snap, "What do you want?"

His laughter fades into a sigh. "I want you to do me a favor."

I'm instantly intrigued. "Do tell, both the favor and what's in it for me."

Nix drags a hand through his floppy brown hair, expression worried. "I want you to keep an eye on Kinsey when I'm gone. In return, I'll give you a part in a movie when you get out."

I hide my surprise by taking a sip of water, then take another one while I collect my thoughts. "First of all, I don't want to be in one of your crap movies. Second, does this mean you're leaving? Never mind, obviously you are. And third, Kinsey hates me and I'm not her biggest fan, either, so what makes you think I'd have anything to do with her?"

"Because even though you're a crazy bitch, I think you're an honest one."

If only he knew.

"You had a different opinion in group yesterday."

"Yeah, but that was before."

My eyes narrow. "I'm five seconds past being over this conversation."

For the first time, Nix looks straight at me, like I'm an actual person instead of an extra in his life. "You really don't give a shit about anything, do you?"

"Nope, I don't."

Instead of giving up, he pulls out the big guns. And big guns they are. "Then you probably won't care that Dr. Chastain pays nightly visits to Kinsey's cabin."

Something akin to dread washes over me, followed by a dollop of disbelief, and finally the acidic burn of jealousy.

Unbelievable.

I make a show of unplugging my ears. "I must have

heatstroke, because I think you just told me Doc and Kinsey are getting it on."

Nix's nostrils flare. "I did."

It's not true.

Definitely not true.

Is it true?

I clear my throat. "I thought you and Kinsey were banging."

"We aren't—haven't."

He looks away, but not fast enough to hide the emotion in his eyes. I feel a familiar swell of pleasure, like a child unwrapping their favorite lollypop. Only my candy is secrets. The special triggers everyone carries that when pressed, explode lives.

Nix is in love with Kinsey Kemper. Puppies, hearts, and chocolate love. *Have my babies* and *grow old with me* love.

Gross. And oddly sweet.

While I'm considering what to do with my new candy, he says, "I'm leaving tomorrow. Kinsey has another couple of weeks." He looks at me imploringly. "She has issues, I know, but she's not a bad person once you get to know her. I'm worried she's being taken advantage of."

"Have you considered asking her what's going on?"

He nods curtly. "She denied it, but that doesn't mean it's not happening. She's covering for him."

Do you think I would abuse my power?

As I remember Chastain's words, Nix continues morosely, "This is difficult for me to say, because I really believe Dr. Chastain saved my life. I feel better than I have in twenty years. I just... don't know what to think."

Neither do I, but I'm not about to admit that. "You're forgetting that I don't care. Christ, if you're that worried, grow some balls and hire a lawyer. Pretty sure doctors shouldn't be screwing their patients."

"It's not that simple."

"Not my problem."

His shoulders slump in defeat; a moment later, anger brings him to his feet. He storms past me, throwing over his shoulder, "Have a shitty life, Mia."

The front door slams behind him. My lips curl in distaste as an unfamiliar feeling washes through me. Shame? No...

Guilt.

"Goddammit." I storm outside after him. He's already halfway to his cabin, three down from mine.

"Fine!" I yell.

Nix stops and spins around. He stares at me for several weighted moments, then nods before resuming his walk.

The door of the cabin beside mine opens and a shirtless Callum walks outside, head swiveling between Nix's back and me.

"What was that about?"

I pout. "Bastard wouldn't airdrop booze for me when he gets out."

His brows rise. "Oh, that's right. He's out tomorrow. Keep forgetting." He chuckles. "Did you really ask him to airdrop alcohol?"

"Hell yes, I did. If I'd known this was a dry town, I would've never gotten in that car."

Grinning, Callum glances at his watch. "You're late."

"Shit!"

I'm ten fast steps toward the facility when Callum calls out behind me. "Ohhh, Miiiaaaa? Aren't you forgetting something?"

I shove my middle finger in the air and keep walking, ignoring the laughter that rings out.

At the back door of the Fish Tank, I pull off my gravel-ridden running socks and drop them on the cement, then step inside and stride down the left hallway.

The office door is open, Dr. Chastain already seated in his customary chair.

"Amelia," he says, looking up with a frown. "You're late."

I sink into the opposite chair and blink innocently. "I got my period and had to drop into medical for some tampons."

"You're a good liar," he says after a moment, "but you'd do well to remember I'm a better one."

I laugh to cover a twinge of unease. "Can't hustle a hustler?"

Those icy eyes don't blink. "Exactly."

I vow to think of a fate worse than castration. Jameson is in for a world of pain for putting me in this nut farm.

6

RABBIT HOLE
DAY 8

DR. CHASTAIN CONSULTS the notepad resting on his lap. Not for the first time, I wonder what's written there. Has he reached a diagnosis? Does he have a plan?

I think about the end goal—my mental health—and what that looks like to Chastain. Amelia Sloan, Bleeding Heart Philanthropist? Or is his endgame to have me walk out of here an emotional mess?

This isn't my first trip down Psychiatry Lane, obviously. And really, all therapists want the same thing: to rip open my scars and make me confront my deepest fears. What none of them have understood is I don't *have* any fears.

"I'd like to talk about Donovan Vicks, your first love."

Memory provides me with the physique of a young man, tan and muscled from his chosen sport of water polo. Chlorine-faded blond hair, almost white, that shines like a halo in the sun. Dimples to either side of his smile. Blue eyes, dark like the ocean he loved.

"He kissed like a Mack truck," I say, watching dust

motes dance near the window. "Put flowers in my locker almost every day."

"Did you lose your virginity to him?"

My mind races, still thinking about endgames. Can I fake a transformation to Amelia the Tenderhearted? Or will Dr. Chastain keep me here until I finally go insane?

Closing my eyes, I replace the picture of Donovan with the face of my brother. Worried and hopeful. I wonder if he's sleeping any easier, knowing I'm safe.

Am I safe?

I face Dr. Chastain. "Let's make a deal."

Dark brows twitch over calculating, focused eyes. "What kind of deal?"

"You answer my questions honestly, and I'll do the same."

He regards me silently for several moments. "Fine, but I can't promise I'll answer all your questions. If I deem them inappropriate, I'll pass."

"Duly noted."

Clouds pass outside, blotting the sunlight. A chill rises over my bare arms and circles down my chest, tightening my nipples beneath my blue tank top. I don't bother crossing my arms, as it will only draw attention to my chest. And right now, that's the last thing I want.

"My first question is how long am I in for?"

"Thirty days."

Relief melts through my tense shoulders, dropping them. "That's it?"

He frowns. "They didn't tell you during intake?"

"They did, but I didn't believe them."

He pauses, the tiniest of smiles on his face. "But you believe me?"

I roll my eyes. "Don't let it swell your head, Doc."

Chuckling, he adjusts his glasses. "Okay, it's my turn. What did you love about Donovan?"

"His smile," I answer honestly. "At least in the beginning. After a while, I started resenting it."

"Why?"

"Because he smiled at everyone. My turn. Where did you go to school?"

"Yale for undergrad, then UCLA." He glances over my shoulder. "My qualifications are on the wall, Amelia."

I've seen the plaques, of course. "They could be fake."

"Are they?"

I study him for tells, but he's either a better liar than I am or he's being honest. The first option is as interesting as it is disturbing.

"They're probably real," I finally answer.

He glances down. "How did your relationship with Donovan end?"

"I paid a girl to get him drunk at a party and seduce him. He took the bait and cheated on me."

Chastain doesn't look surprised by this information, even though there's no way Jameson told him. I've never told anyone.

"How did that feel?"

I shrug. "It sucked. How old are you?"

"Thirty-six. How old were you when you lost your virginity?"

My enjoyment of this game is rapidly dwindling.

"Fourteen," I say rigidly.

"Does that bother you?"

"Why should it?" I snap. "It was my choice. I was curious, so I went to the beach in a tiny bikini and found a surfer to take me home. He lasted five minutes, then yelled at me about the blood on his sheets."

The thing about secrets—receiving them is sheer pleasure, but offering them holds none. Not even when the desired result of eliciting a response from the unflappable doctor is achieved. But what I see in Dr. Chastain's eyes isn't disgust. It's pity, and it's maddening.

"Have you ever fucked a patient, Doc?"

His nostrils flare. "Absolutely not."

His anger sways the balance of power back in my direction. A warm cloak of satisfaction surrounds me.

"How did you end up in this shithole?" I ask mildly.

"My turn," he says, the dark tone fracturing my superiority. "Did you think not wearing a bra would affect me?"

Against all efforts of will, I blush. "I don't know, maybe," I say, then flinch at the vulnerability I've exposed.

He pulls off his glasses, tossing them atop the notepad in his lap. In a now familiar gesture, he rubs his forehead with his fingers.

"You asked me how I ended up here, and I'll answer to the best of my ability." His dazzling eyes find mine. "The short of it is that someone helped me once, and I come here once a year to pay back the debt."

"Once a year?" I ask, confused.

"There are generally six of us who rotate throughout the

year. There's some overlap with patients, obviously, because inpatient schedules are on an as-need basis."

"How long have you been here this go-around?"

To my surprise, he answers without hesitance. "Four weeks. When Kinsey leaves two weeks from now, my rotation will end."

I mull this over. "So you'll be leaving eight days before I do."

He nods. "Dr. Reynolds will be taking my place, but we'll have extensive meetings prior to the transition."

"Meetings about me and the others."

"Yes."

My face feels weird. Cold or numb. What is this feeling? I know only that I don't want to talk to anyone else. Bemused by my own reaction, I tell him the truth.

"I don't want another doctor."

"There's nothing to worry about, Amelia. Dr. Reynolds is very skilled."

"I don't care. I don't want another doctor. I want *you*."

He looks down at the notepad. Though he doesn't move, tension radiates from his frame. Another man might run his hands through his hair. Sigh or fidget.

I hit a nerve. Only I have no idea which one or why.

"We should end here today," he says finally.

"What?" I blurt. "It's been twenty minutes."

He nods, still not looking up. "I apologize, but today's session is over."

I will myself to move, to pull together the pieces of my dignity, but I can't. How can such simple words have a physical impact?

Jameson's face floats through my mind, his features flinching as I swore on our mother and Phillip that the car wreck had been an accident.

Was this how he'd felt?

"Amelia," says Chastain, a warning note in his voice.

"No," I say through gritted teeth. "Fuck no. What kind of therapist are you?"

His head whips up, the fire in his eyes so unexpected—*astounding, beautiful, magnetic*—that I gasp.

"A good one," he says rigidly, "who knows his own limitations, can process complex emotion, and make healthy choices."

"I'll talk about my mother," I say without thinking. "I'll tell you why I jumped off the roof the night she died."

He springs to his feet, notepad clenched in one hand. His glasses slip to the floor, landing on the carpet. That he doesn't seem to notice or care is proof of how much I've unsettled him.

"Either you leave, or I call security to escort you."

Who is this new version of Dr. Chastain? For certain, he isn't a robot anymore, his chest heaving, eyes glittering with anger and frustration.

What have I done?

I stand on shaky legs. There isn't much space between our chairs; less than a foot separate our bodies. I lift my chin to stare at him. Blazing blue eyes. Ticking jaw.

I feel small. Weak. But I don't have enough fight left to remedy it. He's too overwhelming, the smell of him dizzying.

Unable to help myself, I gaze at his lips, which soften and open. "Leave, please," he whispers.

My eyes burn. Am I going to cry? Why?

What the hell is wrong with me?

"I'm sorry," I say, ducking my head as I step unsteadily past him.

I make it to the door and am reaching for the knob when he speaks.

"You have nothing to apologize for, Amelia. The fault is mine."

Why does that make me feel so much worse?

I leave his office, walk blindly into the Fish Tank, and sit down on one of the couches. My skin crawls. My heart pounds. I press the heels of my hands into my eyes and swallow the knot in my throat.

"What's the matter with you?"

I look up at Kinsey, who sits with a magazine on the couch opposite mine. Her breasts and ass are barely contained in a pink halter top and white shorts. Platinum hair is piled high on her head, and the smell of peach body spray is overpowering.

As hard as she is to miss, I hadn't noticed her in the room.

"I'm losing my mind," I answer.

She frowns—or at least, I think she does. It's hard to tell with all the Botox.

"Shouldn't you still be in therapy? Or did you run away?"

"He kicked me out."

Her eyes widen. "Holy shit, really?"

I nod, and she smirks.

"I'm actually kind of impressed. No one's ever seen Leo anything but, you know, all 'I'm a superhuman shrink unaffected by everything.' Bravo, *chiquita*."

I don't know what to focus on. Perhaps the fact she's never spoken so many words to me before, or that she sounds almost *nice?* But only one word sticks between my ears.

"Leo?" I echo.

Kinsey nods, her attention back on her magazine. "Leonardo. Hot name for a hot man, right? I'd do him for sure."

My chest squeezes and I eventually recognized the urge to laugh. So I do, chuckling as I drop my head back to stare at the nearest glassy black bowl on the ceiling.

I tell the cameras, "If I wasn't crazy before, I definitely am now. Good work, Doc."

Kinsey giggles. "You're funny, Mia."

I eye her skeptically. "Why are you being nice to me?"

She glances up from her magazine. "Nix said you're actually pretty cool. Do you want me to do your makeup for his going-away party tonight?"

Nope, definitely not.

"Sure," I force out.

DROWNING, NOT WAVING
DAY 8

Kinsey doing my makeup transitions into her doing my hair, then insisting I borrow some of her clothes because according to her I dress like a slob. Unlike my small wardrobe of basics—mainly T-shirts, tanks, and shorts—she has everything from sequined minidresses to designer jeans crammed into her narrow closet.

The result? I look like a high-end hooker.

I sit on Kinsey's bed squirming in my miniskirt as she curls her hair and prattles on about how much she misses the outside world. Topping the list: Brazilian waxes, pedicures, massages, and her teacup Chihuahua, aptly named Teacup.

I listen with half an ear, offering *Yeahs* and *Rights* at appropriate times, while the rest of my thoughts spiral in darker directions. If what Nix suspected is true, then Kinsey and Dr. Chastain screw on the very bed I'm sitting on. A repulsive line of thought, but one I can't extinguish.

I wonder if he's a missionary man, always in control, or

if he loses his mind and body to passion. Does he talk dirty? Use his teeth? Does he like his woman meek and obedient or feisty?

"Why is your face red?"

I bury my thoughts and meet Kinsey's curious eyes. "We're in the desert in the middle of August. Are you ready?"

I watch her struggle not to point out that the cabin's small air conditioner is on, but apparently she really wants to be my friend.

Bully for me.

"I'm all set," she says with a grin. "Do you like my outfit?"

I make my lips stretch in a smile. "You look amazing."

Kinsey chats the entire walk to the facility, her topics ranging from the dry air that's wreaking havoc on her cuticles, to the temptation of a night swim—against the rules—to Callum's incredible abs, to how excited she is that we're hanging out.

I continue my shtick of pretending to listen. The bulk of my focus is split between not tripping in the ridiculous stilettos she made me wear and the evening sky. The western horizon still clings to a weak memory of sunlight, but overhead, millions of stars twinkle like tiny diamonds.

"It's really beautiful here," I say.

Kinsey, momentarily silent, shoots me a look of disbelief. Clearly my comment doesn't dignify a response, because she keeps walking. I follow with a sigh, around the pool and into the Fish Tank.

Frank and another of the group facilitators, Charlene,

stand near one of the couches, heads bent together as they speak quietly. When they hear the door, followed immediately by our pointed heels, they jerk away from each other.

"Hello, ladies," says Charlene with a fake smile. "You both look lovely this evening."

I'm not fond of Charlene; she runs the group on Mondays and Wednesdays and always comes across as condescending. I think she's thrilled to be in a perceived authority role over people like Kinsey, Nix, and Callum. People like me.

There's a calculating gleam in Charlene's eyes as they fix on my face. I open my mouth to praise her for squeezing her gargantuan thighs into her stockings, but sharp nails bite into my forearm.

Kinsey drags me across the Fish Tank with a cheery, "Thanks, see you at the party!"

Once we're out of earshot, I yank my arm away. "What the hell?" I hiss.

"You were going to say something stupid. I was just saving your ass. You insult Charlene and that bitch will make your life hell."

My mouth gapes.

Kinsey smirks. "I'm not as stupid as I look, *chiquita*. Come on, let's go drink sparkling cider and pretend it's champagne."

"Just when I think shit can't get any weirder..."

She laughs. "This is going to be so much fun."

I think we have different definitions of fun, because the second we walk into the room where our group sessions are held, I almost bolt. Not because of the decorations, which are of the recycled, dollar-store variety, or the supermarket sheet cake on a table. What fills me with panic isn't even the number of people. Pretty much every staff member is here, including the two onsite nurses, kitchen and cleaning staff, and several security guards I've seen prowling the grounds.

The reason my knees lock, freezing me near the door as Kinsey squeals and traipses toward Nix, is that not once had I contemplated Dr. Chastain's attendance. But he's here, standing with one of the nurses, Nora, near the table with beverages.

"Close your mouth," Callum whispers, his arms coming around me from behind.

I'm so numb that his presumption doesn't bother me like it normally would. Turning in his arms to make them fall, I whisper back, "I wasn't prepared to see him. He kicked me out of his office today."

Callum's lips twitch. "Kinsey told Nix, who told everyone else after you left group today." He laughs at my disgusted expression. "By the way, what the bloody fuck are you wearing?"

I growl at him. "Not a word, Rivers."

His tawny brows rise. "Not even to tell you how hot you—"

I smack his hard chest, dancing back when he reaches for me, and run straight into someone. "Sorry, I—" My mouth snaps closed.

Dr. Chastain nods. "Amelia." He glances past me. "Callum." Blue eyes flicker back to me, landing and flying away like a butterfly kiss. "Enjoy the festivities."

As he strides toward the door, Nix calls, "Dr. C, you're leaving?"

His suited frame pauses and turns, and on his face is an expression I've never seen him wear. Pride. Happiness. A grin that transforms him into a man with the gravitational pull of a damn sun.

"Congratulations again, Jason," he says warmly. "I hope to hear from you soon."

Kinsey squeals and Nix hoots, picking her up by the waist and swinging her around the room. When I look back at the doorway, Chastain is gone.

———

I'M A STUPID, stupid woman. Only someone stupid, or crazy, would sneak out of a party at their rehab to stalk their therapist.

Not that my decision is surprising. Not to me, anyway. And as I approach the closed office door, wreathed with light from within, I realize it probably won't surprise him, either.

My brain screams at me to turn around, but my hand lifts and knocks on the wood.

"Come in."

Stop, you idiot. Run.

I walk inside, then close the door and sink against its support. I'm out of breath, like I just sprinted a mile.

Holy shit, I'm a mess.

On the other side of the room, Chastain leans against his desk, slim hips squared. His suit jacked is tossed across one of the leather chairs. My chair. His tie is loosened, the top buttons of his shirt undone. Stubble shadows his jaw, drawing dangerous attention to his full lips.

My mouth goes dry.

I want to destroy him.

"Amelia," he says wearily, "what do you need?"

A dangerous question. But I'm not so far gone that I'll tell him the truth.

"I don't know. I never do. I just… act."

His brows lift over the slim, dark frames of his glasses. "Were you hoping to catch me dozing? Maybe so you could shave my head?"

Smart doctor. When I don't say anything, he answers my silent question. "You stare at my hair quite frequently. The way I comb it irritates you, doesn't it?"

I snort, then slap a hand over my mouth to stifle a giggle. Giggling is inexcusable. Little girls and women like Kinsey giggle. I do not.

Dr. Chastain's lips curve a tiny bit, his eyes challenging.

I fucking giggle.

Waving both hands in the direction of his immaculate hair, I ask belligerently, "How do you even get the part so straight? Do you spend an hour every morning with a comb?"

To my shock, he chuckles, lips parting in a soft smile. And *dammit*, it's a gorgeous smile.

"And how long did it take *you*"—he waves a hand in mirror of my action—"to get like *that*?"

I glance down at the sparkly top and miniskirt. "It's better you don't know."

"Kinsey's clothes, I'm assuming?"

Why, does she play dress up for you? Have you peeled this skirt off her?

I nod, my tongue stuck to the roof of my mouth.

"Amelia," he says mutedly, all humor gone. "Why are you here?"

My eyes bounce around the office, avoiding his piercing stare. "Callum said you stay on the property somewhere."

His brows draw together in confusion. "Yes, there are staff cabins."

I nod jerkily. "That's great. I mean, convenient."

"Amelia," he begins warningly.

Staring at the carpet before my feet, I bite my lip to halt the word-vomit. It spews out anyway. "Will you let me mess up your hair? Please?"

He doesn't move, but I feel the razored edge of his focus. "What does it feel like, that urge?"

I shake my head wildly. "Like an itch. Inside me. My bones. This need to do something dangerous."

"Messing up my hair is dangerous?" he asks carefully.

Touching you would be dangerous.

"Yes," I whisper.

Ten feet separate us—a paltry distance—but I'm held tenuously in place by his eyes. They aren't kind or guileless, but they're familiar. Too familiar. Like some part of my psyche recognizes some part of his. We're alike. We have secrets. We keep parts of ourselves hidden.

I wonder if anyone has seen those hidden parts of him, and whether I want to.

Oh, I want to.

But I also know, without doubt, there would be a heavy price to pay.

The door at my back reverberates with a light knock. Through the wood, a female voice asks, "Leo? Are you still here?"

My lips shape his name. *Leo.* His gaze drops to my mouth. Then he clears his throat.

"Yes, Nora, come in."

I step away from the door as it opens, a smile plastered on my face for the pretty redheaded nurse.

"I was just leaving," I say before her surprise turns to suspicion.

"Sorry to interrupt," she says, nervous eyes darting to Leo. *Leo.* "I can come back."

"That's quite all right," he confirms.

Nora blushes. It's not a good look, her blotchy cheeks framed by red hair. Immediately, I feel petty for the thought. She's never been anything but kind to me.

"Good night, Dr. Chastain," I say brightly. "Thanks again for your advice."

He nods, stone-faced. "I hope you'll think about what I said."

What has he said? Nothing. Everything.

I have no idea what he's referring to, but I nod back and make my escape. Halfway across the Fish Tank, a thought barrels into me. Leo touching Nora. Making her blush all over, making her cry out his name.

"Mia?" questions Callum.

He and Preston stand on the other side of the Fish Tank. Beyond them, voices and music drift from the party.

"Are you okay?" Preston asks softly.

No.

"I will be," I say and kick off my shoes. "Come here, Preston."

He blinks those beautiful green eyes and obeys. Behind him, Callum's brows arch in surprise.

"What about me?" he asks lightly.

I shrug. "You can come, too."

When Preston is close enough, I grab his hand and thread our fingers together. His breathing accelerates, coming in nervous pants.

"What are we doing?" he asks. Scared. Excited.

"Whatever I want," I whisper back. "Ready?"

His throat bobs and he nods. I grin, plant a quick kiss on his smooth cheek, then drag him out the back door of the Fish Tank. By the time the dark waters of the pool loom before us, we're running.

Preston gurgles in alarm.

I laugh and leap into emptiness, taking him with me.

8

─────────

SACRIFICES

DAY 8 - 9

WHILE PRESTON SCRAMBLES to get out of the pool in his heavy clothes, I float in the deep end, arms and legs waving, and gaze at the endless night sky. I imagine the water around me full of stars. I'm high above. *Free.*

My ears are underwater, but before long, I hear the muted reverberations of my name being called. Urgent voices. Then angry ones. I'm sure they're arguing about who will dive in to get me.

Then *his* voice, lower and softer than the rest, but somehow clearer.

"Amelia."

I blow out three short, forceful breaths, then suck air deep into my lungs. Then I fold my body and sink. Another type of freedom, a watery cocoon. No voices here. I come to rest on the floor of the pool, my legs crossed and my miniskirt around my waist.

Dark. Silent.

My first underwater meditation was at thirteen. It hadn't

ended well, but practice makes perfect. I know my limits. Know how to listen to my heartbeat for signs of distress. When my lungs begin to burn, I release a slow stream of bubbles. Ridding myself of carbon monoxide. Savoring my depleting oxygen. White spots dance in my vision. Tiny stars.

A strong, masculine hand grabs my arm, and I open my eyes.

The disappointment is crushing.

Callum drags me to the surface, then to the side of the pool. "What the fuck, Mia?" he gasps, clutching me tightly to him. His warm hand smooths over my head, his stubbled cheek tickling mine. He whispers, "You scare me."

"I scare me, too," I say and finally look across the water, to where a group of people stands.

Dr. Chastain is gone.

Callum leads me to my cabin, away from Charlene's angry blathering. *Disciplinary meeting. There will be consequences.* He guides me into my bathroom and lets me drip while he turns on the shower and adjusts the dials.

Before diving into the pool after me he'd stripped to his boxers, which now cling wetly to his muscled ass and legs. The silky fabric also does little to hide what the tabloids have nicknamed *Callum's Cannon.*

When he turns from the shower, he catches me staring at his ass. I expect him to smirk, or make a joke, but he doesn't.

"Do you need help getting undressed?" he asks slowly and precisely.

I know the tone well. "You think I'm crazy."

He shakes his head. "I think you have a lot of pain trapped inside you." His eyes make a slow map of my features. "Something happened to you. Something bad."

The surface of my secrets shifts, buckling against ice.

"Something bad happens to everyone." I pull off my top. It plops wetly on the ground, where it's joined shortly by the miniskirt and my underwear.

"Jesus, Mia," hisses Callum, eyes hungry as they travel my body. "You really know how to push a guy to his breaking point."

My specialty.

I walk past him, making sure to graze his bare back with my breasts, then step into the shower. Hot water cascades over me, pulling a sigh of relief from my throat.

Blinking at Callum through the spray, I say, "Go ahead and break. No one's stopping you."

His jaw hardens as he takes a rigid step toward me. A finger traces my nipple, pebbled beneath the water, before trailing down my belly. Just when I think I have him, he stalls, breathing heavily, and takes a large step backward.

Wincing, he squeezes his heavy erection with one hand, then gives me a sad smile. "I've had my heart broken too many times. And you"—he shakes his head slowly—"I think you might ruin me."

I ignore the second disappointment—or is it the third?—of the evening. "I'm not offering love, just sex."

"That's my problem," he says with a small shrug. "I don't know the difference."

I feel no pleasure at this secret, no desire to take what

he's offered me and turn it against him. I don't want to break Callum.

Huh.

"Thank you for diving in after me."

The sadness leaves his smile. "You're welcome." He turns away but pauses with his hand on the doorframe. "Let him in. He really wants to help you. You scared the shit out of him tonight."

My heart thumps hard, ever reminding me of my limitations. My sickness.

"Good night, Callum."

"Sweet dreams, Mia."

I pull the shower curtain closed.

At 10:00 a.m., I walk into Dr. Chastain's office and sit listlessly in my chair. My mind is hazy, my body lethargic. I slept through my usual run with Callum and the change of routine has me off-kilter. I don't want to be here.

There's nowhere else I want to be.

"Amelia."

"Leo."

He sighs but doesn't correct me. "You look tired this morning."

I shrug. "Bad dreams."

His pen scratches on paper. "Will you tell me about them?"

I consider lying but don't have the energy. "I was getting married." I snort. "Total nightmare."

"Why was it a nightmare?" he asks softly.

"I don't know. There was this… feeling."

"Did it feel like you were making a mistake?"

"No."

"Then what?"

Realizing it's too late to backpedal, I blurt, "I was happy. Completely, utterly ecstatic."

There's a weighted pause. "Why was it a nightmare?"

I close my eyes. "You know why."

"You had a dream you were getting married, and in the dream you were happy." Patient, measured tone. "Why is that a nightmare?"

"Don't make me say it," I whisper.

"I think you should."

I press my fingers into my eyes. "I woke up! There, asshole. Happy now? It was a nightmare because *I woke up!*"

"How did that make you feel?"

Annoyed. Angry. Heartbroken.

But I keep my mouth shut.

"Is there a reason you won't look at me?"

I lower my hands to my lap but don't lift my eyes. "Because your face pisses me off," I snap.

"And why is that?"

Let him in. He wants to help you.

"I don't trust you," I answer—both him and Callum's voice in my head.

"How can I earn your trust?"

I shake my head. "I don't know. You can't."

"Do you trust anyone?"

"Jameson."

"Even though he was the one who contacted us?"

"Yes. He was only trying to help me. Protect me."

"And what do you think I'm trying to do?"

Through my teeth, I say, "Break me."

He doesn't reply. Minutes tick by on the antique wall clock. *Tick. Tick.* The sky is overcast, the normally bright room shadowed. I consider whether or not I'm still dreaming. Tossing and turning in my bed, trading one nightmare for another.

Absorbed in my chaotic thoughts, I don't notice Chastain has moved until I feel his hands on my jean-clad knees, spreading them apart. I stiffen, my eyes snapping of their own volition to his face. He takes advantage of my pause, settling between my legs. Closer than he's ever been.

Not nearly close enough.

"Give me your hands," he says, offering both of his, palms up.

"What are you doing?" I breathe.

He says nothing, watching me and waiting. The glasses are gone, and his eyes are soft and a little wary. His pulse jumps against the skin of his throat. Like candy I want to suck.

I put my cold fingers in his warm ones.

Slowly, he lifts my hands to his head. Even with him kneeling, my arms aren't quite long enough to reach. I hold my breath as he moves forward until we're nearly chest to chest.

His breath teases my cheek. "Go ahead, Amelia."

I don't recognize the whimper that comes from me as I

sink my fingers into his perfect hair. It's softer than I imagined, barely any product in it. I drag my fingernails across his scalp, tugging and twisting the strands. He sucks in a breath, his eyes closing and chin dropping.

I take hair in my fists and yank his face up. Startled eyes meet mine. More than anything, ever, I want to kiss him.

"Don't," he says.

For some godforsaken reason, I listen. With a final tug on his hair, I release him and sink back into my chair. He lowers onto his heels, eyes still wide and startled, like he doesn't understand what just happened. Dark hair in wild disarray. Hands clenched on his knees.

By his dilated pupils, I assume he's hard beneath the concealing flaps of his jacket. The thought doesn't thrill me like it should. Instead, I feel unsettled.

"I still don't trust you," I say, because the moment is too real. Too heavy.

Hadn't I wanted this?

I had, but I don't anymore.

"You're making me crazy," I add.

Chastain moves to his feet, turning quickly. Long strides carry him around his desk, where he sits heavily in the rolling chair. I watch him stare blankly at the desk until I can't stand the silence anymore.

"I can hold my breath for two minutes and twenty-three seconds."

He looks up. "Yes, I know."

My eyes narrow. "Fucking Jameson. Did he tell you my favorite food, too?"

"Ceviche," he says with a twitch of lips.

My own mouth curves. "Favorite movie?"

He grimaces. "*Reservoir Dogs*."

"Hey! It's a great movie!"

He laughs. *Really* laughs, his head tilted back and shoulders shaking. My smile grows until my cheeks ache.

"Whatever, Doc. I kind of like this game, seeing how well my twin knows me. How about this. Have I ever gone skydiving?"

"Twenty-six times," he answers, still smiling.

"Most embarrassing moment?"

He frowns, thinking, then his eyes clear. "You got your period in the eighth grade in the middle of class"—he pauses for dramatic effect—"in white pants."

"Son of a bitch!" I shriek. "I'm committing twin-icide the second I see that dickhead."

His smile softens. "Why do you think Jameson wanted me to know so much about you?"

I roll my eyes. "Yeah, yeah. I get it. He trusts you, so I should trust you."

"Do you think you can?"

I meet his calm, assessing gaze. "Maybe. If you tell me a secret."

He crosses his arms over his chest. "What kind of secret?"

"Your biggest one."

His lips curve, though not in humor. "I don't think so, but I'll tell you something personal. How's that?"

"I'll tell you after I hear it."

He concedes with a nod. "When I was thirteen, my older brother committed suicide. I didn't put the pieces together until college, but now I know he suffered from untreated bipolar disorder."

No pleasure this time, either.

At my silence, he continues, "I knew there was something wrong with him, but my mother didn't believe in mental illness. She believed in prayer. I'll always regret not listening to my instincts, not pushing harder for him to see a doctor."

There's no bitterness in his voice, which strikes me as a small miracle. *How does he not hate her?* If it were Jameson we were talking about, no matter how much time had passed, I'd still be postal.

"That's why you went into this field?"

He nods. "His name was Vincent. Vince."

There is, of course, a part of me that wants to pry further. To see how far he'll let me open him up, how deep he'll let me peer inside.

I'm not a changed woman after eight days in treatment. The itch for danger will come back—it always does—but right now, I'm content.

I take a deep breath. "Do you want me to tell you about the night my mother died?"

"Please."

So I do.

9

MEMORY LANE
DAY 9

Ensconced in the playroom with a mountain of Legos, Jameson and I listen to our parents in the next room.

"Please, Harrison, you know I'm phobic about water. Will you take him?"

"We've talked about this," replies my father sternly. "He needs to learn to swim. Jameson and Mia started lessons when they were one. I don't know why it's so different with Phillip."

"Phillip isn't fearless like them. Water makes him nervous, too."

"He's too young to be afraid. Clearly he's picking up on your fear."

"I don't think so. I'm very careful not to project—"

"Deal with it, Julia. I'm not putting a damned fence around the pool. You're the adult. Take Phillip to the swim lesson. I have work to do."

Jameson and I trade glances as our mother's footsteps pass the playroom door and go down the stairs.

"He's afraid of water?" whispers Jameson.

I shrug. "That's stupid."

Jameson frowns. "Don't call Phillip stupid."

"Fine, I'll call you stupid."

"I'm not stupid. You're stupid. I hate you."

I stick my tongue out. "Hate you too."

Minutes later, our mother comes back upstairs and pokes her head into the playroom. She's wearing a raincoat since it's been storming all day.

"Hi, lovebugs. I'm going to take Phillip swimming."

"Can I come?" I ask.

My mother smiles. "Not tonight, Amelia."

"But I can help!" I insist. "I'm not afraid of water!"

Jameson pinches me and I squeal, then punch him hard in the shoulder. He wails and throws a handful of Legos at my head.

"I'm going to watch TV," he announces, running from the room before I can retaliate.

"He pinched me first," I tell my mother.

"I saw. I'll have a talk with him later."

Oddly, she doesn't look angry. She normally hates it when we fight. She's constantly telling us how blessed we are to have siblings. Which, of course, falls on deaf ears.

"I really can help Phillip swim," I say, brushing Legos off my lap as I stand. I walk into her open arms, taking a deep breath of her flowery scent. She drops a kiss on my head.

"I appreciate that, lovebug, but you know what would be an even bigger help?"

I crane my neck to see her face—golden hair, warm hazel eyes, and a big smile for me.

"What, Mommy?"

She taps my nose with her index finger. "Clean up this play-room before we get home."

"Mom," I whine, "why am I being punished? Jameson started it."

With a tender swipe of fingers over my cheek, she replies, "Taking care of the gifts others have given us isn't a punishment. It's a privilege."

Knowing she's about to remind me of the bajillion kids who don't have toys to play with, I stomp away from her.

"Fine," I grumble, kicking a flattened soccer ball across the room.

"Thank you, Amelia."

I look up from a pile of twisted, naked Barbies. "If I clean up, can I have ice cream after dinner?"

She laughs, eyes sparkling. "My little deal-maker. Of course. Ice cream it is."

"None for Jameson?"

She winks. "We'll see. Be back soon. Love you, Amelia."

"Love you, too, Mommy."

"THE LESSON WAS at six and they were always home by seven fifteen," I say vacantly. "By eight, Jameson and I were starving. We asked my dad for dinner, but he yelled at us, so we sat together on the couch downstairs and waited."

"Your father didn't realize how late it was?" asks Chastain.

I shake my head. "When he was working on a case, he tended to lose track of time."

"Please, continue."

I clear my throat. "Jameson answered the door. Two cops. We weren't stupid. We knew something had happened to Mom and Phillip. I remember thinking they must have drowned, because they were both afraid of water. But it had rained while they were at swim class and the roads were slick. Some kid in his daddy's Mercedes took a turn too fast and spun out, hitting them. They went off the road."

"Was Phillip in a car seat?"

My breath hitches; darkness crowds my mind. "Yes, but the car hit the back passenger side directly. Mom died when the airbag malfunctioned and her head hit the steering wheel, breaking her neck. She shouldn't have died, really. Neither of them should have. Bad luck."

"I'm sorry, Amelia."

He sounds like he means it, but I also know he's waiting for the rest.

"A neighbor came over to watch us so Dad could go with the officers. Mrs. Clemens, I think her name was. Nice lady. Held Jameson while he cried."

"You didn't cry?"

"Not then. I told them I was going upstairs to my room, then put on my bathing suit."

"Ah," he says, like some puzzle piece has fallen into place. "It was too easy to just jump in the swimming pool, wasn't it?"

I blink burning, dry eyes. "Yes," I say in a voice I don't know—raw and raspy. "I wanted to be close to them. I wanted to feel afraid."

"But you didn't."

"No, I didn't. But I tried. I went into the attic and out the window onto the roof. It wasn't the first time I'd gone up there, but I'd never jumped off before. The pool wasn't that far. I thought I could make it."

"But the possibility of not making it?"

"Yes, smartypants. That's why I did it."

He doesn't acknowledge my nickname, not that I expected him to. "And you broke your arm?"

I nod. "Nearly cracked my head on the lip of the pool. Flinging my arm out gave me the winning inch."

After a small pause, he asks, "Have you had any other close calls?"

"You know I have," I say, eyeing him. "I'm sure Jameson told you."

"I know about the cliff-diving in San Diego when you were pulled into the rocks by rip currents, and I know about the base jump into the Cave of Swallows when your chute malfunctioned."

I smile grimly, nodding at him to continue.

"I know you've bungee jumped, skydived, parasailed, rock climbed, have earned a number of speeding tickets. How many car accidents?"

"Just the one that landed me here." I lean forward. "Which *was* an accident, by the way. My flip-flop got caught under the brake pedal. Criminally stupid, but not suicidal."

"What about the other accident?"

I frown. "There was no other accident."

Chastain opens a drawer in his desk and pulls out a

thick file. *Mine.* He flips through it until he finds a single sheet of paper.

"March 3, 2016. You were involved in a twenty-car pileup on the 405 after a semi lost control and jackknifed."

I shake my head. "Wrong patient, boss. That wasn't me."

He reaches into the file and pulls out an eight-by-ten photograph, holding it up for me to see. I stare at it uncomprehendingly—it's my face, bruised and bandaged. I'm wearing a neck brace and a hospital gown.

I have zero recollection of it. Jerking to my feet, I cross the room and snatch the picture from his hand.

"You don't remember that photo being taken?"

My stomach clenches and a chill radiates down my spine. "No. *No.*" I force myself to look up, to focus on his face. "Where did you get this? Are you sure it's not from my accident last month?"

"It's time stamped," he answers softly.

In the bottom corner of the photograph is printed the date. *03.03.16.* But it doesn't make sense. It's impossible. In March of 2016, I was…

I was…

I sway on my feet. Blood rushes in my ears, drowning out ambient noise. Cold sweat breaks out all over my body.

"I don't feel so good, Doc," I whisper.

Chastain jumps from his chair and grabs me just as my knees buckle. He lowers me to the floor, then brushes the hair from my face.

"Amelia? You need to trust me, and if you can't trust

me, trust Jameson. You're here because of the accident in March two years ago."

"You're lying," I say through harsh breaths. "A trick. I'm dreaming."

"Breathe. Just breathe."

With his arm under my knees, he lifts me onto his lap and holds me tightly. Fingers stroke my hair and down my back. I start shaking and can't stop.

"Did I die?" I ask shrilly. "Is this… after? You're the devil?"

He exhales sharply. "You didn't die, though sometimes I do feel like the devil where you're concerned. We'll figure this out, Amelia. Together. I promise."

I tuck my face into his chest, clinging to him like he's the last rock in the goddamn ocean. "I don't believe you."

"Then I'll have to believe enough for both of us."

"I'm broken," I whisper.

His lips graze the top of my head. "Everyone's broken. Some of us are just better at gluing the pieces back together."

I laugh, still shaking. Teeth chattering. Unhinged.

"Well, at least I don't want to fuck you anymore."

"Oh? Why's that?"

I lift my head, finding his electric eyes. "I don't fuck people I like, much less people I trust."

He grins like I just told him he won the lottery. "You trust me."

I scowl. "I've never had a man this excited to be off my sex radar. I think I'm insulted. Help me up. I don't want to be in your lap if it's not doing anything for you."

He bites his lips to dampen his smile but can't mask the sparkle of amusement in his eyes.

With some awkward navigating, we manage to get to our feet. I pull down my T-shirt from where it rode up my stomach, and Chastain tugs at his tie.

"Do you feel better?" he asks.

"A little discombobulated, but yes. Clearly the only cure for a mental breakdown is reminding me you don't want to get in my pants. Nothing like a blow to the ego to put things in perspective."

He bites his lower lip so hard it turns white. I roll my eyes. "Laugh at me, Leo. Do it."

He does.

I frown at him the whole time, pretending I don't love the deep, infectious sound of his laughter. Finally, he quiets.

"Are we done for today?" I wait for his nod, then blurt, "Amnesia?"

His humor fades fast. "Selective, post-traumatic amnesia, yes."

I hug my arms to my chest. "I have a bad feeling about this. What if I'm not supposed to remember? This is fucking surreal. And Jameson knows about this?"

He nods again. "It's why he called us. You're safe, Amelia. I've got you."

"Is that what you think?" I ask sadly, then shake my head and walk to the door. "No one's got me, Doc. Too many missing pieces."

LOVE AND WAR
DAY 9

"Amnesia?"

"Yeah." I take a drag of a contraband cigarette. "Wild, right?"

"Dude," Callum says heavily. The tip of his cigarette glows in the darkness. "Wild."

"For real."

We trade wry glances at our juvenile vocabulary.

Callum pivots to face me, turning his shoulder against the back wall of his cabin. "What do you think happened?"

"Like you said, something bad." I blow a stream of smoke toward the starry sky, then flick the cigarette to the ground and smother it with my shoe. "Or maybe nothing?"

I don't like the question in my voice, but can't help it. I wouldn't be here if it was nothing. I just hope it wasn't something hugely tragic. Had someone been in the car with me? Had anyone died?

We stand silently for several minutes, each of us lost in

thoughts. Callum finishes his cigarette and pops the cherry out before tossing the butt.

"I had a restraining order put out on me."

I tense. "You don't have to—"

"It's okay. I want to." He sighs. "Another model. Her name was Frenchie."

"That's unfortunate."

He snorts. "Yeah, everyone called her French. Anyway, we fell into bed after a photoshoot last April. The chemistry was unbelievable. We ended up spending a weekend together. I fell in love."

I don't say anything, mainly because I hear the curl of sarcasm in the last word.

"I thought she felt the same way," he continues, a thousand miles of regret in his voice.

I feel a sympathetic squeeze in my chest. *Poor Callum.*

"She blew you off?" I make myself ask.

He nods, features tight in the moonlight. "She had a boyfriend. I couldn't handle it. Long story short, I tried to break them up. I thought if she was single, she'd remember how good we were together. Obviously, she saw my actions in a different light."

I scuff dirt with the toe of my shoe. "You stalked her?"

"Yep, although I really didn't see it that way. I thought I was loving her." He pauses. "I have obsessive love disorder."

I consider saying something flippant, like there are millions of women who'd welcome being obsessively loved by him, but I bite my tongue.

"Do you know what real love feels like?" he asks, voice

tight with need. "Dr. C has described it, but I think a woman's perspective would really help me."

I listen to my heart, which is suddenly beating hard. Anxiety tingles down my arms.

I shouldn't have smoked that cigarette.

"I'm the wrong person to ask," I say finally. "I mean, I love my brother, and I can tell you what I know about that."

He stares at me, silent and rapt.

"It, uh, makes me feel anchored. Jameson is like a weight that pulls me down, holding me to the world. I feel comfort when I think of him. And, um, I guess a big part of it is that he knows everything about me. All my flaws. And he still loves me."

"How do you know?"

"I just do. I feel this… bond. Trust, I guess. No matter what happens, or how much we fight, he loves me and I love him. That's all I've got, sorry."

"That sounds nice."

I glance at him, seeing his soft smile. "Yeah, it is."

Studying his perfect features, ethereal in the moonlight, I wonder how it's possible that Callum doesn't know what love feels like.

"What about your parents?"

He shrugs a shoulder. "Foster kid."

I wince. "Sorry."

Callum waves away my apology. "But you've never been in love?"

My heart kicks my ribs again. "I thought I was. Two times. My high school boyfriend and my ex-fiancé, Kevin."

"Will you tell me? Describe how you felt about Kevin?"

He sounds so freaking needy, I can't deny him. But the truth comes like knives from my throat. "Kevin wanted to take care of me. I wanted to let him, and I tried to take care of him, too. He loved the version of me that was perfect wife material. I was seduced by the idea of being that person."

"That doesn't sound healthy," he says dryly.

I huff. "Yeah, well, this isn't Camp Healthy People."

He snickers and I grin back at him.

"In the end, we were both acting. I don't think we really knew each other at all. I found him banging our next-door neighbor."

"Ouch."

"I was angry, obviously. But I wasn't heartbroken. I didn't feel that empty, hopeless feeling people talk about. I dumped his record collection on the front lawn and set it on fire."

Callum barks a laugh. "Holy shit, Mia. Remind me not to get on your bad side."

I bump his shoulder with mine. "I like you, you're safe."

Silence descends once more, but without its previous strain. We watch the sky. Spy a few shooting stars. A breeze kicks up, tickling our exposed skin with warm drafts.

"I'm getting better," he says mutedly, almost to himself. "Some things Dr. C has told me are finally making sense."

"Like what?"

"Hard to explain." He tilts his head toward me. "The fact I'm not obsessing over you is pretty amazing. It's almost enough to make me fall in love with you."

"Me?" I scoff. "Buddy, I'm ten miles of bad road. You'd be better off with Kinsey."

Instead of laughing, he says gravely, "You really don't see yourself at all."

I scowl. "Quit it. We both know I'm a hot mess."

"Are you?" he asks cryptically. "I don't think you're crazy. I think you're complicated, and passionate, and terrified of the depth at which you feel things. It's easier for you to pretend you don't feel anything at all. A coping mechanism."

"Wrong." I cross my arms over my chest, wishing I had another cigarette. We smoked his last two. "The problem isn't that I can't feel anything, it's that I can't feel *fear*. And believe me, I've tried. I've put myself in horrible situations. Dangerous ones. Short of strolling naked into a biker bar, I've walked some shady lines. Scared the shit out of everyone who cared about me. Everyone except myself."

"Because you don't care about yourself," he states sadly.

"Meh," I say dismissively, having heard that assessment many times. I counter it with the same logic I always use. "If I didn't care about myself, I'd simply jump without a parachute."

"Self-loathing and being suicidal are different," he says gently. "This I know."

I rub my face roughly. "Fine, Dr. Rivers. You win." Peering at him over my fingers, I snarl, "I liked you better when you weren't playing therapist. Chastain's bad enough."

He laughs. "He's growing on you, isn't he?"

"Like a sexy fungus."

Callum thinks this is hysterical and bends in half with the force of his laughter. I try to hold my frown, but my lips quirk. Eventually he recovers, standing to wipe his streaming eyes.

"Don't try to seduce him."

My brows rise. "Why not?"

All traces of laughter vanish from his face. "For both of your sakes. I don't want Dr. C to lose everything because of you."

I open and close my mouth a few times before finding my voice. "You're making a rather large assumption on his behalf."

Callum stares at me, eyes fathomless in the shadows. "It's not an assumption."

My pulse makes itself known again, this time between my legs. Ignoring the insistent throb, I say, "Just because you want to bone me doesn't—"

"Let me put it to you this way," he interjects. "When we met, you immediately triggered my obsessive disorder. A part of that means I become hyperaware of potential challengers. Competition. I've seen him look at you when he thinks no one's watching." He pinches the bridge of his nose. "I shouldn't be telling you this."

Unnerved more than I care to admit, I feign affront. "I'm not going to seduce my therapist, no matter how hot he is. That's low, even for me."

"Good," he grinds out.

"Happy?" I snap.

"Yes!"

Our gazes lock in an angry battle. It lasts ten seconds before we grin and succumb to laughter.

I nudge his shoulder. "I'm going to bed. Wanna come?"

He groans. "Fuck you, Goldie."

I waggle my eyebrows. "That's the offer."

Chuckling, he turns away. "I like you too much to have sex with you," he throws over his shoulder.

"Hey, that's my line!"

His laughter fades as he rounds the corner of the cabin. When I hear the open and close of his door, I relax against the wall, still warm from the heat of the day.

My body hums with the need for sleep, but my head spins like a carnival ride. Complete with disorientation and nausea.

Since my session this morning, all I can think about is the accident I can't remember. I spent hours holed up in my cabin, skipping lunch to piece together the months of 2016.

I have a vague recollection of a Christmas party, then New Year's. In February, I caught Kevin cheating and left his dumb ass. The next event I remember is white water rafting with some friends in June.

Between March and mid-June, there's nothing.

Nothing.

11

SMOKE AND MIRRORS
DAY 10

IT MUST BE after midnight by the time I rouse myself from the void of questions in my mind. The night is darker than before, the moon nearly set, and the air temperature almost classifies as chilly.

Hugging my arms to my chest, I shuffle around Callum's cabin toward mine. My sneakers scuff against fine gravel and the occasional larger rock.

I'm five steps from my door when I hear a feminine squeal. Freezing mid-step, I strain my ears for a repeat of the sound, and when it doesn't come, I tell myself I imagined it.

Then it happens again. This time, the squeal is followed by a low moan. Eyes scanning the cabins, I see only one with light shining behind the curtains.

Kinsey's.

My limbs tingle. Like an automaton, I turn and walk past Callum's cabin, Nix's now vacant one, and come to a stop.

"Please, please, please…"

The low chant reaches my ears through the partially open door.

Why is the door open?

Driven by a need to know if my worst assumption is true, I tiptoe to the narrow swath of light. I'm sure my heart is pounding, but I can't feel it. All I feel is the overwhelming compulsion to know.

I have a clear view of the bed and Dr. Chastain's back. Beneath him, Kinsey thrashes and moans. I barely notice they're both clothed. I just see *him*. On top of *her*.

Then Kinsey whimpers. "Please don't make me. Please, I don't want to, I don't want to…"

Finally, I feel something. A whole lot of something.

My sailing fist slams the door open. "What the fucking fuck!" I yell. "Get off her!"

Chastain jerks back, sliding off the bed and whirling around. His glasses are askew, his hair in disarray.

Motherfucker.

I hate him.

Totally. Irrevocably.

My palms slam into his chest before I'm even aware of crossing the room. "What the fuck do you think you're doing?" I scream at him.

He glances back at Kinsey, who's looking groggily around the room. She seems really out of it. Glazed eyes. Bedraggled hair and rumpled, barely there pajamas.

"Did you *drug* her?" I screech, shoving him roughly. It doesn't matter that he's a wall of solid muscle and barely moves. "You're scum! A fucking monster!"

"Amelia," he snaps, cheekbones flushing with anger. "Return to your cabin. Now."

Hysterical laughter bubbles in my throat. "Are you nuts? There's no way I'm leaving you with her!"

"Amelia, it's all right," says a woman behind me.

Turning, I see Nurse Nora standing near the kitchen, a clipboard in her arms and an anxious look on her face.

Adrenaline drains away in a rush, leaving me shaky and cold. "What the hell is happening here?" I ask her.

Kinsey moans, her head thrashing from side to side. Out of the corner of my eye I see Chastain move back to the bed.

"Night terrors," answers Nora gently. "We've been monitoring her sleep since she arrived."

My head shakes automatically. "What? No. Someone would have heard something. Woken up. Nix never said…" I trail off, feeling more than a few cards short of a deck.

Nora clears her throat daintily, glancing at Chastain. Without looking up, he nods brusquely.

Nora says, "The cabins are soundproofed but wired for sound in case of situations like these. Some of the most profound therapy happens during these hours. Kinsey's progress over the past months has been extraordinary."

Dots connect into lines in my head. "The only reason I heard something was because the door was open."

Nora turns scarlet. "My fault."

My gaze veers to the bed, to Kinsey's blankly staring eyes and tortured expression. "She isn't awake?"

"No," answers Chastain in a clipped tone. Icy eyes meet mine; beneath the ice, though, there's a firestorm. "Are you satisfied? If so, please leave."

Shame curls through me, shadowed by a strange sense of loss.

I accused him of rape.

"I... I—"

"Don't bother apologizing," he says coldly. "Go."

I go.

I DREAM of the day I died. Or rather, the day I wish I'd died.

The sky is a pale, washed-out blue typical of Los Angeles. The air is warm and heavy, smelling of smog and wasted lives.

Two caskets sit side by side, poised above the dark cavities that will house them forever. One full-sized, one child-sized. Their matching mahogany surfaces are so polished they catch the sun through the trees and send glare periodically into my eyes.

The weather is a mockery. This isn't real.

Nothing's real.

"What does it feel like?" Chastain asks.

He sits in the uncomfortable wooden folding chair to my left, dressed in a dark suit with a crisp white shirt. He's not wearing glasses and his hair is mussed and natural, like he just rolled out of bed. No razor-sharp part in sight.

I know I'm dreaming. He's not really here. Neither am I—at least, I'm not here as I was, a seven-year-old in an ill-fitting black dress and shoes that pinched my toes. Shoes that were dug out of my closet from where they'd been gathering dust since Christmas. There hadn't been time or the desire to buy new ones.

I take a deep breath, letting it out slowly, then wipe damp palms on my knees. "Like emptiness."

"Is that what you imagine death feels like?"

I glance around, seeing only blurry faces. Apparently as a child I hadn't paid much attention to the other attendees. I briefly wonder why the two chairs on the other side of me are empty—on this horrible day, they were occupied by my father and Jameson.

"Amelia?"

"I don't know what death feels like," I answer belatedly. "I mean, not really."

"You've come close before…"

I think of the Cave of Swallows and my malfunctioning parachute. The moments in which my backup chute hadn't responded to my desperate tugs.

"Weightlessness, maybe."

He nods contemplatively. "Where are your brother and father?"

"I don't know," I say crossly. "This is a dream."

"Don't you think it's interesting they're not here?"

I tell Dream-Chastain, "I think I hate you."

He smiles like I've only seen him smile once before, at Nix's farewell party, giving me a glimpse of a younger, more carefree man. Leo, not Dr. Chastain.

The knowledge hurts for some reason.

When I don't speak, he says musingly, "Perhaps they're not here because in this difficult time, you were alone. Left to process your feelings without the support of loved ones."

I smile tightly at him. "This dream sucks. Can you at least take your shirt off or something?"

He chuckles, deep and amused. "No."

I throw my hands up in a wordless plea. "Fine. You're right. My grandparents were all dead by this point. My aunts and uncles tried to help, but I wasn't exactly receptive to sympathy."

"Why not?" He pauses. "You think you should have died instead of your mother and brother?"

"No. Yes. I don't know."

"The rational adult says no, the emotional child says yes."

"Whatever you say, Doc."

He smiles again. "It's not me saying anything, Amelia. You're speaking to yourself through me. Your guilt has driven you to become the adult you are today. With no one to tell you as a child that the accident wasn't your fault, you've carried misplaced shame all your life."

"It wasn't my fault," I whisper unconvincingly.

"And if you'd been at the swim lesson with them?"

Searing pain slices my heart. Words pour from me, unbidden. "My mom wouldn't have panicked and left early when Phillip swallowed some water. They wouldn't have been on the road when that dickwad decided to take a joy ride."

Chastain is silent for a long time. Long enough that I watch the shadowy funeral guests file past the caskets and leave. Long enough that I see the caskets being cranked gently into their earthen beds.

Finally, he says, "It's not your fault. I'm sorry no one

was there to tell you that then. But I'm here now. And I'll tell you every day until you believe it."

"Why?" I breathe, not even knowing the real question I'm asking.

Dream-Chastain knows, though. "Because we're only as sick as our secrets. It's time for you to let someone else take care of them for you."

I close my eyes against a swell of tears. "I don't trust you," I mumble.

I can hear the smile in his next words.

"Yes, you do."

12

____

GROWING PAINS

DAY 10

I PURPOSEFULLY SLEEP through my standing appointment with Chastain. I'm honestly not ready to face him.

Embarrassed? *Check*. Ashamed? *Check*.

I'm also weirded out by his starring role in my dream last night. It's making me question things I'd rather not question. Like, what if the dream means I do, in fact, trust him? What do I do about my attraction to him? And the biggest mind-fuck of the bunch: am I actually attracted to him, or have I manufactured my obsession in order to place distance between us?

Groaning, I roll out of bed and stumble into the shower. The hot water is delicious; I imagine it rinsing off the taint of last night's mortification. I wash my hair three times.

After toweling off and dressing, I give my wan reflection a stare. The woman in the mirror doesn't look young. Sure, her skin isn't wrinkled, and the spattering of prematurely white strands of hair are camouflaged by varying shades of blond, but her eyes are dark and haunted.

Hunted.

I'm being stalked by an unnamed beast. Ghosts and memories, both those accessible and those hiding beneath the fog of forgetting.

When I leave my cabin around noon, I almost trip over Tiffany, who's sitting cross-legged on my stoop. Her black hair is pulled up into a stump of a ponytail. Strands cling with sweat to her neck and around her pale ears.

She doesn't turn around when I close the door behind me. "Uhh, hello?"

"I ate a whole pizza once," she says in a flat tone.

I blink. "Say what?"

"A whole pizza, a pint of ice cream, and a super-sized bag of potato chips."

Oh Lord.

It doesn't take a genius to figure out which end it all came out. She must be here for an eating disorder. A girl I went to high school with suffered from anorexia; she was hospitalized multiple times and nearly died. I briefly wonder what happened to her. If she made it past twenty-five.

My limbs strangely heavy, I walk slowly around Tiffany to see her face. It's streaked with tears, mascara streaks fanning from her lower lashes.

"Why are you telling me this?" I ask, forcing the accusation from my tone.

I'm not heartless.

She sniffs. "I don't know. I heard you last night—I'm right next door to Kinsey and you were"—a watery smile appears—"really loud. I heard how you put yourself on the line for her. To defend her."

I shake my head. "I was an idiot. It wasn't what I thought it was."

"I know. I've seen Dr. Chastain and Nora go in a bunch of times." She glanced up at me. "I don't sleep well. I go for night walks sometimes. Don't tell anyone."

"I won't," I say before I can even process the secret. The impulse to use it as a weapon is nowhere to be felt.

She shrugs. "So, anyway, I guess I just wanted to, you know, talk to you."

I sit down, leaving a foot or so of space between us, and squint at the labyrinth. "Is that Kinsey?" I ask in stupefaction.

Tiffany snorts. "She's been doing it for an hour. Walking in and out, in and out. Maybe she thinks it's a magic portal back to Teacup."

I bite my lips on a laugh. Tiffany studies me from red-rimmed hazel eyes, her lips teasing up at the corners.

"So everyone thinks you and Dr. C. have a thing."

My ears ring and I tense. "We don't. Not even a little bit."

"Why'd you jump into the pool?"

"Because I could. What is this, twenty questions?"

Tiffany pushes a few stray hairs from her forehead, her eyes steady on mine. Searching. Hoping. "Mia? Will you tell me the truth?"

I look away. "About what?"

"For starters, the pool."

This conversation is going downhill fast without brakes. I can feel the cliff coming. The jumping off point.

Do I trust Tiffany? Hell with a capital No.

But does it matter?

"He scares me. So I wanted to scare him back."

I don't filter the words. Don't think about them. I just let them free from the lockbox of my head.

"Dr. C.? Why?"

She sounds truly surprised. And I suppose she would be —everyone loves Chastain, after all. He's a goddamn wizard.

I feel the muscles in my neck and back quivering with tension, and I know I'm not capable of sharing more. Not with Tiffany. Not with Chastain.

Barely with myself.

He sees me.

Rather than give a bullshit answer, I say, "I can't tell you right now."

Tiffany puts a small, delicate hand on my knee. "It's okay, I understand."

Beating back a reflex to hurt her takes so much effort I feel lightheaded. "Thanks," I choke out. "Can we, uh, pick this up later?"

Tiffany nods, all sympathy and camaraderie. Like I give a shit.

Do I give a shit?

"I need some coffee," I tell her as I stand, "then I have to take a lashing from Chastain for not showing this morning."

"He's not here."

I freeze. "What do you mean, *he's not here?*"

Tiffany stands, too, lifting her arms and sniffing her armpits. The Crazy House dissolves polite boundaries like that.

"My session is at seven thirty, so I'm the first every day. There was a note on the door that said he'd be back tomorrow, but he'd be watching the group session remotely. Basically, don't fuck up."

"Huh," is all I can manage.

Tiffany jumps off the stoop and heads toward her cabin.

"Tiffany?" I call out and wait for her to turn around. "Why were you crying?"

I can't see her eyes, which are shaded by her hand, but I can see the small lift of her mouth.

"I'm six months without a relapse. I was feeling emotional about it, but after talking to you I feel better." She waves and saunters off.

Greaaat. In my experience, there's only one surefire way a person feels instantly better about their problems— talking to someone who they think has bigger ones.

With a sour feeling in my belly, I head toward the Fish Tank. As I bypass the labyrinth, Kinsey waves at me.

"Hey, Mia! Charlene wants to see you." She glances at her Rolex. "Right now. Better hurry! That bitch is mean."

It takes my brain a minute to remember why I knew this was coming.

The pool incident.

Kinsey walks on, a bounce in her step I've never seen until now.

"Seems like everyone's getting better," I grumble and head inside to face the music.

———

CHARLENE DOESN'T BOTHER DISGUISING her satisfaction at having me on the wrong end of a disciplinary hearing. She, Frank, and the third group moderator, Ruben, sit behind a long table, while I face them in an unbalanced plastic chair that squeaks threateningly every time I shift my weight. It's a petty tactic, but I have to admit it's working.

I'm literally and figuratively on edge.

"… not what you did, but that you involved another patient. Inciting rebellion is a serious offense." Charlene glares at me with righteous indignation.

Frank and Ruben exchange a glance. At least I'm not the only one who thinks this is ridiculous.

I swallow back what I really want to say to her. "You're right. I'm sorry. It won't happen again."

Apparently an apology wasn't the right move. Charlene's face darkens with an angry flush. I kind of wish my father were here. Dodging accountability is his specialty.

Frank speaks up, "Thank you for apologizing, Mia. That's a great first step."

Ruben nods in agreement.

Charlene smiles. Not a good sign.

"Unfortunately, actions have more power than words. To make restitution for your offense, you'll mop the Fish Tank and adjacent hallways tonight."

I merely smile. "Sure. Sounds fair."

Charlene is seconds from a meltdown, which gives me immense satisfaction. She expected me to throw a fit. She thinks I should be horrified at the prospect of doing menial chores. That mopping a floor is beneath me.

Oh, she thinks she knows me.

How fun.

13

———————

GROUP INSANITY

DAY 10

IT'S incredible that Chastain hasn't mysteriously disappeared before now. Seeing four to five crazies a day, I'd need a break for sure. I do have to give the guy some credit, if not a healthy dose of respect. His schedule is brutal, but he's never seemed distracted or tired. Frustrated, yes, but I think I might bring out the worst in him.

He sees Tiffany from 7:30 to 8:30. Nix's slot, from 8:45 to 9:45, is currently empty. I torture the poor doc from 10:00 to 11:00, Preston's session is from 11:15 to 12:15, and Callum's is from 1:45 to 2:45. Kinsey's therapy is from 3:00 to 4:00, which I'll admit annoyed the crap out of me initially. I thought it indicated preferential treatment. Having seen what happens to her at night, though, the scheduling now makes sense. Clearly the woman doesn't get much quality sleep.

Breakfast hours are from 7:00 to 8:30, lunch is from 12:30 to 1:30, and dinner is from 6:00 to 7:30. I've never seen Chastain in the cafeteria, so I imagine he eats alone in his office, munching on sad sandwiches while regretting all his life choices.

Group therapy, where I'm sitting now, is from 4:00 to 5:15. An hour and fifteen minutes of forced conversation and bonding. As Chastain normally watches the sessions from his office computer, that means the man works from around 6:30 or 7 a.m. to nearly 6 p.m.

Definitely not a life I'd relish.

I pick at a hangnail on my thumb, thinking about what Tiffany told me—that Chastain is watching remotely—while our moderator Ruben gives us today's group focus.

"We're going to take a journey today from the book of somatic therapy, exploring the interaction between mind and body in the context of the past. I want each of you to think of an event that occurred in adolescence, roughly age ten to nineteen. I'll give you a few minutes."

Tiffany's hand shoots up. "Like, what type of event? Something good or bad?"

Ruben shrugs, smiling. "Whatever you think of first."

It doesn't take long for a memory to surface, one that makes me drop my chin to hide my smirk. I was a terror in high school, the queen of pranks. But I only ever targeted those who deserved it. Bullies. Snobs. Misogynistic pricks.

The rest of the group fidgets and sighs as they dredge through their formative years. When everyone finally settles, it's with expressions of embarrassment or discomfort.

"Okay, who wants to go first?"

We all trade glances, and Tiffany eventually raises her hand. Defiant tilt to her chin. Embarrassed flush on her cheeks. Not a good omen for what's about to come out of her mouth.

Ruben nods, and Tiffany fiddles with the multitude of earrings marching up the lobe of her right ear. "Okay, so, when I was twelve I got my period for the first time. I called my best friend and told her, and she said her mom told her that periods make you fat."

Kinsey and I simultaneously grunt in disgust.

"Go on," urges Ruben.

"I asked my friend what I was supposed to do. She said her mom made her drink these smoothies the entire time she's bleeding. So I got the recipe and started drinking them the next day." She pauses. "All I wanted was chocolate and pizza for a week. It was the first time I realized how much control food had in my life."

Shifting on my chair, I decide for the billionth time that I fucking hate group therapy. I look at Ruben, waiting for him to warn her not to divulge details too near to her particular diagnosis, but he merely smiles.

In a flash of understanding, I realize why Oasis has that particular rule—it makes us develop bonds and trust each other before we spill our secrets. Which given enough time is apparently a foregone conclusion.

Clever bastards.

"Great, Tiffany. Now I want you to think about what you felt during that conversation."

She licks her lips. "Hungry."

Callum laughs, but Ruben shoots him a silencing glance. "Go on."

"And, um, scared. I had cramps, too, so I was in pain."

Ruben nods sagely, glancing at each of us in turn. "I want everyone to think about this phrase: *neurons that fire together, wire together*. What this means is that when uncomfortable or traumatic moments in childhood are linked to an action—say, smoking a cigarette or eating or taking a drug—your brain wires itself to always connect those emotions to the corresponding coping mechanism."

I frown as his words drop in the dark, deep well of my memory, and wonder if this explains why I hate rain and don't associate sex with emotional intimacy. After all, it was raining when my mother and brother died and I lost my virginity to a stranger.

What a mind-fuck.

"Mia, why don't you go next?"

My head jerks up, my mind completely blank. I can't remember what memory I was going to share.

"What are you thinking about?" urges Ruben.

I cross my legs. Then uncross them and bounce my knees. "The first time I ate kielbasa sausage. I got the stomach flu that night. To this day I can't stand the sight of the stuff."

There are soft chuffs of laughter around me. Ruben's dark eyes regard me knowingly; they don't have the piercing power of Chastain's icy blues, but they're in the ballpark.

"And what were you feeling the night you jumped into the pool after-hours with Preston?"

I chew my lip. "Antsy. Hot."

"And?"

I glance at Callum, who gives me a little nod of encouragement.

I mutter, "Annoyed."

What I don't say—can't—is that I was out of my head with jealousy after seeing Nora blushing at a smiling Chastain.

Stupid, Mia. So stupid.

"Do you see any parallels in your life of similar occurrences?"

I sigh, resigned. Of course I do. I've never been accused of lacking brain cells. Every time I've done something reckless, it's because I'm feeling something I don't want to feel. I don't skydive when I'm happy.

"Yes," I answer, not elaborating.

Ruben, either sensing my unease or that he's not going to get more from me, shifts his attention to Preston.

I listen to the rest of the stories with half an ear. Preston was caught jerking off in the shower by his dad, who told him he'd never fuck a real woman. Kinsey fell on her face during her first red carpet walk as a teenager and had to deal with weeks of tabloids exploiting the images. Callum was bullied at school for being too tall and skinny.

Very different lives, same story. Shame, secrets, and humiliations that shaped our self-identities. That led us to starvation, self-harm—Preston showed me his arms—and love addiction.

My personal poison doesn't fit in any of the standard boxes, but it's nevertheless real. A corrupt seed was planted in me on that rainy night when instead of crying from loss,

I'd jumped off the roof and felt, for brief seconds, close to my mother and brother.

Escaping reality is my ultimate high—chasing that elusive feeling until I achieve my goal. Freedom from memory. From pain.

Do I want to die? No.

Do I want to live?

That's harder to answer.

By the time group therapy wraps up, a bad idea is firmly embedded in my mind.

14

SCOURING

DAY 10

At 9:00 p.m. on the dot, the head of the cleaning staff, Margaret, meets me in the Fish Tank. She's a no-nonsense woman with dark hair slicked back in a tight bun and frown lines bracketing her mouth.

Having clearly played this part in a resident's punishment before, she gives me perfunctory instructions. Where to dump and refill the water—in a back room she unlocks for me—how much time I should spend in each area—twenty minutes—and a warning—she'll be inspecting my work in the morning. She finally looks me up and down, huffs, and saunters away with the keyring at her waist jingling.

I actually don't mind the labor. It soothes the burn in my bones, though doesn't entirely suppress it. By the time one hallway is done, and the Fish Tank's floors gleam, I'm sweating, my hair curling damply against my temples.

I've saved the final hallway for last. When I've mopped all the way from the locked door at the end—presumably the security monitoring station—to Chastain's door, I stop and lean against a wall to rest. And, if I'm honest, to rethink my plan to pick the lock and find my file.

My fingers toy with a set of hairpins in my pocket. Maybe I won't be able to get in, my skills too rusty. Maybe the lock is too complex, its simplistic design merely camouflage to lure deviants like me.

The desire to know the truth of my missing months battles an equally potent desire to leave whatever memories I've buried where they are.

I stare at the door until the itch returns, driving me forward to press my ear against the wood. There's no light on inside, but I'm not stupid. And *thank fuck*, because my plan turns to smoke when I hear his voice.

"... I know it's hard, Marianne... I'm sorry... Yes, of course, I'd love to talk to him."

There's a long silence wherein I hear his muted footsteps pacing. When he speaks again, he's so close to the door that I jump, my heart leaping to my throat.

"Hey there, buddy... I miss you, too! How's school?" Whatever is said makes him chuckle. I melt into the door as the rich sound flows through the wood.

"You did? That's awesome, Vince! I can't wait to see you in action." Another laugh. "I'll get on a surfboard if you get on ice skates... Really? Okay, it's a deal... I love you, too, and miss you so much, but I'll be home soon, okay? Will you put your mom back on the phone?"

My breathing is shallow and uneven. I screw my eyes shut, searching for a loophole, something to prove that what I'm hearing isn't true. That Leo Chastain isn't married with a child. But there's no relief. Of course he named his son Vince, after his brother.

"Hey," he says softly. *Intimately.* He laughs. "Yes, I told him that. I'll have to take surfing lessons so I don't make a fool of myself in front of my kid… You think so? Well, I'd like to see you on a surfboard, too. It's a date… Okay, give my love to Vince and Celia. I'll see you guys soon. Love you, too. Bye."

My eyes are still closed, all of my attention focused on the piercing ache in my chest, when the wood beneath my ear disappears.

I yelp, grabbing for the doorframe and missing, and land hard on my knees before Chastain.

"Fuck!" he hollers. "You scared the shit out of me, Amelia! What the fuck are you doing here?"

Kill me, I beg the universe.

I'm ignored.

I hazard a look up. "Do you know any cuss words besides fuck and shit? I can teach you a few if you'd like."

He grabs my bare arm and hauls me to my feet. I yank my arm away, and there's a moment that he doesn't let go, that we're stretched apart like dancers.

He releases me with a grunt, taking a step backward. The only light on in the room is the lamp on his desk, which wreathes his hair while shadowing his expression.

"I'm going to ask you one more time: what are you doing here? Were you trying to get into my office?"

"No need to shout," I snap, moving to the side so he can see the mop and bucket. "I'm serving out my sentence for the crime of jumping into the pool."

His gaze dissects my flushed face, my damp hair, and my bare legs and sneakers.

"Where did you go today?" I ask, when what I really want to ask is, *Who were you talking to? Why don't you wear a wedding ring?*

"None of your business," he says, just like I knew he would.

I tuck a loose strand of hair behind my ear. "Okay, well, sorry for surprising you. I was just leaning against your door taking a break. No harm no foul."

My legs are half-numb as I move to collect the mop bucket. I make it two steps before his voice freezes me.

"Amelia. Do you remember what I told you about lying?"

I turn around slowly. It takes every ounce of control I have to merely raise my eyebrows. "That I shouldn't bother because you're a better liar than I am?"

His frame fills the doorway, his face and eyes becoming clear in the hallway's lights. I can't decipher his expression, but his gaze is unnervingly intent.

This man. *This fucking man.* Why does he have to be so goddamn beautiful?

"I still haven't forgiven you for your assumptions about Kinsey and myself."

I blink in surprise. "Okay."

Still with his eyes trained on mine, he asks, "Is your fascination with me due to the fact you can't read me? That you can't find any weaknesses to exploit?"

I laugh to disguise my spiking blood pressure. "Good Lord, are you high?"

"Answer the question, Amelia."

I glance down the hallway. *Where the fuck is a bystander when you need one?*

I'm unravelling, on shifting earth. He's too close to the truth. A truth I haven't even admitted to myself yet.

"I'm not comfortable with this conversation," I say stiffly.

"I'm not comfortable with *you*," he snaps, then goes rigid, mouth thinned and jaw clenched.

My eyes fly to his face. "What? What the hell does that mean?"

"Nothing."

Anger is a hot, bright blessing, soothing away the rough edges of my emotions. I point a shaking finger at his chest. "Fuck that. Fuck you. I haven't done anything to you. And trust me, there are about a million things I want—and could—do to you!"

"Like what?" he bites out.

I step right up to him, my face tilted just inches from his and my accusing finger wedged between us. "I want to ruin your fucking life!"

His gaze flies over my face. "Why?" he asks mutedly, as though he really wants to know.

Because I want you.

Because I trust you.

Because you see *me.*

I take a shaky step back, then another, until a safe three feet separate us. Only then do I notice his hands clenched at his sides. The rapid rise and fall of his chest.

Finally, I confront his eyes. And in them, my worst nightmare is confirmed. No longer ice, but fire—desire.

"You don't wear a wedding ring!" I blurt.

He frowns. "I'm not married." Then his expression clears. "You were listening at the door."

"Yes, dumbass," I say belligerently.

He shakes his head. When he looks at me again the fire is gone, and he's once again the cool and collected Dr. Chastain.

"This conversation is over. My personal life is none of your business, nor will it ever be. Please refrain in the future from eavesdropping on my private conversations."

The words are a bucket of cold water on my face and heart. *Nor will it ever be.* I can't decide whether his proclamation makes me hate him or respect him even more.

I nod rigidly. "Good night, Dr. Chastain."

With a final, searing glance, he kicks the door closed between us.

15

HERE COMES THE GROUND
DAY 11

Nineteen more days. Four hundred and fifty-six more hours. Seventeen sessions of therapy to go. Eleven of them with Dr. Chastain.

For the first time since arriving at Oasis, I'm not sure I'm going to make it the full thirty days. I can't shake a feeling of impending doom. It lurks around me, hiding just outside my peripheral vision. Biding its time before unleashing disaster.

I can no longer clearly envision my life in the real world, though I suppose I wasn't really living, merely sustaining the impression of life. I had fun in college, I think. Wild days bled into wilder nights. Concerts and festivals. Traveling in vans clouded with pot smoke. Dying my hair blue and piercing my navel.

Drifting... Jameson my only anchor in the world.

Empty inside.

Alone.

After college, I remember holding two or three odd jobs at a time to avoid asking my father or Jameson for money. Dingy apartments with peeling paint on the cabinetry. Then the craftsman Kevin and I had shared, before cheating and record-burning. After, homeless and crashing in Jameson's spare bedroom. Feeling sick all the time, both physically and emotionally. Watching reruns of *Battlestar Galactica* and eating frozen waffles by the box.

A human train wreck.

What happened to me?

"Can you share with me the last memory you have prior to March 3, 2016?"

I pick at the frayed edges of my shorts, not looking up. Avoiding his X-ray eyes. Memory comes begrudgingly. Polluted. Distorted. Dug with pain from unyielding ground.

"I woke up at Jameson's. But I... I don't know why I was there. I think I had my own apartment by then—it had been a few months since the breakup. I remember Jameson was getting ready for work. He made me toast. It had lots of nuts and too much butter. The smell made me sick."

Pen scratches paper. "You mentioned you'd been feeling sick after leaving Kevin. Did you ever see a doctor?"

"No. It wasn't anything, really. Dizziness. Fatigue." I shrug. "Just... life catching up, I guess."

There's a long beat of silence.

"You look tired, Amelia. Did you sleep all right?"

I'm so fogged, I can't even muster anger. Of course I'm tired. Our confrontation last night is surreal in the light of day, but I hadn't fallen asleep until four in the morning.

I no longer know if the heat I saw in his eyes was real or not. For the last thirty minutes, there's been no sign of it. Not that I'm looking—I haven't looked at him once.

"More bad dreams," I answer noncommittally.

"Anything specific?"

I massage my temples. "Swimming in the middle of the ocean. Feeling tired, about to give up. In another one I was stranded on the side of a cliff with no rope. I must have been thrashing around or something, because my muscles were sore this morning. Oh, and eating an ice cream cone, only every time I tried to taste it, the single scoop fell into a dirty sidewalk gutter."

"What's your favorite ice cream?"

I blink, my eyes flickering up. "What does that have to do with anything?"

"Just answer the question."

"Pistachio gelato."

Expensive fabric rustles as he shifts in his chair. "When was the last time you had it?"

I shrug. "I don't know. A couple of years, maybe."

"Why so long? Why deny yourself something you love?"

"I'm watching my figure," I snap, though without heat. "Jesus, Doc, where is this conversation going?"

Chastain sighs. "All right. Let's refocus. Tell me a little more about Kevin. How did you two meet?"

I groan. "This guy again?"

"Humor me."

I inspect my fingernails, bare of polish and short. "He plays recreational ice hockey with my brother. Jameson was always inviting me to come watch their games. I always had excuses because who wants to watch a bunch of grown men reliving their college years?"

Chastain makes a sound of amusement. "Go on."

"Anyway, I was bored one Sunday night and went."

"Do you have a weakness for hockey players?" he asks dryly.

I look up, confused and startled, then remember telling him about Kyle, the Canadian hockey player I'd had a brief affair with.

A wan smile cracks my lips. "I guess. Something about the aggression. And those big shoulder pads."

Chastain's eyes flare with laughter. "So you met Kevin after the game?"

"Yes. He asked me out. I said no."

"You said no?"

I narrow my eyes. "Is there an echo in here?"

He smiles slightly, conceding with a nod. "So I'll assume he got your number, probably from Jameson." At my nod, he continues, "And after going on a date with him, you refused his calls for a few weeks before finally answering."

I look away, ignoring the disquiet I feel at how well he has me pegged. Waving a hand nonchalantly, I motion for him to continue.

"You gave him another shot. He wooed you. Chased you. You enjoyed being the object of his obsession. Were you planning on hurting him?"

"Initially," I admit quietly. "But he… we… everything about it was so normal, you know? I got used to it. Used to how he treated me."

"Did you stop skydiving? Base jumping? Pushing your body to limits?"

"Yes," I whisper.

"Did you talk about starting a family?"

I screw my eyes shut. "Yes."

"How did you feel about that?"

"Excited." The word comes out half-strangled.

Chastain is silent for so long, I open my eyes to see if he's still there. He is—watching me with patient, surprisingly kind eyes.

"Had you stopped using birth control?"

The question rocks me back in my chair. Memories clamor for attention, creating a collage of confusion in my mind. Leaving a drugstore with a brown bag. Stopping by Kevin's favorite espresso bar to grab his preferred drink and a couple of pastries.

Walking through the house with his drink, looking for him. Hearing the sounds no woman wants to hear. From our bedroom. In our bed. Running for the nearest bathroom. Vomiting up the bagel I'd had for breakfast.

Darkness falls through me, snaking tendrils that dim my vision.

"Oh, Jesus," I whisper. "Oh, God, no. No."

"I think it's time, Amelia."

His voice resonates oddly. My skin flutters, panic skating along my nerves.

"I don't... don't remember."

"Yes, you do. You're safe here. You're with me."

With me.

Inside me.

Everything explodes. My mind. My heart. My life. I rock forward, clutching my head with my fingers.

"I was... I..."

"Yes," he says gently. "You were pregnant."

16

RUN RUN RUN
DAY 11 - 12

I DON'T FEEL the scrape of spiny desert brush on my ankles and calves. I don't feel the burn in my muscles, working beyond the limits of their endurance. I don't hear the footsteps racing after me, the voice calling my name.

What stops me isn't my protesting limbs, my wildly thrumming pulse, or the shoe I lost somewhere along the way. Not my screaming, gasping lungs. My burning, sand-scoured eyes.

Not my breaking heart.

It's the chain-link fence around Oasis that brings me to an abrupt and painful halt.

My fingers curl around metal links and my knees give out. I taste blood where I bit through my lip on impact.

"Amelia!" An anguished, masculine yell.

Sand flies up behind me as he skids to a stop. I feel the vibration of his knees hitting the earth. Fingers curl around my shoulders.

"It's okay," he says between panting breaths. "I've got you."

The darkness funnels to dangerous density, spinning toward its target with poisoned tip. My body follows, a puppet to the primal demand. I register the blue of his eyes, tortured and red from the run. His handsome, flushed face. The perfect hair no longer perfect but sticking in all directions. The swipe of his tongue across a full lower lip.

I lunge forward and kiss him. Hard enough that I feel the press of his teeth, the warm give of his dry lips. He gasps. I take advantage, driving forward, dipping my tongue into his mouth. Tasting him harshly, completely. Drinking him down.

It's seconds. A lifetime. Then his hands on my shoulders wrench me back.

"No," he says breathlessly.

Another level of me breaks.

I swing both arms, kick my legs, landing blows wherever I can reach as hard as I can. I'm screaming.

"Liar! Fucking liar! Oh God, oh God. I wrote *Daddy* on his cup. I hadn't even taken the test yet, but I knew. Goddammit!"

Chastain finally subdues me by hogtying me with his arms and legs. I'm flooded with his scent. Hot, clean skin. The tantalizing musk of sweat.

"Let it go, Amelia. Let it out."

I'm tumbling.

Freefall.

No parachute.

I was on my way to my favorite gelateria, a couple of

freeway exits away from Jameson's. The night before, he'd joked I should name the baby Gelato or Gelata because I couldn't go a day without the stuff.

I was in a good mood. Singing along to a popular song on the radio. The windows were down, the sun shining.

Brake lights. A chorus of honks. Screeching tires. Time slowing to a crawl. A white wall swinging across the highway several cars ahead of me.

Nowhere to turn. Slamming on the brakes while cranking the steering wheel as hard as I could to the left. Spinning.

Drifting.

Impact.

Pain. Both indistinct and sharp.

"The only reason you're alive today is because you turned," Chastain says into my ringing ear. "That split-second decision caused you to hit the guardrail instead of the semi head-on."

"I should have died." My voice is scratchy from abuse. Broken, just like me.

"If you should have died, you would have. But you didn't. You're here. And you're safe."

I laugh. A horrible, wretched sound. Leaning back—slowly, so he doesn't think I'm going to attack him again—I find his eyes with mine.

"Take it back, Leo."

He shakes his head, tears glistening in his eyes. Fire melting ice. "I'm so sorry, but I can't."

This time the darkness is gentle, a sweep of silken feathers. Calm filters through me. And resolve.

"Are we done for the day?" I ask blankly.

He frowns concernedly. "Amelia—"

"I said, are we done for the day?"

He hesitates, torn, then nods and releases me. I reach for the fence and pull myself up, not feeling the bite of sharp metal links. When I'm standing, I look down at the man on his knees before me.

"Congratulations, Dr. Chastain. You've won."

His brows pinch together. "Please, Amelia—"

I cut him off. "Eleven days until you leave. Eight more days of therapy. Tomorrow we can talk about my stay in the hospital and what happened there. Then we can spend a few days discussing all the reasons why I shouldn't blame myself. And finally, we'll end on an uplifting note. The life I can rebuild when I get out of here." I tilt my head. "Isn't that your agenda?"

He reaches for me, but I sidestep. His hand falls and he looks down.

As I begin the long trek back to the facility, I call over my shoulder, "Don't forget to make that appointment for surfing lessons. And for fuck's sake, man up and ask the mother of your child to marry you."

FUNNY THING, the power of the mind to protect itself. Even funnier—the machinations of the heart. Between those two forces, how and where can the Self exist?

My roommate in college was a meditation junkie, always going to retreats in the mountains and listening to podcasts from gurus around the world. I went to a retreat with her once at one of those campsites for the rich, with cabins and a full-service spa and a community hall for listening to lectures from highly paid speakers.

Only one memory sticks out from that weekend, a few words spoken by a guest speaker. A Tibetan Buddhist, I remember his eyes most of all. Fathomless, dark. A calm lake under moonlight.

After the lecture, I stood in line with fifty others to thank him. When it was my turn, I asked, "Where do I find myself?"

He smiled and said, "Wherever you're not looking."

At the time, the answer annoyed me. Why did spiritual people always have to be so fucking vague, smiling like they have a secret they're not willing to share?

I don't have any answers now, even less than I had before. But at least I finally understand what he meant. Because now, right now—as I lie in the dirt behind my cabin watching the stars, as my mind sews itself back together—I'm not looking. I'm nothing.

And I can feel it. What the Buddhist called No-Self. The acknowledgement that if all things change, and change is a constant, it follows that there can be no permanent, unchanging Self.

I understand.

I am changed.

IT HITS me at 4:00 a.m. when I'm curled on my side in bed. My arms, tucked over my stomach, begin to shake. Then my legs, my shoulders. A soul-quake, tectonic plates of Self ripping apart.

I'm only dimly aware of Tiffany and Kinsey on the bed with me, holding me between them and murmuring words of comfort. I hear Callum's voice, too, threaded with worry.

What's happening to her?

Should we get the doc?

What if she's having a seizure?

"It's not a seizure," snaps Kinsey. There's a gravity in her voice I've never heard. "She's grieving."

Grieving.

Such a small word. Such a commonplace emotion. We grieve everything, don't we? Death. Time's passage. The loss of an animal or person. The end of a favorite TV drama.

But grief is a process. There are stages and adjustments and gradual acceptance. I robbed myself of the natural cycle. The rhythmic wave of loss—the pound, the push, and finally the soothing caress—is instead a tsunami blotting out the sky, tearing apart everything in its path. I can't see anything; I feel everything.

Scars rip open, and there, in the deepest part of my psyche, I see them. My mother and brother. Spaghetti crowning Phillip's head because it was more fun to play with it than eat it. My mom's laughter, bright and sunny, floating across the backyard as Jameson and I tried to teach Phillip how to do a somersault. A thousand moments, a thousand memories.

Flashing lights.

Caskets.
My father's hoarse cry.
Jameson's sobs.
And now mine.
The tsunami passes, taking parts of me with it.

17

THE LABYRINTH
DAY 12

I DON'T KNOW whether Dr. Chastain expects me to show up to therapy today, but I do. I'm running on hate for the world and an hour's worth of shitty sleep, but I have to see him. Need to see him.

I shuffle into his office and fall into my chair. "Morning, Doc."

Concerned blue eyes scan my face. "If you want to take today off—"

"Nope, I'm good," I say quickly.

I'm not good and probably look worse. Wrinkled pajama pants, a threadbare T-shirt and bedhead to the max. I can only imagine the dark circles under my eyes since I didn't bother with a mirror.

When Chastain doesn't immediately speak, I ask, "What's on the agenda today? More revelations? Hmm, let me guess—this whole place is really a smokescreen for a government-funded social experiment to determine..." I frown. "Ah, forget it, I can't think of anything. My head hurts."

Chastain shifts, adjusting his glasses. "Would you like to go for a walk?"

I tilt my head, considering. "Interesting tactic, Doc. I like it. Change of scenery to combat my present, negative associations with this office."

He's silent. Watching me. Expression as gentle as I've seen it, without any expectations for my behavior. Today, I can do or say anything I want and he'll let me. Well... *almost* anything. If I told him all the things I want to do to him, how I burn with the need for him to make me forget, he'd probably have me sedated.

I drag myself to my feet. "Okay, let's go. But I need to change."

Chastain stands as well, his gaze lowering to my feet. "I didn't take you for a fuzzy-slipper kind of woman."

I snort. "Every woman is a fuzzy-slipper kind of woman."

Infinitesimal curve of lips. "Duly noted. After you, Amelia."

We walk side by side to my cabin, not speaking. Chastain waits outside as I trade pajama pants for cut-off shorts and slippers for sneakers. After tugging a baseball hat onto my head and grabbing sunglasses, I join him on the stoop.

"Do you want to change, too?" I ask skeptically, eyeing his dark slacks, Italian loafers, and pristine white dress shirt.

He glances at me. "I'll be fine." He nods toward the labyrinth. "Have you tried it yet?"

I wrinkle my nose. "Walking in circles, going nowhere? Yeah, I'm pretty well versed in that practice."

He smiles softly. "I'll take that as a no. Come on."

At the entrance to the labyrinth, he shocks the hell out of me by taking my hand. His grip is warm and dry; mine, I'm sure, is the opposite. In fact, I'm suddenly cold and clammy everywhere.

"I don't think—"

"Labyrinths have been constructed and used since ancient times," he says, tugging me forward. Since not following means releasing his hand, I let him guide me through the entrance. A brief squeeze of my fingers conveys his approval.

As our footsteps find a matching rhythm, he continues, "They're often confused with mazes, but a labyrinth is different. There is only one path—the one leading in is the same one that leads out. The inherent purpose of a labyrinth is to mirror and enhance a journey inward to the deepest parts of ourselves. Once there, we reflect, then travel outward with greater understanding of who we are."

"Sounds like New Age bullshit," I quip, but I'm nevertheless seduced by his deep, calm voice and the steady press of his palm on mine.

The labyrinth itself isn't much to look at, basically a bunch of dirt molded into low borders around the curving path. In the center, there's a single stone bench shaded by a massive Joshua tree. In spite of myself, the farther we walk the calmer I feel. Our progress inward slowly becomes less about the destination.

"You feel it," he says softly. "Your breathing is deeper and your shoulders have relaxed."

I angle a surprised glance at his profile, the small smile on his lips. Because I'm an ornery bitch, I say, "You know that exercise lowers blood pressure and produces endorphins, right?"

His smile only grows. "Walking a labyrinth is symbolic. Yes, your body is responding to fresh air and exercise, but your mind is responding as well. It's the mind that travels inward more so than the body." Blue eyes flash to my face. "If you can, describe to me what you're feeling right now."

Unable to summon a pithy response, I look down at the path under our feet. Small pebbles crunch under our shoes, and a delicate breeze combats the pressing heat of the sun. We're alone out here. Alone in the world but together. His hand no longer feels separate from mine but like an extension of my body.

"I feel…" I swallow hard. "Insulated. Like there's a fog protecting me from how broken my heart is. It's still there, this pounding ache in my chest, but I'm not overwhelmed by it."

"Good."

"All that can be explained by how little sleep I got last night," I grumble.

"Maybe, but does it matter? Why not simply embrace the feeling? You're safe here, Amelia. There's no judgement, no need for pretenses. Moving inward, *toward* the pain, might seem counterintuitive, but when we do we find that even the deepest grief holds a kernel of light. There is always the possibility of healing. Always."

We finally reach the center. Chastain leads me to the bench and we sit in the shade, unspeaking for long minutes. At length, he asks, "How do you feel now?"

"Like I could sit here for the rest of my life," I say honestly.

He smiles, his gaze fixed in the distance. Our still joined hands rest on my bare knee. He hasn't tried to release me and even if he did, I'm not sure I'd let him. His presence is the only force keeping me afloat.

"Will you tell me a secret?" I ask, the words escaping of their own volition.

Silence reigns for so long I almost take back the request.

"I often think about what my brother would be like today if he were alive. If he'd gotten the help he needed. Sometimes, I have dreams about him so vivid that when I wake up, for a few minutes I think he's still here."

The words filter through me like new snowfall, soft and delicate. "Another," I whisper.

"Most days, I have no idea what to say to you. None of my usual techniques have worked, which has been incredibly difficult for me to adjust to. I've never treated someone so completely impermeable and at the same time so transparent. And I'm deeply afraid it was too soon for you to remember. That I've caused you irreparable harm."

I lick my lips and taste the first wave of silent, salty tears. "If it were a girl, I was going to name her Julia, after my mother. A boy would have been Jackson. I never told Jameson because I... I had this feeling. This fear. I can't explain it. Maybe it's something all women feel when they have life inside them—this vague dread that something bad is right around the corner. I don't know. But now, I wonder if that feeling was because I knew deep down I didn't deserve something so amazing in my life. That it was going to be taken away."

The tears come harder. Silent heaves convulsing my torso. Chastain shifts, his fingers leaving mine, but before I can feel the loss, his arms come around me. I tuck my head beneath his chin and melt into him. The only safe place in my world.

"I'm sorry, Amelia," he murmurs. "I'm so very, very sorry. But you're wrong. What happened was a terrible accident. You deserved that child, just as you deserve every happiness life has to offer. Someday, you'll have it. I promise."

"I don't believe you," I rasp.

"You will."

18

____

COOL WATERS

DAY 15

Two weeks after the accident, I woke up in the hospital. My multiple injuries on their own hadn't been life-threatening, but I'd been kept heavily sedated until then. Apparently whenever they'd roused me before, I'd been extremely confused, easily agitated—read: prone to violence—and in general a pain in the ass.

When I was lucid and mellow for a solid twenty-four hours, a kind-faced grief counselor told me the news of my miscarriage. Irreparable trauma. No heartbeat.

I told her I had no idea what she was talking about—I hadn't been pregnant.

Afterward, Jameson came in and tried again to tell me what happened. He was crying. Sobbing really. So sorry for me because he knew how much I wanted the baby, even if it was douchebag Kevin's. He wished he'd bought me extra gelato the night before the accident, when I'd made him run out to appease my craving. He felt responsible.

Which was silly—I'd never been pregnant.

122

There were times during my sojourn in the hospital that I doubted my sanity. The grief counsellor kept coming back. Every day, she'd sit quietly beside my bed. Every day, she'd tell me she was there to listen if I wanted to talk.

If it hadn't been such a deranged proposition, I might have decided I was the victim of an elaborate prank. Except broken bones aren't funny. Neither is being told you miscarried your baby at eleven weeks.

I really didn't remember.

When I was released, Jameson took me back to his condo. Now, I have a vague recollection of a bottle of pain pills. I took a lot of them. Too many. Mainly because I felt like I was dreaming and needed to wake up. Because everyone believed the same lie. I was sick of being treated like porcelain and I needed an out. Escape from this bad drama.

Oops.

"A suicide attempt isn't an *oops*," says Leo softly.

Leo.

I can't think of him as Chastain anymore. Not since losing myself and finding myself and kissing him. He tasted like cool water on hot rocks. Burning stars in a freezing firmament. I can't get the taste of him out of my head. Know I won't—not for a long, long time.

Nor will I forget the experience in the labyrinth yesterday. The exchange of secrets, the long walk into them and into him. My tears on his shirt and the imprint of his hand in mine. The long walk out, the pure exhaustion of having purged poison from a deep wound.

I slept for fourteen hours straight.

There's no sign today of the uncertainty he revealed about my treatment. We're back to business. At least on his end.

When I don't answer his leading statement, he eventually asks, "What do you remember next?"

I sigh. "You."

He nods. "Do you remember where you were?"

"UCLA. Psychiatric Unit."

Leo waits for me to continue, but I don't. I know now why I felt an inexplicable bond between us. Not a magical connection or simply attraction, after all, but buried memory.

We have a history, Leo and I. He was the Psychiatric Fellow in charge of my case at UCLA. Diagnosed me within hours. Discharged me three days later. Met with Jameson and my father and explained what was happening. That they shouldn't push me to remember. That I needed support and normalcy. That the mind had a way of healing itself.

Or, in my case, breaking itself.

"Though it's not unheard of for a patient to have both retrograde and anterograde amnesia post-trauma, your situation was unique. In most cases, memory of events prior to the trauma come back, while those after the trauma rarely do."

I understand what he's getting at even though I don't want to. "So you think I had some crazy form of denial, not amnesia."

"Yes, in a sense. The phenomenon is called confabulation. The accident triggered an exaggerated stress response.

Coupled with your head injury, it's likely your memory retrieval was blocked by an adaptive response to avoid stress."

"I love it when you talk smart to me."

His lips quirk. A tiny twitch. I hate that the sight of it warms the cold place inside me. *Hate hate hate* how his effect on me keeps growing day by day.

"You lied to me," I say mildly, staring out the window behind his desk.

"You weren't ready to hear the truth."

"Yeah, yeah." I pause, chewing my lip. "I still don't understand why I blacked *you* out, too."

He shrugs. "The mind is a mysterious domain. It could be because you associated me with the trauma of taking the pain pills."

I frown and shift in my chair.

"It makes you uncomfortable thinking about the attempt, doesn't it?"

"Well, yes," I snap. "I really didn't want to die. I didn't think of it like that. I just wanted to wake up. I really thought that was the solution. Shit… I sound crazy."

"You shouldn't have been discharged from the hospital," he says gravely. "I'm sorry you weren't properly diagnosed, Amelia."

I shake my head. "It's not their fault. I probably looked and sounded normal. I'm good at hiding the crazy."

"You're not crazy," he says, then pauses. "Well, maybe ten percent or so."

I glance sharply at him. His eyes twinkle at me. *Fuck.* A smile teases my lips, the first genuine one in days.

His eyebrows lift. "Now that that's out of the way, let's talk about why the accident wasn't your fault, shall we?"

I groan.

Then I laugh.

Smartass.

"DID YOU HEAR?" asks Kinsey.

"Hear what?"

She glances over her shoulder, footsteps never faltering on the path of the labyrinth. We've been at it for an hour. I'm counting the seconds until she has to leave for her three o'clock therapy session.

"We're getting new blood today. They're intaking him right now. Apparently he's a real mess."

"Great."

She stops and I almost career into her back. "You could at least *try* to sound excited."

My eyebrows shoot up. "Why should I be excited? Whoever he is, he's probably in a world of pain. None of us want to be here—you do realize that, right?"

She glares. "If I didn't like you so much, I'd think you're a bitch."

"Ditto."

Kinsey laughs and gives me an impromptu hug. She's a lot stronger than she looks, and I wheeze for air until she releases me. It's almost painful to admit, but I actually do like her. She's unabashedly… Kinsey. I still don't know why exactly she's here; I'm the last person who would try to pry it out of her, which is probably why she won't leave me alone.

"Oh! Gotta go! I want to grab a coffee before my alone time with Dr. Hotness." With a giggle, she scurries past me in her espadrille wedges that likely cost more than I made in wages last year.

Relieved to have an excuse to get out of the sun, I head toward my cabin. I veer aside at the last second when I see Callum and Preston playing checkers on the small stoop next door.

Standing over them, I put my hands on my hips. "Seriously, you two? You're stalking the new guy, aren't you?"

Preston grins sheepishly. Callum frowns at the checkerboard. "You bastard, you're going to win again."

Preston laughs. "I write complex computer code for a living. Did you think I wouldn't kick your ass at checkers?"

Callum grunts. "I figured I'd at least have a chance."

I kick Callum's boot and he snorts, then swings an arm out, grabbing my legs. I topple, screeching, but moments later end up neatly deposited beside him.

"Shhh," he hisses. "Here he comes."

I turn and see Leo and Ruth, the other nurse, escorting a man out of the Fish Tank. Longish brown hair hangs around his downturned face, concealing his features. He's almost as tall as Leo and walks with the confident gait of a mature man. One who knows how to swagger without looking like he's trying.

"Not a model," whispers Callum.

Judging by the tattoos covering most of the skin of his arms, I have to agree.

"Why does it matter who he is?" I gripe, though I'll admit, I'm intrigued.

My gaze veers to Leo, his profile teasing me as he speaks softly to the man. The group passes the meditation garden, making their way around the labyrinth, and finally moves onto the path leading directly past us.

"Definitely a musician," murmurs Preston when they're about ten feet away.

Like he heard the words, the man looks up. Dark eyes land on Preston, snap to Callum, then zero in on me. They widen, then narrow.

My ribs squeeze my next breath.

"Uh-oh," I whisper.

"Mia?" he barks.

"What the fuck?" whispers Callum, his arm tightening around me. "You know this guy?"

I'm caught in the dark, angry stare, frozen with my eyes blown wide. Shame prickles down my spine.

"Um, yeah," I whisper. "His name is Declan Foster. We were... friends in college."

Leo saves the day, his hold on Declan's tattooed arm firming as he guides Oasis' newest addition past us and into the next cabin. Icy blue eyes spear mine, then disappear.

When the door closes with a thump, Callum sighs. "It's never dull with you around, Goldie."

"Har har." I turn my head to meet his stare; something in my expression kills his humor. "Did the universe put a target on the back of my head or something? *Time's up, Mia, here comes Karma!*"

Preston's soft, slightly awed voice interjects, "I remember who he is now. The guitarist of Amy Falls." His eyes find mine over Callum's shoulder. "Amy… Amelia…"

I wince. "It's a coincidence."

It has to be. Who names their band after someone they dated—in the loosest sense—for three weeks? Ridiculous.

"Ridiculous," I say aloud, just to confirm it.

The majority of those three weeks were spent in a drug-fueled sex fest. Ten years later, I remember only the haziest details. Sure, I've thought about him occasionally over the years. Mainly when I heard one of his songs on the radio.

"Whatever happened, he's got a grudge," Callum mutters.

"We were kids," I retort, but it only sounds like I'm trying to convince myself.

Callum gives me a squeeze. "At least you've only got two weeks left."

Two weeks is a long goddamn time.

19

SMOKESCREENS

DAY 16

"Do we have to talk about it?"

"Yes, Amelia. It's important."

My knee starts to bounce. I press my hand into the bare skin, driving my heel to the floor. "Fine. It hurts, Doc. It's a cornucopia of fucked-up feelings. I want to cry and never stop, and at the same time I feel like I don't deserve to cry."

"Why's that?"

I find his eyes. They anchor me; allow me to take a deep breath. Despite the chaos in my mind and heart, I do trust him. I might be a little in love with him, but I've come to terms with it. I'm likely not his first patient, or the last, to have these confusing feelings.

"I made myself forget the baby to avoid the pain of losing…" I swallow thickly, "him or her. I feel guilty, like I gave up my right to mourn. It's been almost two years."

"Why do you think time matters?"

"It matters."

"What if I told you the pain of my brother's death is still

very much real for me? That you will always mourn, and miss, your mother and brother?"

My shoulders tense. "I'd probably say it's time to jump out of an airplane."

"Do you want to jump out of an airplane?"

I sigh. "Leo, come on. Just because you cracked the nut that is my head doesn't mean I'm a completely different person. Ten percent crazy still, remember?"

He doesn't smile. "Who said I wanted you to be different?"

The dim bulb in my heart flickers, then dies on his next question.

"Did Declan Foster want you to be different?"

My knee stops bouncing. "I figured we had another day or two before he came up," I mutter.

He pauses, removing his glasses. I can't believe he's never realized that pulling off his glasses is his tell. Almost, I want to let him know. Maybe I'll divulge the intel on our last day, when I don't have to see him ever again.

The thought hurts, throbbing dully somewhere in the vicinity of my dead heart.

"It's relevant now," he says with a snap to his voice. "The monitors caught him coming out of your cabin in the middle of the night."

"Doc, are you jealous?" I ask, forcing levity.

Frigid eyes narrow. "Do I really need to tell you how disruptive a sexual relationship can be to rehabilitation—both yours and Declan's?"

A familiar excitement courses through my veins. This is a game I know how to play, one that will hopefully take my mind off my own baggage for a little while. Leo thinks he doesn't have any weaknesses for me to exploit? Bullshit. His weakness is that he *cares*.

I shrug, smiling blandly. "What's the harm in letting off a little steam? Declan isn't like Callum. Sex won't hurt him."

Leo sits utterly still, lips in a thin line. Finally, he releases a slow breath. The spark in his eyes fades. His shoulders relax.

Dammit.

I slump in my chair, defeated. "You're a fucking fortress, Doc," I grumble.

He taps his lower lip with his pen, eyeing me. "I know you didn't have sex, Amelia."

I huff. "No, you don't."

"Declan told me this morning what happened. That he confronted you about what you did."

Jerk.

Yeah, it hadn't been pretty. The man carried a serious grudge about me disappearing after our fling. And disappear I had—giving him a fake number and skipping town. I'd just graduated and nothing was keeping me in the Bay Area anymore. But if our middle-of-the-night reunion was any indication, Declan and I have about as much potential as Kinsey's failed acting career.

We've both been through a lot in the last decade, and the sex-crazed maniacs we were in our early twenties are dead and buried—or at least whatever chemistry we had certainly is. He didn't tell me why he's in the Funny Farm except for *a break from everyone*. The yellow tint to the whites of his eyes nevertheless points to an addiction to drinks of the adult variety. He certainly wouldn't be the first rock star to cross the line from parties to dependence.

After he tore me a new one for disappearing on him all those years ago and I apologized, he cooled off enough to thank me for inspiring several songs. I didn't bother asking what they were about—not hard to guess they weren't the flattering kind.

All in all, he was in my cabin for maybe a half hour. Once the past was out of the way, it became quickly apparent we had nothing to talk about.

I pinch the bridge of my nose, feeling a headache coming on. "I use people. You know this. I know this. What do you want me to say?"

"You avoid emotional intimacy. Why?"

My jaw clenches. "Oh, I don't know… lack of examples in my life of healthy adult relationships. Romance books that offer unrealistic ideals. The media. My dad jumping in the sack with an endless stream of bimbos after Mom. Losing my virginity to a nobody, being cheated on, et cetera." I jerk forward, jabbing a finger in his direction. "Or maybe I'm just a liberated woman. Why does sex have to be some big, emotional investment? Maybe you're living in the wrong century, Doc. Slut-shaming is passé."

Leo regards me a long moment with something akin to tenderness in his eyes. Or maybe it's pity.

"Have you ever had sex with someone you love, Amelia?"

"Yes. It was appropriately mind-shattering. Emotionally orgasmic."

He keeps staring, waiting.

I glare back.

Hooking the pen to his pad of paper, he drops both to the floor. The glasses follow, though more gently.

"Can I tell you a story?" he asks softly.

Bemused by the abrupt shift, I nod. When he starts talking, though, I immediately wish I could retract my assent.

"When I was in graduate school, there was a woman in one of my classes. Beautiful and bright. She smiled all the time and every day had a different flower in her hair. I finally found the courage to ask her on a date. We fell in love. It was the best year and a half of my life until she dumped me."

I blink. "*She* dumped *you*?"

He smiles wryly. "As I'm sure you realize by now, I'm not the most flexible or easygoing man. She was a self-professed bohemian. She'd decided to drop out of grad school and pursue a longtime passion for sculpting. And women. I was devastated."

I shake my head, dumbfounded. "Wait—*women*? Holy shit, that's some serious drama."

He just smiles. "As far as breakups go, ours was amicable. How was I supposed to fault her for following her dreams? Or for that matter, realizing she preferred having long-term relationships with women?"

I wince. "Ouch."

"Yes, well, I didn't hear from her for close to a year. And when I did..." He falls silent, eyelashes dropping to shadow his eyes. "It was her partner, Celia, who made Marianne call me."

Celia... Marianne...

I shoot straight in my chair. "She had your kid? Vince?"

Leo nods.

"She was pregnant when you broke up and didn't tell you? That's..." I pause, considering. As far as I know, Kevin still doesn't have a clue I was pregnant with his child, however briefly. Before the accident, I was even seriously considering how I could prevent him from ever knowing.

I finally admit, "I guess I can't throw stones, can I?"

Leo regards me knowingly. "Ask me if I regret having my heart torn out by Marianne. If I regret one moment of that relationship."

"I get it," I say sourly. "You don't regret opening yourself up to love and you scored an awesome kid out of it. Good on you, Doc. You're emotionally stable. I bet you love after-sex cuddling and giving your lady foot massages, too."

"Amelia," he says chidingly. "My point—as you know— is that I healed. Having my heart broken was the worst pain I'd experienced since losing my brother. But I healed. You can heal, too."

I can't help but chirp, "Are you offering to heal me?"

I almost miss it. But I don't. The heated glimmer in his eyes. The sharp rise of his chest. The brief glance at my mouth.

I really don't know why I keep torturing myself. Or him. Or maybe I do—he's my distraction. A fantasy rarely entertained and certainly unrealistic. Stability. Family. Love.

Leo glances at his watch.

I speak before he can. "Time's up."

Nodding, he stands. I follow, my arm brushing the sleeve of his suit jacket as I pass him. My skin tingles at the intersection of our two worlds.

Worlds that will never fully overlap.

"Amelia."

I stop with my hand on the doorknob. "Yes?"

"There's nothing scarier in the world than intimacy. If you really want to conquer fear, show someone all of yourself."

I leave without answering.

I already have.

20

BASOPHOBIA

DAY 18

FRIDAY AFTERNOON IN GROUP, we're told there's going to be a special, surprise event that evening. Frank excitedly informs us it's a tradition held every year on August 18. Why the specific date? Why, it's Dr. Leo Chastain's birthday. And what are we doing, you wonder? We're going *camping*.

Woo-freaking-hoo!

Kinsey is horrified, Callum is stoked, Declan and Preston are indifferent. Tiffany asks for specifics like she's plotting a bank robbery. I'm… *eh*. I actually enjoy camping, and given the money this place generates, I doubt we'll be sleeping in tumbleweeds.

Maybe if I didn't think there'd be chaperones up our asses, I'd enjoy the idea a bit more. Roasting marshmallows around a campfire with Charlene the Shark monitoring our every word doesn't sound anything like a good time, even if Chastain is there sans suit, looking all sexy and outdoorsy.

"There's a short hike, about three miles, to the campsite," Frank continues, enthusiasm undimmed by our collective lack of it. "You'll need to pack necessities for two nights in the wilderness. Prepare for high nineties during the day and potentially mid-fifties at night."

"Hold up," snaps Kinsey. "You didn't say anything about *two* nights."

Frank is momentarily baffled. "I didn't? My fault, then. It's a weekend event. We'll hike back Sunday."

"Kill me," mutters Tiffany.

Frank shows the first signs of irritation. "This is a privilege, and every year the residents have a great time. Try to reserve your judgement. Oh, and pack a bathing suit because there's a small hot spring in the area."

Callum pumps a fist in the air. "Rad."

Even Declan cracks a half smile, looking around 70 percent alive.

Sensing someone's stare, I look down to find Kinsey's stormy gaze trained on me. She's clearly annoyed I'm not mirroring her disgruntlement. I shrug; she huffs and rolls her eyes. Whatever. Either she'll get used to the idea that I'm not her sidekick or she'll leave me alone. With some surprise, I realize I hope it's the former. She's almost... a friend.

"Any more questions?" asks Frank, cocking a brow at Tiffany, who nods.

"How many chaperones will there be?"

I perk up, interested in the answer.

Frank's eyes narrow. "Why?"

"Just curious."

We're all a little shocked when Frank falls for Tiffany's

I'm-super-cute-and-innocent face. He relaxes, smiling. "Just me and Dr. C, which incidentally means you'll all be helping haul supplies and set up the tents."

Cue Kinsey's dramatic groan.

Frank continues, sending each of us pointed looks. "Where we're going, there are no services within twenty miles. You set out on your own, you'll get lost, dehydrated, and eaten by some coyotes. Maybe we notice you missing in time to commission a search party, maybe we don't. Maybe we can't find you and cut a shitload of red tape to get a chopper out here. But you'll probably be dead by then."

The room is quiet, even Kinsey's shocked stare locked on Frank's face. I laugh, loud and abrupt, startling everyone.

"Something funny, Mia?" Frank asks, frowning.

Still smiling, I shrug. "Just appreciating your badassery in a new light, Frank."

His turn for a shocked expression. "Oh. Well, er…" With a cough, he promptly ignores me. "Okay, that's it, guys. Go pack."

I'm out the door first, walking fast. By the time we cross the Fish Tank, I hear Kinsey bitching to Tiffany. Probably about the impending lack of hot water and blow dryers.

Immediately, I feel a spike of shame.

"What are you frowning about?" asks Callum, reaching past me to hold the door open. We step into sunlight, our hands leaping to shade our eyes from the glare off the pool.

"Ugh, I'm annoyed that you were right."

He barks a short laugh. "About what?"

I squint at him, catching Declan's interested look over his shoulder. "You told me to dump my baggage and I'd feel better, and you were right." Before he can say *I told you so*, I grumble, "I'm just not sure I like the better version of me."

"Why?" Declan's dark eyes scan mine as he walks up to us.

I focus on Callum's easy grin, and he answers for me. "Because *feeeeelings*," he sings loudly. "Oh so many *feeeeelings*!"

I roll my eyes, heaving a sigh.

"Is that why?" asks Declan.

For a badass rock star, he looks all kinds of innocent right now, his body vibrating with curiosity and his eyes beseeching mine. But like I told Leo, I'm still 10 percent crazy. Since I'm awake approximately fifteen to sixteen hours a day, that means I'm allowed a good hour and a half of bad behavior. I haven't met today's quota yet.

I stop walking, the men halting with me. Staring Declan dead in the eye, I say, "What you really want to know is whether I've forgiven myself for the heinous shit I've done, so you can have some hope for the same. Sorry, bud. My opinion of myself has only declined since I got here."

"Jesus, Mia," mutters Callum, then tells Declan, "Don't listen to her. She just had a huge breakthrough with the doc and is a little shell-shocked. Think of it like this: we spent years building these protective cocoons around ourselves with lies and denial, and here, we work to break free of the shell. What's inside, though, is—"

Declan and I share a glance, then dissolve into laughter.

Callum glares at us. "You guys suck."

Declan claps him on the back. "Good on you, bro. You're a beautiful butterfly now."

Callum snorts. "Fuck you."

Behind us, the door to the Fish Tank opens. Kinsey, Tiffany, and Preston walk through, followed by Frank.

Shooting us a frown, Frank yells, "Did I say enjoy a social hour, or pack your damned bags?"

"On it!" shouts Callum.

I glance at Declan. "Welcome to Crazy Town."

OUR EXCITEMENT at being beyond the fence is short-lived. Hiking three miles across relatively flat ground should—theoretically—be a piece of cake. Callum and I could probably make it to the campsite in less than an hour, even toting backpacks and duffels with supplies. Unfortunately, we're not alone, and at the rate we're going, we'll be setting up tents in the dark.

I actually feel bad for Kinsey and Tiffany. After a mere mile, they already look ragged, their hair limp, faces bright red, and their steps faltering. Even Frank with his extra cushioning and Preston with his stick limbs are having no problem keeping pace. Declan isn't doing too bad for a detoxing alcoholic, either. And naturally, Leo looks unfairly perfect in running pants, sneakers, and a white tee.

Despite my physical fitness, I'm still feeling the additional pounds I'm hauling. Loose strands of hair stick to my neck and face, and my calves and shoulders burn. Leo, on the other hand, might as well be walking on a treadmill in an air-conditioned gym. He's barely sweating, carrying just as many supplies as Callum, and looks like any other hot-as-fuck guy taking a leisurely stroll. The cherry on top of my sexual frustration is his stupid hair. Completely wind-blown, dark strands everywhere and no part in sight, it's a visceral reminder of what it felt like to drag my fingers through it.

I spend most of the hike wishing my attraction to him were based solely on physical allure. My libido has never been the boss of me. But sadly, when I look at him—too often, too long—all I see is the calm point in a storm. I want to tackle him, crawl inside his skin, and stay safe and warm until everything isn't so frightening anymore.

I'm so fucked.

21

MOON-LIGHT

DAY 18

WE MAKE it to the campsite before dark. Barely. The spot shows clear signs of use—a central fire pit boasting a blackened tripod for hanging pots, a few makeshift benches of sun-bleached wood atop rocks, and a generous area of mostly flat, shrub-free ground for the tents.

The sky is a hazy watercolor of purples and reds, and the distant mountains reflect the last fire of sunset. The sight is a breathtaking reminder of how vast the universe is, how small we are. As I unload my pack and stretch sore muscles, I feel the rare blessing of contentedness. For the moment, at least, there's nowhere else I need or want to be.

While Kinsey and Tiffany nurse their sore feet, the rest of us put up the tents in the last light of day. Three tents total, spaced about ten feet apart in a semicircle. Frank is bunking with Callum and Preston, Leo will share with Declan, and the three women have the last. When I see the tight fit of sleeping bags in our tent, however, I consider the appeal of sleeping beneath the sky.

That idea fades fast as the sun dips below the horizon and the temperature drops. As the rest of us pull on sweatshirts and pants, Frank starts a fire in the rock-bordered pit. Leo appears with dinner—a campfire pot and freeze-dried packages that he mixes with water. There are good-natured grumbles around camp about the rustic fare; that is, until the stew begins to heat, sending up a mouthwatering scent.

Darkness settles like a heavy blanket, the moon not yet risen. Despite its inherent stillness, the desert sings at night. Gentle gusts of wind carry to our ears the chorus of crickets, the muted flap of wings overheard, the hoots of owls, and the occasional patter of small critter feet. When it blows just right, we can even hear a trickle of water from the nearby hot springs.

Two high-powered halogen lamps illuminate the entirety of the camp as we gather for a meal of stew, fresh sourdough bread, and apples. Whether in reverence for nature or outright fatigue, when we speak, our voices are near-whispers.

I focus on my food, listening to the mellow chatter around me. A few times, I glance up to find Leo's eyes on me from across the fire. My crazy is in hibernation, though, because I can't hold his gaze for more than a second before looking away. It's too hard with him looking so unprofessional and... normal. The emotional distance between us feels blurred on my end, though I doubt he's experiencing the same confusion.

I'm his patient and he's my therapist. That's it. But right here, right now, as he smiles at something Callum is saying and the firelight flickers over relaxed, happy faces, I'm having trouble convincing myself we're not simply a group of friends on a weekend camping trip. Even focusing on Kinsey and Tiffany doesn't help—the exercise, fresh air, and full bellies have given both women blissful countenances.

I'm relieved when Frank asks me to help clean up dinner. I throw myself into the task of scrubbing the dishes and utensils with biodegradable soap and packing them away in a duffel behind one of the tents. I hide in the dark as long as possible, until Callum's voice finds me.

"Mia! Take off the apron. It's time for s'mores and Truth or Dare!"

Dragging my feet, I head back to the fire. One of the halogen lights has been turned off; the other is far enough away, set between two tents, that the night presses close. The campfire presses back, flickering brightly against the seven faces turned in my direction.

"I'm tired," I say artlessly.

Frank speaks first. "By all means, you can—"

"Hell no!" interjects Kinsey. "Girl, get your ass over here. I'm reliving the youth I never had!"

And then comes the ultimate torture in the form of a deep, teasing tone. "Are you scared, Amelia?"

My eyes snap to Leo. *Yes, you asshat. And do you really want to play? Did you forget how badly I want to break you?* His smile slowly fades, though his gaze doesn't waver from my face. Steady challenge issues from his shadowed eyes.

Declan, who's sitting beside Leo, looks between the two of us, his brows lifting. Then he laughs. "Doc, your balls are definitely bigger than mine. If she were looking at me like that, I'd probably beg for my life."

"Pleeease, Mia?" begs Kinsey.

"Yeah, come on," adds Tiffany.

Callum squawks like a chicken. I break eye contact with Leo and stomp forward. Plopping cross-legged on the ground, I snatch a marshmallow from a pack and stab it with a stick.

"Commence the bonding," I announce, then point my stick-impaled marshmallow around me. "But don't say I didn't warn you."

"Oh, oh, I'll start!" chirps Kinsey. Her knees bounce as she chews her lip in thought. "Mia, truth or dare."

I flip her off and everyone laughs. "Truth."

"Really?" whispers Callum, surprised at my choice.

I'm surprised, too. It just slipped out.

Frank clears his throat loudly. "Do we need to lay down some ground rules?"

Kinsey waves him off. "No. I'll go easy. So, Mia... most embarrassing memory, please."

"Boring," mutters Declan.

I don't even have to think about the answer. "When I was in eighth grade, I got my period for the first time in the middle of class while wearing white pants. I didn't know it had happened until I stood up and a boy behind me screamed that I'd pooped blood and was dying."

When the laughter fades, I look around the group, squashing my first impulse to pick Leo. "Tiffany, truth or dare?"

"Dare."

"Hmm. Okay, I dare you to braid Frank's beard."

Both Tiffany and Frank groan in protest, but the result is worth it. The attention is off me, and Frank's biker-long beard sits in a perfect French braid.

Declan goes next, then Callum, then Preston. Frank dares Declan to eat a raw egg, which is produced from a cooler and downed with disappointing ease. Callum and Preston both choose truth, but the mood stays light, both the questions and their answers funny.

"Okay, um, Doctor Chastain?" asks Preston hesitantly. "Truth or dare?"

"Truth."

"Do you have any hobbies? If so, what are they?"

"Come on, P-man!" exclaims Callum. "That's totally lame."

Preston shrugs indifferently.

"Yes, I do have hobbies," answers Leo. "I like to hike, mountain bike, kayak... really anything outdoors. Let's see, I also collect books—first editions—and my favorite evenings are spent reading at home, listening to jazz and smoking an imported cigar."

Everyone gets a kick out of the response, especially Kinsey. "Do you also enjoy romantic dinners and sunset walks on the beach?"

Leo grins, eyes sparkling. My stomach tightens and drops to my toes. I can't take it anymore. I just can't.

I leap to my feet. "I'm going to bed," I announce and beeline for the tent amidst surprised protest.

Not until I'm inside do I realize I should probably pee, maybe brush my teeth... *Fuck it.* I drop face-first onto my sleeping bag and pull the hood of my sweatshirt up to block the sound of voices.

It takes a while, but eventually my body overrules my brain and delivers me to sleep.

22

—————————————

MOON-BRIGHT

DAY 18

A PAINFUL, pressing need in my bladder jolts me awake at an undermined hour. Kinsey and Tiffany are passed out beside me and the camp is quiet. The walls of the tent glow, backlit, and it takes me a few seconds to realize it's not the lamps but the moon.

Carefully maneuvering to my feet, I step over Tiffany's legs and unzip the door. Thankfully, the tent is new and the sound muted. Outside is a different world from the one I left. Brightened by moonlight, the landscape is both beautiful and alien, like something out of a science fiction movie. Shadows abound, giving wavering aspects to small, spiny plants and making giants out of boulders. At least there's no need for a flashlight.

Warmth still radiates upward from the sun-baked ground, but the air is delightfully chilly. I pick my way through the sparse brush to a location safely distant from camp and quickly take care of business. As I'm walking back, I hear something that stalls my feet.

The gurgle of water.

Do I think about coyotes? Snakes? Getting lost? No, I don't. There's no voice of caution. No monitor of reason. No fear at all. My mind is as empty and dark as the space between stars.

It's not hard to find the small trail, worn by many feet over the course of years. My steps are unhurried, my heartbeat steady. Everyone's asleep. What's the harm in exploring? Maybe taking a skinny-dip in the hot springs? It wouldn't be the first time.

As my eyes adjust fully to the night, the moon becomes an inverse sun. So bright. So clear. The scent of sulfur increases, teasing my nose and ramping up my excitement. I make my way up a short incline and around an outcropping of rocks. Before me is a perfect, dark pool of water, maybe seven feet across. Steam rises from the surface.

A startled intake of breath tells me I'm not alone. When I see the sole occupant, his broad, bare shoulders glistening wetly, I'm not surprised. *Why am I not surprised?* On the heels of that thought is another: *Of course, I'm dreaming.*

"Amelia," he says, voice rigid.

I don't ask for permission before I toe off my sneakers and socks and whip my sweatshirt over my head. There are sounds in the night, but all I can hear is his breathing, suddenly loud. All I can feel is the assault on my sensitive skin as my jeans come off, then my shirt, and finally my bra and underwear.

Dream-Leo looks down and mutters, "Could have used a warning."

Dream-me replies, "Where's the fun in that?"

Water swirls and laps as he moves through the pool and offers me a hand, his gaze carefully averted. "It can be a little slippery."

The contact of his fingers is a revelation. Another follows when first one foot, then the other, hit the water.

Oh my God, I'm not dreaming.

"Holy shit, that's hot."

Despite his firm grip, I slip. And since this isn't a dream, I don't slide magically into his arms. Leo tries to catch me, but I fall sideways, accidentally kicking him in the junk— *crap, he's naked*—and going headfirst underwater.

I come up coughing, expelling a nose-full of water. "I'm so sorry," I gasp.

Leo is as far away from me as he can be while still remaining in the pool. His shoulders are rounded defensively, and I'm pretty sure he's checking to make sure his balls are still there.

"Glancing blow," he wheezes. "I'll live."

"Sorry," I repeat feebly.

He doesn't say anything else, his eyes closed in a prolonged wince. I shift on the natural rock seat, unable to recall a time I felt this unbelievably awkward. At least my skin doesn't feel like it's melting off anymore. The downside is I'm achingly aware that I'm naked. And. So. Is. He.

"Sorry to crash your party," I murmur. "Believe it or not, I really thought I was dreaming." Not until Leo goes unnaturally still do I realize what I've said. I force a laugh. "Whoops. Let's pretend I didn't say that."

He drops his head back against a smooth rock, arms falling to his sides and eyes opening to the sky.

"Fucking fuck. *Fuck.* Son of a… fuck."

His whispered words belatedly register in my ears. A queer calm drifts through me, stilling my thoughts, while an equally potent spike of adrenaline makes my heart race, my breath shallow, and my fingertips tingle.

"Truth or dare, Leo?"

His head snaps down. "What?"

"You heard me."

A pause, then a whisper of, "Don't do this."

I'm a horrible person. A slave to impulse. A user and a *breaker*, and he's the ultimate prize. There's a high chance that if I push this—push *him* until he shatters—he'll never forgive me. Or himself. Then again, it's not like we have a future together. And he's leaving in four days.

What to do… What to do… New, healthy Amelia? Or old, impulsive Amelia?

Four days.

My chest tightens at the thought of never seeing him again. I can't do it—I can't not. So I end up answering the question for him. For both of us.

"Dare."

I push from the rock and stand. Water sluices from my chest, my wet hair. Cool air tightens my nipples and lifts goose bumps. But none of those sensations compare to what I feel when I see the look on Leo's face.

Agony.

The proof of his desire brings such relief my knees almost buckle. I take a weak step forward, then another. There's a slight slope to where he sits, and the water drops below my navel. His gaze restlessly scans every moonlit inch of me that's revealed. Fierce need tightens his features, echoed by bunched shoulders and hands that I know are coiled into fists beneath the water.

"I didn't imagine it," I whisper.

"No, you didn't," he says hoarsely, like the admittance is painful. I'm certain it is, but I can't process how fucked up this is because my joy is so immense.

I take another step, every second stretching to a hundred as I capture every detail. The rapid rise and fall of his chest. Clenched jaw. Sweat beading on his brow. Lowered brows over eyes that look silver in the moonlight. Warm breeze, cool air, hot water, pulse fluttering and swollen between my legs. I vow to remember this forever.

On my last step, my thighs brush against his knees. Two seconds pass—*an eternity*—before his legs slowly part. One more surrender, one more crack. I stay where I am and lift a hand to his face, dancing my fingers down his jaw to his mouth. His lips part and my index finger slides inside. He sucks the tip, then bites it.

I almost collapse again.

"Leo," I whimper.

He shatters.

His hands find my hips, yanking me forward. My knees are wrenched apart, then my ass claimed as he pulls me atop him. My senses fragment, overcome. Hot skin slick against mine, his fingers tangled in my hair. A hiss from his lips as I rub against him, teasing us both. *Thick. Hard. Long.*

I bite his neck, then lick his earlobe and murmur, "How can something that feels so good be wrong?"

His teeth find my shoulder, clamping hard enough that I

jerk. Pain pushes my pleasure higher. I'm so close to climaxing, it would be funny under different circumstances.

"Maybe it's good *because* it's wrong," he whispers against my skin. "Maybe you've rubbed off on me."

"You don't believe that."

His hand, anchored in my hair, drags my head back until he can look me in the eyes. Our faces are so close I feel his breath on my lips, which tingle in anticipation of tasting him again.

"Tell me the truth," I plead mindlessly.

His fingers tighten, spreading fiery sensation through my scalp. "The truth? Fine. I've wanted you from the first moment I saw you. Damn you, Amelia. Damn your sarcasm, your lies, your eyes that tell me more than your mouth ever has, your scent that drives me crazy, and your beautiful, wounded heart. You're goddamn perfect and I'm going straight to hell."

And he kisses me.

23

RISE AND SHINE
DAY 18-19

I KNOW the world is still turning, that the moon will eventually set and this night will end. It will then be a dream in truth—scattered impressions, stolen time too perfect to be real. And never to happen again.

But none of that matters when Leo's lips meet mine. However lurid my imagination has been where he's concerned, I missed the mark by a long shot. Beneath his suits and control and cutting intellect, he's a fucking *animal*. But so am I.

When he pulls my hair, I pull his back. When he bites my nipples, I dig my nails into his arms. And when in the flurry of our movements the head of his cock comes against my entrance, I grab its thick base and impale myself inch by torturous inch.

He groans, long and low, when he reaches the end of me. I sit utterly still, panting and wincing in discomfort. I'm not even sure he's all the way in, but I sure as hell hope so.

"Um… just give me a sec—"

Leo flexes his hips. My body catches fire, every nerve ending exploding into sparks.

"Oh God, Leo—"

One hand anchoring my hip, he growls, "This is what you wanted, so take it."

I almost come from those words alone, and again when he thrusts hard enough I see stars. I'm so wet for him the water around us doesn't matter, and finally, on his third thrust, my body adjusts and the pain fades.

"You feel perfect," he murmurs. "So fucking hot and tight. Better than I ever imagined."

Completely out of my mind and body, I moan like a harlot. I've never been with a man as depraved as me, and the realization of who I'm with—and that he'll never be mine—almost ruins the best sex of my life.

Leo Chastain is a filthy fucking unicorn. I'm never going to get past this, past him. *This is a huge mistake.*

All thought is swept away as he finds a devastating rhythm and claims my mouth again, his tongue sweeping deep. He kisses me like he owns me, like he'll never get enough. We slide against the smooth edge of the pool, his powerful legs doing all the work. Wrecking me. Unraveling me.

My orgasm unfolds slowly. Deceptively mild tremors that build, and build, until he has to cover my mouth to stifle my cries. My nails dig deep into his shoulders, a litany of his name pouring against his fingers. Instead of speeding up like most men would do, he slows and lets me grind against him.

"Take it," he demands. "Let me see you move."

So I do, riding him in tight little circles, my clit finding the perfect pressure against his pelvis. I own my pleasure, let go of my inhibitions—not that I have many—and give up any and all notion of guarding my heart where this man is concerned. Frankly, right now I don't give a shit.

He's at least eight inches deep, a dirty-talking, hair-pulling fiend wrapped up in a suit-wearing, control-freak package. I'm ruined for life.

But what a sweet way to go out.

I climax on a soundless scream as he whispers in my ear how much he wishes I were riding his face. That he can feel me gripping him like a vise, that right now my pussy belongs to him. As I come down, transitioning to a boneless sack of sweat and endorphins in his arms, he licks sweat from my neck then nuzzles my skin. Our arms locked tightly around each other, our hearts pound out the same fast and furious rhythm. I imagine them trying to break apart from our bodies and join.

I eventually realize he's still hard as a rock inside me.

"Leo?" I whisper, wiggling a little.

His head lifts, a lazy yet savage smile on his face. "Did you think we were done? I'm just getting started." The smile falls as his thumb brushes my lower lip. "I'll have to go easy on you. Your mouth is already swollen, and I don't think we can swing a bee-sting explanation."

I shake my head quickly, pressing fingers into his lips. "Don't. I mean, okay, go easy on the kissing, but don't talk about… it. There's nothing to talk about. We're on the same page."

"And what page is that?" he asks, an eyebrow cocked.

"Don't make me say it. Please, let me dream as long as I can before I wake up."

His eyes roam my face. Finally, there's an infinitesimal shift in his expression. "Tonight, then." He brushes a soft kiss over my lips. "But I promise you're going to feel me for weeks."

Grateful to have skirted the topic of our inevitable implosion, I swirl my hips lazily. "I don't know if I believe you."

Strong fingers spread my ass, and his thumb presses proprietarily against a spot no man has gone before. I jerk forward with a squeal.

Leo's smile is pure wickedness. Does he relent? Not in the least. And by the time we return to camp hours later—me first, him forty minutes behind me—every hole on my body has taken him in one way or another.

I have a new hole, too. Wide enough for a 747, straight through my heart.

THE MOON IS SETTING when I finally hear Leo return to camp. I wonder if the lust has worn off enough that he's panicking over all the ways we could be discovered.

I wonder if I care.

Rolling onto my side, I almost scream when I see Tiffany's eyes open and watching me. When my heart stops trying to break my rib cage, I exhale slowly.

"Didn't mean to wake you," I whisper. "Needed to pee."

She blinks, calm and alarmingly alert. "Did you forget my issues with insomnia?"

If I didn't have twenty years of practice lying, I might start sobbing. Instead, I cock an eyebrow. "Fine, so I went for a walk. What are you, the tent police?"

"You don't have to do that, Mia," she whispers back. "Besides, your hair is wet and you stink of sulfur. It's okay. I won't tell anyone. I think it's awesome, actually. You and Doc are like Romeo and Juliet."

Oh, Fucking, Hell.

I circle the Truth Drain one last time. "Nothing happened. Yes, I followed him, found him in the hot springs. Tried to put the moves on him. Failed. Did you really think the unimpeachable Dr. Chastain would risk his career for some crazy pussy?"

She rolls her eyes. "The better question is, do I think he's hopelessly attracted to you in a weirdly intense and tragic way? Why, yes, I do."

I stare at her until my eyes water. Blinking, I rasp, "Thank you for not saying anything. But I don't want to talk about it. Not now, not tomorrow, not ever. I'm keeping this secret until the grave. If you have any respect for him at all, you will too."

"Of course I will," she hisses with affront. "I'd never betray either of you."

Sensing her sincerity, my expression softens. "Thanks."

I roll over to stare at the wall of the tent and try my damnedest to think about something other than our last, lingering kiss, and the fact it tasted so bitterly of goodbye.

"Even Romeo and Juliet are together at the end," whispers Tiffany.

I bite my tongue.

24

THUNDERSTORMS

DAY 19

Tiffany and Kinsey are gone when I finally wake up to a hot, bright tent and the sounds of clanking poles, scuffing shoes, and low voices. Yawning, I sit up and rub my eyes, then unzip the door and peer outside.

What I see doesn't make any sense. Callum and Declan are breaking down the other two tents, talking and laughing. Frank is crouched by the fire pit raking sand over the embers. I look around for Tiffany, Preston, and Kinsey, and finally spot them walking back from the direction of the hot springs. My embarrassment lasts only a second before memories of last night hijack my mind and body.

Covering my face with my hands, I try to shake the visions away. My legs over his shoulders, his mouth ravenous between them. All his slick, hard heat punching the back of my throat. His finger claiming my ass, heightening our pleasure as he propped me against the rocks and rode me from behind.

How at the end, he helped me get dressed with gentle

hands, saying nothing, then gave me a slow, lingering kiss and sent me back to camp.

"You feeling okay?" asks Callum. "Tiffany said we needed to let you sleep because you were up all night. You're not sick, are you?"

My fingers part, exposing one eye. "Just had trouble sleeping," I mumble. "Why are we packing up? I thought we were staying two nights."

Callum's brows go up. "You must have been really out of it to not hear anything this morning."

Panic rising, my numb hands drop to my lap. "What are you talking about?"

Callum rakes a hand through his hair. "A jeep came out and picked Dr. C up just after dawn. No idea what happened. Frank doesn't know either. We're all worried it's his family or something. Declan said when he woke up Doc was on the satellite phone." He sighs heavily. "I don't think he's coming back, Mia."

White noise roars in my ears. "What do you mean, not coming back?"

"Declan overheard him saying something about Dr. Reynolds starting immediately." He gazes toward the horizon. "Shit, I really hope his kid is okay."

So do I.

But there's an insidious voice inside me that won't shut up, and it's convinced there's nothing wrong with Leo's son. Nothing at all. What's wrong is what we did. Who he let me see. What he offered and what I gave in return.

The only thing wrong is me.

OASIS FINALLY COMES INTO VIEW, all the glass shimmering like a mirage in the afternoon sun. I don't remember the hike except for Tiffany forcing me to drink water from her canteen a few times. I don't feel the heat, don't feel the blister on my right heel. Don't feel resentful, confused, afraid, or crazy.

If there's anything floating through the white haze of my mind, it's resignation. Acceptance. Thanks to Leo Chastain, I've lost the ability to lie to myself. I shattered him—just like I wanted to—and it doesn't feel good at all.

I was wrong in worrying he'd blame me. I know that now. When Leo snapped out of his moonlight-induced madness, he likely choked on shame and self-loathing. No doubt he's taking 100 percent of the blame onto himself. It's who he is. I'd expect nothing else from a man who carries around guilt for his brother's suicide—which he had absolutely nothing to do with and no control over.

In his mind, he broke the most sacred rule in his book. He lost his precious control and jeopardized not only his career but my treatment.

Truth tastes like ash on my tongue.

It's *my* fault.

I did this to him.

"Hey, space-cadet."

I look at Declan, whose silent presence has been beside me for a while. "Yeah?"

"Whatever you're thinking, it can't be that bad."

A spike of misplaced anger shoots through me. "Just

because we fucked a thousand years ago doesn't mean you know me."

Shock drops his mouth. "Whoa, what the hell? I was just being nice."

"Fuck, I'm sorry." Fatigue and hunger whiten my vision momentarily. "I don't feel that good."

"Want me to take your bag?" he asks.

We're close enough to Oasis now that I can see the single figure standing just inside the open front doors. He turns fast and disappears, but I know it's him.

I unsling the duffel from my back, then shimmy out of my backpack. "Yes, actually. Can you drop my bag at my cabin?"

Looking confused and concerned, Declan nods and grabs the bags. My body feels immediately lighter. Faster.

Fast.

I take off running, ignoring the shouts behind me. Closer… closer. My sneakers hit the asphalt driveway, but I don't slow. Not on the stairs, which I take in one leap. Not when the sudden shade and cool air of the facility shocks my system. The Fish Tank is empty now, but I know where he is.

I don't stop running until I'm at his door. Don't knock before I wrench it open.

"Leo—" His name stutters and dies in my throat.

A woman sits behind the desk. Leo turns slowly from the wall where he's removing the frames with his credentials. His eyes meet mine blankly, then veer to the woman.

"Gretchen, meet Amelia Sloan."

Neither comment on the fact I'm panting, drenched in sweat, and covered in dirt from my run.

"Are you all right, dear?" asks Gretchen.

Dr. Reynolds, my new therapist.

It takes three tries for me to find my voice. "Yes, um… I heard you were leaving, Dr. Chastain, and wanted to say goodbye. I hope everything's okay at home?"

He nods. Distant. Professional. "Thank you. Everything's fine. My son had a severe asthma attack and was taken to the hospital, but he's okay now. Since Dr. Reynolds was arriving today anyway, I'm going to leave a few days early."

I shouldn't know he's lying, but I do. This man has never lied to me. Not once. Until this moment. I stare at him, waiting for him to look at me. But he doesn't.

My choices are clear: make a scene, or act like a mature woman who cares about other people, especially him, and doesn't want him to suffer. The way Dr. Reynolds is looking at me—with sympathy and compassion—makes me want to vomit. She clearly thinks I'm wigging out because I'm some wacko in love with my therapist.

She's right, but still… fuck her and her sympathy.

I swallow past a dry throat. "Okay. Well, take care. Thank you for everything." I stammer on the last word. To my horror, tears fill my eyes. Waving at the man who isn't even looking at me, I blurt, "Have a safe trip!"

I hightail it out of there, my sneakers squeaking rapidly over tile. I make it out the back door and as far as the pool. Without a second thought, I jump. Cool water takes me into its embrace, flowing around me, above me, inside me. It dulls the jagged edges of my pain.

Leo regrets what happened. I don't. He's running from the shame of it. I'm content to relive it in dreams for years to come. He surrendered to physical desire.

I surrendered my heart.

Does losing Leo hurt worse than the revelation of losing my child? Oddly, it doesn't. At least not in the same way. After all, you can't lose something you never truly had.

25

STEP TO THE EDGE
DAY 22

TUESDAY. 10:25 a.m. Eight more days of this place, then I'll be free to live my life. I don't know what that looks like yet, but I do know that whatever direction I go, it's a different trajectory than it was twenty-one days ago. So that's something, I guess.

The door to Dr. Reynold's office—*his office*—is open. I pause outside, then blink at what I see. The layout is the same. So are the desk, bookshelves, filing cabinets, and the several quality art reproductions on the walls. But the weathered leather armchairs are gone, replaced by wing-back chairs upholstered in an attractive taupe. Between them is a small coffee table with a succulent and a box of tissues. An electric oil warmer sits on a side table, shooting small geysers of lavender-scented vapor into the air.

All the changes, coupled with the addition of fresh flowers on the desk and a potted ficus in a corner, erase Leo almost entirely. I can't decide whether it's a relief or a new level of torture.

"Come on in, Mia."

Dr. Reynolds sits in one of the new chairs, smiling at me, a blank notepad on her lap. A small part of me wants to correct her—*my name is Amelia*—but a larger part likes that the name belongs to him.

"Morning," I mumble, then make my way to the chair opposite hers and sit.

"I heard you weren't feeling well yesterday. How are you doing today?"

"Better, thank you. Guess it was one of those twelve-hour bugs."

Yeah, if there's a twelve-hour bug that makes you cry until your eyes swell closed. I spent the majority of Sunday and Monday curled in my bathtub with a pillow and blanket, as the bathroom is the only area in our cabins not wired for sound. Tiffany and Kinsey brought me smoothies, snacks, and contraband chocolate at intervals. I'm not sure if Kinsey knows what went down or not; if she does, she's keeping quiet.

"I'm glad to hear you've recovered." Dr. Reynolds has a warm, clear voice, the kind that makes me think of kindergarten teachers. A *trustworthy* voice. "Let's jump right in, shall we? I'd like to talk about the relationship between you and Dr. Chastain."

The blood drains from my head, leaving me momentarily dizzy. "Excuse me?"

She smiles softly. "His notes made it clear that the two of you formed a close bond in a short period of time. It's remarkable, the progress you made together."

I have no idea what she's talking about, but I nod like I do. "I guess so."

"To be perfectly honest, Mia, I'm wondering what he did to earn your trust. I read your case file and..." She shrugs delicately.

I almost smile. "You're shocked."

She nods with a guilty smile, though it rings false. "With the kind of trauma you experienced as a child and again two years ago, as well as long-standing behavior patterns including recklessness and narcissistic tendencies, I'm both amazed and baffled by your headway." Losing the smile, she reveals her true self—a sharp, cunning mind that wants to pull me apart and pick at the pieces. "Tell me, what do you think of Dr. Chastain's assessment that you've exhibited increased empathy for others and decreased antagonism since you arrived?"

"Is that a trick question, Dr. Reynolds?"

The maternal smile returns. "Not in the least. I'd simply like to determine *your* opinion of your progress."

With a reflexive sigh, I look past her and out the nearby window. "You're pursuing the sociopath angle," I tell her tiredly. "You think I deceived Chastain into believing I was changing. That I've manufactured the emotions and responses expected of me."

She doesn't respond. I glance at her to see her eyebrows lifted in expectation. I gotta hand it to her, she's working the hardass-therapist archetype pretty flawlessly. Trying to get a rise out of me. To see if I'll break, reveal my own true colors.

I may have changed somewhat—but not that much. She won't get what she wants from me.

"I tried in the beginning," I murmur. "He saw right through it. You want to know why I trusted Chastain? He didn't give me a choice. He kept pushing and pushing from every conceivable direction. He was... easy to talk to. Before I knew it, I forgot how to lie and told the truth instead."

"How did that feel?"

I cock a brow. "Fucking *alarming*. It felt like he had power over me. I didn't like it."

"Didn't, or still don't?"

Ah, there it is. She's not stupid and clearly picked up on my desperate, lovesick vibe when I burst into his office Saturday.

Undaunted, I look her in the eye. "Chastain taught me that relationships—even client and therapist ones—don't have to be a power struggle. That when two people let their guards down, magic happens. *Trust* happens. Did he cross the professional boundary with me in this office? No, he did not. As for whether I crossed it, I'm sure he left detailed notes, as well as his opinion that I was trying to assume control of the 'relationship' by using my sexuality to undermine his authority."

Dr. Reynolds doesn't bother to hide either her surprise or her lingering doubt. Can't say I blame her.

"Well, Mia," she says finally, "that's a very insightful response. Thank you for your candor. You should feel very proud of the hard work you've done. How would you describe your overall state of mind at this stage?"

My heart rate finally begins to slow. To my astonishment, I don't consider lying to her. Whether or not she's a wolf in sheep's clothing, I need some fucking guidance.

"I'm scared."

"Why's that?"

I look at the ceiling to avoid her stare. "I don't know who I am anymore."

"I think that's a perfectly natural response to the trauma you've endured, as well as the therapy process here at Oasis. Let me ask you something else, Mia. Have you considered that not knowing who you are means you can be whoever you want to be?"

My gaze drops to her face. "That's a little abstract."

She smiles like I just told a joke. "Yes, it can be, but we can narrow it down." She pauses to scratch something on the notepad, then looks back up. "There are two primary tasks I want to accomplish with you in your remaining time. May I share?"

I stuff down a sarcastic quip. "By all means."

"First, I want to utilize a method popular in Twelve-Step programs, that of compiling a list of people we've harmed and making a plan for amends or restitution. Then I want to tackle the issue you just brought up, that of identity. We'll talk about what your ideal life looks like—vocation, love, friendship, family, et cetera. We'll also discuss the first steps you'll take toward those goals, as well as determine whether you'll benefit from ongoing therapy."

I sink back into my chair and force a smile.

"Sounds like a plan."

26

COUNTDOWN TO FREEDOM
DAY 22

KINSEY's goodbye party is a more subdued affair than Nix's, Leo's absence an almost palpable undercurrent. I'm certainly not helping elevate the mood—I've spent the last half hour sitting in a chair in the corner, watching but not really seeing the celebration. I'm mostly left alone.

Everyone thinks I'm bummed about Kinsey leaving. And surprisingly, I am. I'm going to miss her… for exactly six days. She lives in L.A., too, and already demanded my phone number and a promise to meet for coffee. Also surprisingly, I'm looking forward to it. I can't recall the last period of my life when I had any close, female friends. Or any friends, really.

God, I'm such a loser.

Declan drops into the chair next to mine. "Hey. Are these things always this depressing? I expected a little more bang for our buck." His gaze lifts to the ceiling. "Pink streamers? Really?"

My smile is wry. "They do it on purpose. Everything here is done on purpose. You'd do well to remember that."

The weight of his gaze hits the side of my face. "Callum asked me if I named the band after you. You know I didn't, right?"

I nod, glancing at him. "You have a little sister named Amy who used to fall a lot."

He blinks in surprise.

"When you guys got famous, I might have Googled it just to make sure."

He chuckles; it fades on a sigh. "Shit, where did everything go so wrong?"

I consider the question as I look around the room. Tiffany and Preston are laughing at whatever ridiculous joke Ruben is telling them. Frank and Dr. Reynolds are chatting with a grinning Kinsey. Callum and Charlene are handing out slices of cake to the rest of the staff.

"I don't think anything went wrong, exactly," I say slowly. "Maybe some of us just feel things more deeply. So deeply we try to make it stop however we can."

He grunts. "Then what's the point, huh? Why are we here?"

I meet his dark, tired eyes. "Because somewhere inside us is a person who wants to live and be happy."

"And are you, Mia? Happy?"

I snort. "No. But that's got nothing to do with Oasis. But you know what? Today I can honestly say I want to live. And that, my friend, is a goddamn miracle."

THE PARTY WINDS down around ten, and Kinsey and I walk arm in arm toward her cabin. She's blissful at the notion of seeing Teacup tomorrow. And calling Nix.

"So… you and Nix, huh?" I tease.

Her arm tightens on mine. "I don't know. Maybe. I guess I didn't realize how much I liked him until he was gone."

Thinking of Nix's feelings for her, I say, "You should see where it goes. Although, statistically speaking, rehab relationships—"

"Shut up," she snaps with a grin. "Even if there's nothing there with Nix, you're not getting rid of me that easily. We're besties now."

I sigh dramatically. She merely giggles and pats my arm. When we reach her cabin, we sit on the small stoop and lapse into companionable silence.

"Mia?"

"Yep?"

"Thank you for not asking why I'm here."

I give her the side-eye. "You're welcome. I hope that doesn't mean you're about to tell me."

She laughs softly. "You bitch. Don't you want to know?"

I shrug. Secrets don't have the pull they used to. I haven't felt the itch since… Stumped, I dig through the last couple of weeks. *Ah, there it is.* Since the day my own secrets swam to the surface and found air.

"I want to tell you," murmurs Kinsey.

I shift to face her, giving her my full attention. "Okay."

"I was abused as a kid. Pretty badly over a two-year period. It was my uncle—my mom's brother. He used to stay with us for a few months at a time. My mom couldn't say no to him. She'd tell my dad he just needed some help getting back on his feet, that he was family, and my dad always fell for it. Anyway, he would sneak into my room at night. Until Dr. Chastain, I'd never told anyone. Shit, I'd buried it so deep I didn't remember a lot of it. I never knew this thing that happened to me when I was little was driving my choices in life. All I knew was that I felt different. Wrong. Hence the night terrors." She pauses. "Doc told me you barged in one night. That you misread the situation and went toe-to-toe with him to protect me."

I squirm in embarrassment. "Uh, yeah. I'm really sorry that happened to you, Kinsey."

She grabs my hand and clamps down hard. "You're a good friend, Mia. I look up to you a lot. We all do."

My jaw drops. "What the fuck for?"

She smiles, shaking her head. "You don't see it, but we do. Your problem—if you have one—is that you're *too* alive. When the rest of us tried to hide and ignore our broken wings, you tried to fly with them."

I'm so stunned, I just stare at her. My heart thunders in my chest. "I slept with him," I blurt. "With Leo. The night we went camping. That's why he bailed, not because of his kid."

Kinsey blinks rapidly, processing, then squeals in laughter and shoves me hard, rocking me on the stoop. Then she falls onto her back, laughing so hard tears stream from her eyes.

"Oh my God, I'm dying," she gasps. "Dying of how awesome this is."

"It's not awesome," I hiss. "I broke the poor man and now he hates me and probably himself. Who does that? Who sleeps with their therapist? And keep your voice down, will you? This is fucking top secret."

Wiping her tears, Kinsey sits up and crosses her heart. "I won't tell anyone, Mia. Promise." She sobers—a little. "Are you going to look him up when you get out? His practice is in L.A."

"No. Fuck no. What could I possibly say? *Hey, Doc, sorry I almost destroyed your credibility and career. How do you feel about dating ex-patients?*" I shudder. "I'd rather stay in Oasis for the rest of my life."

Kinsey's arm wraps around my shoulders. "Hey, you do get that he's equally responsible for what happened, right? He's a grown man. He could have told you to get lost."

Her words, though welcome, do little to soothe the storm inside me. Covering my face with my hands, I mumble, "I don't even know if what I feel is real or some side effect of the therapy. I've never been that vulnerable with anyone who wasn't my brother. It probably messed with my head."

"I don't know the answers, Mia," she murmurs into my hair. "All I know is we aren't the same people we were when we got here. And that you're meeting me for coffee next week. Regret lives in the past and fear in the future, but neither exist in the present. Let's live in the moment, one day at a time."

My hands falling, I glower at her. "I don't even know where to start with that pseudo-spiritual mashup of bullshit."

She smirks. "That's my girl. So tell me, is Leo hung or what?"

I groan. Then I tell her about the freakiest, best sex ever. She listens with wide eyes and when I'm finished says succinctly, "You're screwed."

Tell me something I don't know.

27

GOODBYE
DAY 28

EARLY MONDAY MORNING, I'm roused from weird dreams about surfing on a sand dune by a pounding on the door of my cabin.

"Mia, open up!" shouts a familiar voice.

Stuck in that viscous moment between sleep and waking, I decide I'm still dreaming. The curtains are still dark with night. There's no way Jameson is outside right now.

The door rattles, and his low voice snaps, "Give me the damned key!"

The sound of the door swinging open brings me fully awake. I snap upright, yanking the sheet over my bare chest, to see two dark figures standing in the doorway. One of them flips on the overhead lights.

My eyes bug out. "Jaybird? What the..." My voice fails as I see the man beside him. "Le—Dr. Chastain? What's going on?"

Jameson is across the room in seconds, blocking my

view of Leo. My brother reaches for me, then frowns. "I forgot you sleep naked. Get dressed. We have to go, Meerkat."

I blink dumbly. "Huh?"

A drawer opens and Leo tosses a shirt onto the bed. Feeling like I'm in the Twilight Zone, I watch him move to the closet and pull out my suitcase, then start tossing all my clothes inside. His shoulders are tense, his gaze never once veering my way.

The last cobwebs clear from my mind. "What the hell is going on?" I snap at Jameson. He hands me the shirt, then meets my gaze. What I see in his eyes makes my stomach bottom out.

"Jaybird?" I whisper.

He nods, swallowing and rubbing at his eyes. "It's Dad. He had a massive heart attack last night. He's stable right now but is scheduled for bypass surgery in two days. I couldn't get ahold of anyone here, so I called Dr. Chastain. He was kind enough to drive out with me."

I glance at Leo, not for confirmation, but because I can't help it. I can't believe he's here. For the first time, he's looking back at me. There's no professional mask—just the man, tired and rumpled and sincere.

"I'm sorry, Amelia," he says softly.

I nod numbly, then clear my throat. "Can you both step outside for a sec so I can get dressed?"

They go.

An hour later, I sit in the back of Jameson's Lexus SUV as it eats the miles toward Los Angeles. Dawn is breaking behind us, a kaleidoscope of blue and orange through scattered white clouds.

Everything since getting dressed is a little blurry—Callum and Tiffany outside in their pajamas, giving me tight hugs and pieces of paper with their phone numbers; Charlene's unexpectedly sorrowful face waiting in the Fish Tank; a hug and a kiss on the cheek from Nurse Nora. Then buckling my seatbelt, Jameson behind the wheel. Leo hesitating at the passenger door, then sliding in back beside me.

For the last few miles, every couple of minutes a random thought has come out of my mouth.

"He always loved bacon."

"He played tennis twice a week."

"Just turned sixty last year."

"I skipped his birthday party because he invited his girlfriend."

Finally, I turn my gaze from the passing scenery and look across at Leo. "Is this my fault?"

Jameson barks, "What? Of course not!"

Leo watches me sadly for a few moments, then reaches over and unbuckles my seatbelt. "Come here, Amelia." The arm closest to me lifts, beckoning.

I move toward him like a flower seeking sunlight, sliding across the leather to tuck myself into his side. He finds the middle seatbelt and secures it around me, then hugs me against him.

"It's absolutely not your fault."

My cheek is against his chest, my arms cradled comfortably between us. Leo's chin rests on my head. I don't feel the seatbelt digging into my hip and stomach. I only feel him.

I think I should cry. *Shouldn't I be crying?*

I don't realize I've asked the question aloud until Leo says, "People process the shock of emotional pain in different ways. Some funnel overwhelming feelings into denial, anger, or violence. Others cry, or seek comfort in loved ones, or isolate."

"Where do I belong on that list?" I murmur.

He pauses, a sigh warming my scalp. "You're a survivor. You're not going to run from this. I don't think you can anymore."

"Because of your brilliant work inside my head?"

I'm only half-joking. I honestly don't know how I would have taken this news a month ago. Would I have shown up at the hospital? Maybe. For a few minutes at least. To comfort Jameson, to play the part of caring daughter— poorly, I might add.

And now? I just feel an amorphous sadness. For the past, for the fractured present, for words unsaid and efforts unmade. Despite my lack of relationship with my father, he's still my dad. The only parent I have. And the thought of him suffering, not knowing if his daughter even cares... it hurts. I want to change it.

Leo finally answers my question. "Not me, Amelia," he says gently. "It's because of you."

I breathe in and out, my exhales fanning the strong column of his throat. Despite everything, I feel safe. And that's what finally brings tears to my eyes.

Because he's not mine. Can't be mine.

"It's not fair," I whisper.

His arms tighten around me. He thinks I'm talking about my father. He doesn't know.

Against my hair he whispers back, "I agree."

Silence cocoons us. Need and deep, penetrating loss rise in my veins. A thousand wishful memories pass through my mind.

Leo.

Sunday mornings in bed. Teaching him how to surf. Coffee and croissants at my favorite Venice Beach café. Private smiles and wordless glances full of meaning. Walking our dog. Because of course we'd have a dog. Fights and forgiveness and hunting for the perfect surprise birthday present for his son.

Loving him. Being loved.

These last thoughts are the ones to break the camel's back. A sob tears free; long-suppressed emotion hurls forth. The hunter becomes prey as fear barrels through me. Fear for my father, Jameson, and myself. For Kinsey, Callum, Nix, Tiffany, Preston, Declan. For our futures, for our precarious, precious lives.

I feel it. All of it. I know it's fear because of the metallic taste in my mouth. Because I remember tasting it when Jameson and I opened the door that rainy night to two police officers.

Leo holds me tighter, harder, his arms a wall of false hope. My heart breaks again. More. Differently. Because I gave Leo Chastain what I've given no man before him—the unmitigated truth of myself.

"I'm sorry," he whispers softly, fiercely. "If I could have found you in another time, another place…"

Is he saying…?

Hope soars.

Then it plummets.

"I'll miss you," he finishes. "Please be happy. Your heart is too big and beautiful to be hidden away."

The words are said with finality.

A farewell.

PART 2

THE FLIGHT

28

NEW WORLD

"So, uh, you looked pretty cozy with your therapist in the car. You guys were all whispers and cuddles most of the drive."

I ignore Jameson and focus on the electric buzz of a nearby vending machine. My head feels like it's been through the blender, pounding out retribution for sobbing all over Leo. As much as I would have welcomed them, there were no cuddles or whispers. At least none in line with what Jameson's probing for. Leo was Leo—professional, kind yet fierce, and brutally honest.

"No more accidents or stunts, Amelia. When you feel overwhelmed, remember that feelings aren't facts. The storm will pass. Always. Find something that brings you happiness and give it all your passion."

No suggestion of seeing me again, no asking for my phone number or slipping me his. No response other than platonic, doctorly affection. I almost hate him for his superhuman ability to ignore what happened between us.

Almost.

What's really strange is I don't feel the urge to jump off a cliff or out of an airplane right now. I don't feel like maxing out a credit card or surfing big waves or skipping town for life as a beach bum in Puerto Vallarta. I actually did that once, and it wasn't nearly as glamorous as I'd imagined.

"Are you going to talk to me or just stare at the wall?"

"Stare at the wall."

"It speaks! Hallelujah!"

My lips twitch, too tired to smile. The fluorescents are starting to get to me, pulsing in my periphery, as is the long day of waiting around the hospital. We've been in our dad's room off and on over the last hours. He's on a lot of drugs and not really conscious, but he did open his eyes long enough to see us and smile.

"Thank you, Jaybird," I whisper, dragging my eyes from the vending machine to his face. "For shipping me to that place. I'm sorry for everything I put you through. Especially the last couple of years."

He nods, scanning my features. "You're welcome. Dr. Chastain didn't tell me much, but he did say you remembered everything."

I know he's talking about more than the accident.

My eyes sting. "Yeah, I remembered. Something inside me turned off when Mom and Phillip died, but whatever it is, it's on again. I think Dr. Chastain might have saved my life."

He nods, eyes soft with relief. "I think you might be right. Told you they had the best drugs."

I manage a laugh. "If by drugs you mean therapy, then yes. The best drugs on the West Coast."

ONE DAY LATER, when the surgery is over and my dad is resting comfortably in a recovery room, I call Kinsey and ask if she wants a temporary roommate. Her scream of acceptance almost blows my eardrum out.

I take a cab to a house nestled in the Hollywood Hills, where a newly brunette and natural-looking Kinsey greets me with tears and hugs. I meet the infamous Teacup. The tiny, yapping shithead pisses on my leg within five minutes. But I have to concede he's pretty cute.

FIVE DAYS LATER, Jameson and I take our dad home from the hospital. A sweet-faced and cheerful in-home nurse arrives after us. Her unlucky job for the next six weeks is to manage his medications and assist him in developing better physical and dietary health. He's not a happy camper, but he's alive.

ONE WEEK LATER, I get a full-time job at a new restaurant in Venice. Then I borrow money from Jameson to put a deposit on an apartment within walking distance.

As much as I like her, a week living with Kinsey turned out to be six days too long.

ONE MONTH LATER, I pick up my surfboard from Jameson's house. I haven't felt like surfing yet, but I want it just in case. I also make an appointment with a new therapist recommended by Kinsey. Thankfully, Dr. Wilson isn't anything like Dr. Reynolds. She actually reminds me a bit of my mom.

When I see her every week, I tell the truth. Not because I don't have anything else to lose, but because for the first time in a long time, I do.

TWO MONTHS LATER, I still have a job, an apartment, a therapist, and I surf every morning before work. Dad's doing better, thanks in part to a massive crush on his nurse, Jessica, who still comes by a few times a week to check in. We've also started a new tradition of family breakfast every Sunday at the Malibu house. Sometimes Jessica joins us.

And I've made friends. A few at work and a couple I met out in the water. All women. We do things like see movies and go to concerts and art museums. Activities that once upon a time would have bored me to tears. I kind of like them now.

My best friends, however, are Kinsey and Nix. The odd-yet-somehow-perfect couple drag me out on the town at least once a week. The three of us keep in touch with Callum, who's back in New York, and Tiffany, who's in Massachusetts—I was right about her father being a senator. I also recently saw a flyer for Amy Falls' new tour, and a tabloid photo of a smiling, healthy-looking Declan.

Wherever Preston is, I hope he's okay.

***

My therapist has me journaling a lot, automatic writing being her "thing." My homework is to spend at least ten minutes a day scribbling down anything that comes into my head. It was hard at first—more days than not, I forgot to do it—but now I look forward to journaling at the end of the day. I call it my daily exorcism.

During therapy, we often talk about topics that come up repeatedly in my writing. Fears and uncertainties about the future. Regrets and unresolved issues from the past. In yesterday's session, I made the unwitting mistake of mentioning I was writing about Kevin a lot. Thinking about what kind of girlfriend I was and feeling conflicted about how things ended.

Thanks to my confession, I have new homework. Homework that makes my bones itch. For the first time since leaving Oasis, I want to jump out of an airplane.

I go surfing instead, for hours and hours until I can barely stand when I hit the sand. The itch is still there, but it doesn't control me anymore.

29

COTTON CANDY

TOMORROW IS HALLOWEEN, but you wouldn't know it from the weather. Santa Ana winds—aka the Devil's winds—have been pummeling the city for days, simultaneously pushing temperatures into the mid-nineties and moods down the crapper. At least the surf has been epic.

I spend the early morning hours in the water, soaking in the salt and sun, then run home to shower and change for work. On the small patio outside my front door, I prop my board in the shade, then strip out of my wetsuit and toss it over the small railing to dry. By the time I pull my house key off the thong around my neck, I hear distinctive mewling and scratching from inside.

Smiling, I open the door and look down at Ferdi, our neighborhood stray. He rubs his gargantuan body against my leg then curls around my ankles, almost tripping me. Once I've passed inspection, he sits on his haunches, fixes bright green eyes on my face, and starts his rusty-engine purring.

No one actually knows his name, or if he's ever had one, but he's huge, black and white, and reminds me of Jameson's favorite childhood book, *The Story of Ferdinand*. Like the titular character, Ferdi would rather lie around in the sunshine napping than hunt mice. Probably because he's extremely well fed and therefore as lazy and entitled as any house cat.

Still, he's had his share of trouble in life. One of his ears is missing the top portion, the healed border ragged with scar tissue. A thin scar also bisects his black nose and a corner of his mouth, giving his kitty-grin a lopsided effect.

"Hey, Ferdi," I coo, closing the door and reaching down to scratch between his ears. "Found your way in again, did you?"

I'm on the second floor and the small complex has a coded gate for safety, so I usually leave a window or two open to catch the breeze off the ocean. For all his weight, Ferdi is deceptively agile. One night about a month after I moved in, he made his way onto the roof, sliced through the sagging screen of one of my bedroom windows, and jumped onto my bed.

The rest is history.

Ferdi follows me across the apartment, a sunny, cheerful haven I fell in love with at first sight. After Oasis and the grueling weeks spent between the hospital, Kinsey's pad, and Jameson's spare bedroom, the apartment felt like a gift from the heavens. It still does.

Checking the time on the kitchen microwave, I quickly fix Ferdi his daily serving of the specialty raw food I spend a small fortune on—I don't want him getting any ideas about picking a new buddy. Then I head for the shower to rinse off the lingering salt and sand.

Twenty minutes later, I'm weaving through pedestrian traffic toward the restaurant and thinking about my homework from Dr. Wilson. Mostly, I wonder if it's even possible. I mean, it's not *impossible*. I just really, really don't want to do it.

I have to make amends to Kevin, which includes coming clean about the baby I lost. *Ugh.* Dr. Wilson also said no phone call or letter. I need to do it face-to-face. For resolution. Healing.

Being mentally healthy is fucking hard.

MAGNOLIA CAFÉ—HOUSED in a prime location on the Venice Beach Boardwalk—is deceptively rustic in appearance. No tablecloths, cloth napkins, or fancy glassware. The menus boast basic black print, the single sheet protected in plastic with items like pancakes, cheeseburger, and salad listed at affordable prices. We're open seven days a week from nine to ten, and only in off hours is there no line outside.

Despite its lack of extravagance, minimalistic white decor, and borderline-paltry menu options, Magnolia has been popular since before it even opened. The owner, a restauranteur famous for flower-themed restaurants, has the Midas touch when it comes to location, ambiance, and fare.

The owner and his family are frequent visitors and hands down some of the nicest people I've ever met. They pay amazingly well, offer great benefits, and rumor even has it they let their daughters create the menu.

Freaking *swoon.*

It's Monday afternoon between the lunch and dinner rush, and I'm manning the hostess station while our part-timer, Gloria, takes a break. I don't mind, as the people-watching is unparalleled. Within minutes, I see a man in a leotard on a unicycle, a group of bodybuilders in Speedos, and a hundred different expressions of style and near-nakedness. Skaters weave through the crowd. Punk kids with chains and tattoos smoke cigarettes despite the ban. Adolescent girls flounce around in too much makeup and clothes that would make their parents flip. Hippies float by in clouds of pot smoke.

A group of mystified out-of-towners meander past the café, all of them wearing long-sleeved tops, pants, hats, and sunglasses. Apparently they didn't get the memo that Southern California weather is as fickle as a teen.

"Hi."

I smile at the small figure in the doorway. "Well, hello there."

He's maybe seven or eight years old, gorgeous in an innocent way—the girls haven't gotten ahold of him yet—with a mop of brown curls and dark, expressive eyes in a sun-flushed face. Dressed in swim trunks and a damp T-shirt over his narrow shoulders, I surmise he's spent most of the morning in the ocean.

Expecting his mother or father any second, I glance at the open doorway. Though a steady stream of people pass by on the boardwalk, none seem to be heading our way.

"Are your parents around?" I ask gently.

He nods, grinning so hard two dimples appear in his cheeks. "My dad is. You have cool hair. It's the same color as the cotton candy I got at the pier last week."

I laugh, lifting the braid on my shoulder and feigning a bite of the pastel pink strands—my single remaining act of outward rebellion.

Making a face, I stick out my tongue. "Yuck. Doesn't taste like cotton candy."

Mystery Boy laughs at my expense, the sound sweet and bubbling in my ears.

"Of course it's not cotton candy. It's *hair!*" He looks over his shoulder and waves. "Dad! In here!"

A tall figure rounds the corner, face downturned to his cell phone. One hand effortlessly manages the device while the other absentmindedly brushes through the curls on his son's head.

"Sorry, bud, I'm almost done answering this email. Did you finally decide where to eat?"

The beautiful boy smiles happily at me. "Yep. This is the place. This lady is nice and has pink hair. Hey—why do you look all pale?"

I can't answer him.

30

IMPLOSION

HOLY SHIT, holy shit.

Even as my brain turns to mush, my eyes greedily swallow every inch of the man before me. A man I never thought I'd see again outside my daydreams. But he's here. *Real.* And even more handsome than I remember.

Leo's dark hair is longer than it was months ago, messy and half-dry from a recent swim. Broad shoulders are encased in a faded black T-shirt, highlighting muscular arms. Swim trunks hug his lean hips, leaving his tanned calves bare.

I sway a little toward him, like I'm in free fall and he's the ground. The following seconds stretch for an eternity. The longing I'd thought buried screams like gale-force wind in my ears.

"All good," Leo says, tucking his phone in the pocket of his shorts and looking up.

"Hi," I wheeze.

He blinks, eyes so blue it hurts to look into them. His

lips part on a swiftly drawn breath. "Amelia," he says softly.

The boy—*Vincent*—grabs his dad's hand. "You know her?" he asks brightly. "That's crazy. She looks way too cool for you, Dad! How did you meet a lady with pink hair?"

For the first time since dying it, I experience a moment's regret. It passes, but not before a revelation sinks in. Even outside Oasis—perhaps even more so—I don't belong in Leo's world.

He's still staring at me, though he's regained his poise. The calm and collected doctor. The flush on his cheekbones is merely the sun's doing. The rigidity in his shoulders must be because of how fucking uncomfortable this moment is. Our stolen night together hangs between us, stark in the light of day.

"How are you?" he finally asks. "It's good to see you."

I clear my throat too loudly. "Good! Great, actually. Working here, obviously, and just, you know, living life."

I choke back more word-vomit and mentally slap myself. *Good show, Mia. Really classy.*

Leo, however, only smiles warmly, those infinitely charming crinkles appearing at the corners of his spectacle-free eyes. "How's your father doing?"

"Really great, thanks. Healthy as a horse these days." I make an effort to speak with a normal cadence, but over-shoot the mark and end up sounding stoned.

Fuck my life.

Leo drags a hand over his unshaven jaw, brilliant eyes glinting with laughter. His gaze darts to my crimson cheeks then flickers up.

"I like the hair, by the way. It suits you."

"Enough flirting already!" bleats Vince. "I'm hungry!"

We both chuckle in that stilted, child-said-something-embarrassing way. Snagging a couple of menus, I lead them to a table with a view of the boardwalk. As soon as they're seated, I mumble something about getting them water. Vince's voice stops me before I can escape.

"Do you surf?" he asks, grinning up at me. "You look like a surfer."

I glance at Leo, who's watching me with a soft smile that turns my insides to jelly. "I sure do," I tell Vince. "Almost every day. You look like you surf, too."

"I do? Yes!" He yelps in excitement and a skinny arm jerks across the table. A proudly grinning Leo fist-bumps his adorable son.

I die a little at the cuteness.

As Vince shimmies in his seat, I tell Leo softly, "He's awesome."

Blue eyes twinkle up at me. "He is."

"Hey, Dad! Why doesn't this lady give us lessons?" Without waiting for a reply, he swivels toward me. "He keeps saying he's going to get us lessons but then forgets. He's rich, too. He'll pay you."

How many feelings can you feel at the same time? A goddamn landfill's worth, that's how many. Shock at the proposal. Excitement at the idea of spending time with them. Arousal—Leo Chastain shirtless and wet and in *daylight*? Yes, please. Embarrassment, too, because Vince clearly thinks I'm a broke waitress and could use the money. Which is sadly true.

And shame. Shame that even for the briefest of moments, I forgot that Leo was once my therapist. That he saw me at my worst and knows every dark, twisted corner of my heart and soul.

I'm in hell.

"We can talk about it later, Vince," offers Leo, handing his son a menu. "Let's get some food. I told your mom I'd have you home by four."

Vince shrugs, attention diverted to his stomach.

"Thank you, Amelia," murmurs Leo. "Could we have an iced tea and a lemonade, please?"

"Sure, absolutely." I nod enough times I feel like a lunatic and finally escape to the kitchen.

———

"OH MY GOD, what did you say? What did you do? What were you wearing? Is he still the hottest therapist on legs?"

I shouldn't have called Kinsey. *What was I thinking?* I console myself with the knowledge it would have come out sooner or later. The woman has drama radar. Better to rip off the Band-Aid now than to wait until the wound is festering.

Riiiip.

"After I stared at him like a creepy stalker for a minute, I said *hello.* Then I served them lunch because that's my job. I was wearing leggings and the café's T-shirt, and yes, he's still hot. Five-o'clock shadow, windblown hair, freaking six-foot-two inches of tanned, toned, take-me-home and bend-me-over hotness."

Kinsey sighs dreamily. "Was he wearing his glasses?"

"Nope."

Another sigh. "Did he smile at you?"

Jesus.

"Yes, and he still has all his teeth, too. It's been less than four months, Kins. Not ten years."

She laughs. "Oh, Mia, you're so funny. I miss your face! Come over tonight. Nix and I are ordering Thai in a bit."

I roll my eyes, but I'm smiling. "We had dinner the night before last. Plus, I grabbed food before leaving work."

"Whatever. You're still coming tomorrow night, aren't you? You promised." She says the last in a cajoling singsong.

Ah, yes, the much-anticipated Halloween party. Anticipated on her end, that is. I'd rather stab myself in the eye than hang out at Kinsey's with a shit-ton of Hollywood's young and restless, but she's right. I did promise.

"Yes," I grumble.

"Are you going to tell me what you're dressing up as? The curiosity is killing me."

"Not a chance."

"But—"

"Gotta go! Say hi to Nix and don't forget to use a condom." I hang up before she can reply.

Ferdi's head lifts from my lap, disturbingly perceptive green eyes meeting mine. I sigh. "I guess I should think about a costume, huh?"

Slow blink, which I translate as cat-speak for *Duh.*

31

WALK THE PLANK

"ARE YOU SERIOUS?" deadpans Kinsey.

I look down at myself, then frown at her. "What do you mean? This costume is classic."

"Classic like *boring*." Laughing, she tugs at the zipper of my wetsuit that sits near my throat. "Zombie Surfer? Really?"

I shrug. "Maybe it's not original, but my makeup is on point. I freaking spent two hours watching YouTube tutorials."

Her nose scrunches. "Yeah, the makeup is pretty good. You look freaky."

I know exactly why she's giving me a hard time, but it's more fun to skirt around the issue. Her own costume is a sexy version of Alice in Wonderland, which means Nix is probably the Mad Hatter. With a quick sweep of the room, I confirm that the ratio of exposed skin to clothing is drastically skewed. I, on the other hand, am wearing my scuba wetsuit, which covers me from wrist to ankle and is nice and thick.

The weather took a dive today and it's actually chilly tonight. I'm going to be comfortable hanging outside, where the main party is going on, while everyone else is going to freeze.

Basically, I'm a genius.

Turning back to Kinsey, I open my mouth to compliment her costume—or maybe point out the goosebumps on her arms—but before I can get a word out she grabs the zipper near my neck and yanks it down, exposing my bikini top.

"Dude," I protest.

Kinsey grins at my exposed cleavage. "Much better."

I pull the zipper back up.

She pulls it back down.

It happens three more times before we hear Nix's loud laughter. "Leave the girl alone, Kins!" he says, draping an arm around his girlfriend's shoulder. He squints at me. "Zombie surfer, huh? Cool."

I arch a brow at a scowling Kinsey. "See?"

She's unswayed. "Friendship is about compromise, Mia."

I begrudgingly lower the zipper to my cleavage. "Fine, but only because you told me fifty times how important this party is to you."

Her features soften. "Thanks." She glances around the beautiful backyard. There's a live band playing, a ton of quality Halloween decorations—including performers whose sole goal is to scare the bejeezus out of partygoers. Servers dressed as ghouls carry around trays with themed appetizers, and the bartenders are all dressed up as vampires.

"Does it seem like everyone's having fun?" she asks, glancing nervously between Nix and me.

"Of course, babe!" Nix says quickly.

"I just got here, but there are probably a hundred people in your yard." I point toward a nearby group. "Look, people laughing. Laughing means fun. Oh, and dancing. Dancing is fun, too."

Kinsey nods, tension releasing from her shoulders. Nix kisses her temple. This is the first year her annual party hasn't been geared toward outright depravity. No drugs. No hard alcohol, only beer and wine. The guest list was whittled way down from prior years, too, from a whopping three hundred to a mere one-fifty.

"Thanks, guys, I feel better." Kinsey gives herself a shake and grins up at Nix. "Time to mingle!"

I point in a vague direction. "I'm going to, uh…"

They laugh at me. Kinsey blows me a kiss. "Try to have fun, Mia. And remember, you can't leave before midnight."

I give her an ironic salute. "You got it, boss."

I head for the nearest bar.

AT ELEVEN THIRTY, the party is still going strong. For the most part, it's stayed classy. No broken glass or calls to the cops. That being said, the Incredible Hulk is holding Wonder Woman's hair as she pukes into a bush. A werewolf is fondling Betty Boop's breasts near the fence, and there's a couple in the hot tub who may or may not be having public sex.

I've been camped out on a lounge by the pool for the last hour or so, nursing my third beer, people-watching, and generally enjoying the repellent effect of my scary makeup and covered body. Contrary to the pitying looks from passersby, I'm not bored or lonely. I've been texting with friends at various bars and other parties, hassling Jameson for staying home to hand out candy, and basking in the knowledge that I'm off tomorrow and can sleep in.

"Is this seat taken?" asks a muffled, male voice.

I don't look up to see whatever mask he's wearing. Eyes on my phone, I wave at the empty lounge beside mine. "Nope."

The man settles with a sigh, tossing legs and booted feet onto the lounge. He smells good. Weirdly familiar. Ignoring the urge to glance at him, I text Jameson.

Will Jessica be at the house Sunday?

I think so

Should we start calling her Mom?

Wow

Too soon?

Are you drunk? Leave me alone

Whatever

I might, in fact, be a little drunk.

"Nice night, isn't it?"

"Yes," I mutter distractedly.

"Pretty cold, though."

Mr. Conversation over here.

I lower my phone and look at my companion, prepared to dissuade any notions he has of scoring casual sex. He's dressed as a pirate, complete with eye patch, bandana covering the lower half of his face, and a fancy hat set at an angle that obscures most of his visible eye. A billowing white shirt is unlaced at the throat to expose a tanned neck and a patch of smooth skin. Snug black pants flatter the hell out of his long legs.

Pulling my head from the gutter, I glance up again, trying unsuccessfully to see his face. *Why does he seem so familiar?* I'm two beers past answering that question or considering it for longer than a second or two.

"Do I pass inspection?" he asks with a small chuckle.

That chuckle.

My breath catches. My skin prickles. Reaching forward, I yank the bandana down his face. It snags on his ears and he makes a small, pained noise.

"Sorry not sorry," I breathe.

He laughs, tugging the bandana the rest of the way down and pulling off his hat. The eyepatch is next, flipping up to expose his other bright blue eye. Both of them are now fixed on my face, their expression unreadable.

"Happy Halloween, Amelia."

Not yet recovered from shock, I continue gaping. "What are you doing here?"

"Kinsey sent an invitation to my office last month. I

wasn't going to come—it's not exactly professional—but then I realized you'd probably be here and professionalism flew out the window."

He says it so matter-of-factly, like the words didn't just explode my brain. "What?"

His gaze lowers to my chest. Electricity follows the path of his visual caress. The zipper is still above my breasts, but I suddenly feel more naked than the skinny-dippers currently in the pool.

Leo drags a hand over his mouth, eyes snapping up to mine. "I'm not good at this, so I'm just going to tell you the truth. I've never been more attracted to anyone in my life than I am to you. I thought a few months would change things, but it didn't. Hasn't. I'm not sure what to do about it, or what I'm asking, or if you even—"

"Are you propositioning me?" I blurt.

"I don't know. Maybe." He swallows hard. "I'm not sure I can offer you a normal, uh, situation."

What the WHAT?

His feet hit the ground between our chairs. Propping elbows on his knees, he lowers his head, shaking it like he has no clue how he got here. I want so badly to touch the dark strands, to pull his head up and kiss him until we both go insane, but my emotions are bouncing around like kids on sugar. Not all of them are excited, either. And one of them feels a lot like heartbreak.

"Tell me what to do, Amelia," he says softly. "Tell me what you want."

My libido provides a flashback of the hot springs. Warmth surges through me, coalescing in my breasts and between my legs. I've relived that night so many times I should own stock in batteries.

Do I want more of that?

Hell yes, hollers Vagina. *Best sex ever!*

Wait a darn minute, cautions Heart. *He's asking for sex, not a date.*

A date would mean… well, dating. A potential relationship as equals. Being seen together in public.

He's a respected psychiatrist.

I'm his ex-patient.

"Leo?"

He looks up sharply, eagerly. "Yes?"

I open my mouth, then close it and look away. On the other side of the pool, I spot Kinsey and Nix. They're standing close, smiling and kissing and holding each other. Oblivious to my crisis of conscience, insulated by their love. For some reason, the sight of them calms me. Brain takes advantage, delivering a knock-out punch to Vagina.

When I turn back to Leo, he speaks before I can. "You don't have to answer. I understand. And fuck, I'm *proud* of you. My only excuse is I haven't been thinking clearly since I saw you yesterday. I'm sorry."

I manage a wobbly smile. "Don't be sorry. For anything. You brought me back to life."

He studies me another moment, then nods and stands. "If it's any consolation, you did the same for me."

Watching him walk away lands in the top five worst moments of my life.

32

GREY MATTER

MAKING hard choices in alignment with my highest, healthiest self sounds great in theory. In reality, it sucks. Leo Chastain asked me to be his booty call and I turned him down. Why the hell did I do that? Because of some inner-princess telling me I deserve more? The boring ritual of dinner and a movie before sex? Push and pull and ignoring calls and the usual, stupid games men and women play?

More importantly, what if it's not about me deserving something at all? What if my choice didn't stem from self-respect or some new, misguided sense of dignity but stemmed instead from patriarchal conditioning that tells me I can't trust my impulses? That I'm not allowed to follow my body's desires and have mind-blowing, no-strings-attached sex with my ex-doctor?

"Is that all it would be? Sex?" asks Dr. Wilson, one eyebrow arched.

Winded from my tirade, I sink back into the plush couch in her office. "I don't know how to answer that. I'm not in love with him—I get there was some Stockholmey-ness happening for a while, and that I don't really know him beyond what he shared in our sessions."

"But?"

I look out the window at the closest palm tree. "It's complicated. I have a lot of respect for him. I trust him, feel… safe, I guess, because he's seen the worst of me already."

Dr. Wilson makes a noise of consideration. "Finding acceptance is a powerful motivator in the search for relationships. Unfortunately, he implied that he doesn't want a relationship, likely because of the professional ramifications. Is that something you can live with, or would it make you feel like he was ashamed of you?"

I don't bother answering.

She doesn't know Leo's name or exactly when he treated me, but she's a smart cookie and has rightly gleaned his personality. She's also a nonjudgmental cookie, which is one of the main reasons I've stuck around.

"Have you ever had the hots for a patient, Doc?"

Like I knew she would, she deflects the question. "Therapy can create a strong, pseudo-intimacy between two people. When those people also have physical chemistry, that closeness can be mistaken for something else."

"Love?" I ask rhetorically.

She nods. "Obviously I don't know this man's inner thoughts and can only speak from my experience. But perhaps his conflict is not too dissimilar from yours. A battle between what he wants and what he thinks is expected of him. Consider his parting words on Halloween."

You did the same for me.

I shake my head. "He couldn't have meant I brought him back to life. Right? Maybe he misheard what I said."

The damn eyebrow goes up. "Why do you say that?"

"Because I have self-worth issues," I mutter robotically.

Dr. Wilson smiles softly. "I think it's time to disavow you of the notion that life is simply a series of good or bad choices, Amelia. It's much more than that."

"I know," I parrot.

"Do you?" She waits for me to look at her before continuing. "What if instead of focusing so much on what you *should* and *shouldn't* do or what *is* or *isn't* healthy, you try focusing on what makes you happy?"

We've had this conversation before. Hell, Leo said almost the same thing to me at one point.

"You still don't get it," I say tiredly. "I don't trust the things that make me happy. Except for surfing. And sushi. All the other shit landed me in a world of pain."

"You don't trust yourself *yet*," she replies gently. "That's okay, Amelia. There's no finish line here. We have to wrap up, but I want you to think about something for me when you do your journaling tonight."

"What's that?"

"Perhaps all the skydiving, base-jumping, reckless driving, et cetera, wasn't so much a mission to feel close to your mother and brother, but a search for something else. An aftereffect, if you will."

I stare blankly at her. "Not picking up what you're putting down, Doc."

"How did you feel when you landed on the ground after jumping out of a plane?"

"Invincible," I murmur.

Dr. Wilson smiles. "You never needed fear, Amelia. You just needed to feel safe."

———

WHEN I GET HOME, Ferdi isn't there to greet me. He loves prowling in the early evening, so I'm not surprised so much as pathetically lonely without him.

To stave off my therapy hangover and imminent consumption of an entire frozen pizza, I light a few candles and put on a Miles Davis record before wandering into my bedroom. I trade my casual, wraparound dress for ripped jeans and a navy sweater, then throw my hair into a messy topknot. For exactly 3.2 seconds, I also consider dealing with the pile of laundry on my closet's floor.

Yeah, no.

While the oven preheats, I take my phone to the couch and browse Facebook. Grateful people. Sad people. Angry people. Drooling babies. Cute dogs. Same old, same old.

Then I see a status update from my brother, which is equivalent to a UFO sighting.

Jameson Sloan
Today at 5:04 p.m.

Come support Ice Holes hockey tonight @ Ice Arena,
8:00 p.m. It's the playoffs and we need support!

The fact that he didn't text me to invite me means one of two things. Either he remembers my overt condemnation of grown men beating each other up with sticks and pucks, or Kevin is playing tonight.

My bones start itching. When I told Dr. Wilson about the sensation, she said it means my instincts are trying to talk to me. If that's the case, then right now they're screaming, "Stop procrastinating on making amends, asshole! Talk to Kevin after the game, then you never have to see him again!"

Fuck.

I haul myself off the couch and turn off the oven, then impulsively call my dad. He picks up on the second ring.

"Mia! Jessica and I were just talking about you. Are you going to Jameson's game tonight?"

I'm still not used to how happy he sounds when he hears from me now. But damn, it's nice.

"Uh, are you?" I hedge.

"Yep. We're leaving in a few minutes. Can we pick you up?"

In the background, I hear Jessica say, "Come with us!"

What do they call it when the universe conspires to make something happen? Oh, right.

Bad luck.

33

BARN BURNER

Oh, ice hockey, how I love to hate you. But what female can truly hate such a gorgeous display of masculinity? The sheer physical strength required to skate so fast, so gracefully, is astounding, as is the necessary mental acuity to keep track of a tiny, flying disc.

I haven't been to a game since Kevin and I broke up. Not even to support my brother, who offered at least ten times to kick Kevin off the team. I honestly didn't care and told him as much. It wasn't like watching the games was my favorite pastime.

Though Jameson never mentioned anything else about defending my honor, a few weeks post-breakup I did overhear him explaining to Dad the reason for his scabbed, bruised knuckles. My twin kicked some cheater-ass, almost landing Kevin in the hospital. But because men are weird, apparently the Fight Club reenactment settled the issue—Kevin still plays defense for the Ice Holes.

Jessica and I sit on the top row of bleachers outside the

rink, munching on popcorn drowned in butter and wincing every time someone hits a wall. My dad can't handle being so far from the action and is pressed up against the plexi-glass barrier along with a handful of other enthusiasts, alternately cheering and cussing.

"Should he be getting so worked up?" I ask as I watch him pound on the glass. He's not the only one going apeshit, but I missed whatever happened to cause the hysteria.

Jessica smiles and taps her watch. "He's not allowed to yell more than once every five minutes. If he does, we have to leave."

My eyes widen. "You're savage."

Just then, my dad turns and looks up at us. Jessica holds up five fingers. He grins sheepishly in return, then nods and turns back to the glass.

"Can we keep you?" I ask fervently.

Jessica laughs, blushing a pretty pink. "That depends on your dad, Mia. Oh! Look at Jameson go!"

My brother weaves expertly around opponents, the puck flying just ahead of his stick. Making it look effortless, he feints a few times, does an awesome spin, and slaps the puck into the goal just as the buzzer ends the second period.

"You want anything?" asks Jessica. "I'm gonna hit the ladies' room and grab a soda."

I shake my head. "I'm good, thanks."

She moves agilely down the bleachers as the teams skate off the ice for a breather. The score is 2-1 in favor of the Ice Holes. I watch my brother's teammates congregating on the bench. Three seats down from my brother, Kevin removes his helmet and squirts water into his mouth.

Oddly, seeing his face doesn't escalate my anxiety. I'm not even that nervous. For a long time, my selective memory painted Kevin as some evildoer who deserved slow dismemberment, but like Dr. Wilson is trying to teach me, things aren't usually as simple as *good* and *bad*. Yes, he cheated on me, but I had a part in our demise, too. I was pretending to be someone I wasn't, and that wasn't fair to either of us.

"Amelia!"

I look around the crowded bleachers for the source of the voice but don't see anyone looking at me.

"Over here!"

A skinny arm waves at me from the third row. Attached to the arm is a familiar—and shocking—face, currently grinning from ear to ear. *Vincent*. I gawk for a second, then smile and wave back. Scanning the area, I don't see Leo. Two women bracket Vincent, all of them wearing beanies and jackets. Could it be Marianne and Celia?

What the hell are they all doing here?

My gaze snaps to the opposing team's bench. Like clouds parting, two players shift and #17's jersey comes into view.

CHASTAIN

For the love of God, seriously?

"Are you here to see my dad?"

In the lapse during which my brain half-melted, Vincent climbed the bleachers. There aren't many people on the top rows, so he perches beside my propped feet and smiles up at me.

My vocabulary finally returns. "Uh, no, actually. My brother is on the other team."

His nose scrunches. "Aw, that sucks. We're gonna whoop them in the last period."

I can't help laughing. "Is that right?"

Vincent nods confidently. "My dad almost went pro. He's the best player in the league."

My mind flashes back to one of the sessions at Oasis and Leo asking, *"Do you have a weakness for hockey players?"*

Wow, Universe. Just wow.

"Do you like my dad?"

Focusing on Vincent's face and the bright curiosity there, I nod. "He's pretty cool."

"Yeah. For an old guy. How old are you? Do you have a boyfriend?"

This freaking kid.

"I'm, uh, twenty-eight. And no."

To my endless gratitude, the buzzer interrupts Vincent's next, no-doubt-awkward question. The teams hit the ice, skating around the newly polished surface. I lose sight of #17, but not for long. A figure—familiar even through pads—stops at the glass opposite Vincent's abandoned seat. Through the clear visor, I see Leo's questioning look to the women.

All I can do is watch, a bystander to life's hilarity, as the women turn and point up, as Leo's gaze lifts, scanning, then lands like a blow on my face.

His eyes widen. His mouth drops open.

"There he is!" cries Vincent, standing and waving.

Leo recovers, grinning and waving at his son. My stomach does a little flip, then my ovaries join in with an irrepressible shimmy. Leo's final glance is for me, and it's so full of heat that my toes curl. All my excuses and defenses melt like smoke.

Just like that, I know—I'm getting on the train and riding it until it crashes.

The puck drops and it's instant pandemonium on the ice. Tapping Vincent on the shoulder, I ask over the noise, "Do you think you can give me your dad's phone number?"

"Sure! What for?"

I think fast. "I, um, want to talk to him about those surfing lessons."

Vincent's whole face lights up. "Awesome!"

The lie doesn't sit well, but the truth isn't an option. I only hope that when this bites me in the ass, it won't hurt too badly. And won't hurt anyone else at all.

Putting my guilt aside, I smile at Vincent as I enter Leo's number in my phone, then promise I'll do my best to convince his dad about the lessons. I doubt Leo will go for it, but at least it's a promise I can keep.

34

CAREFUL WHAT YOU WISH FOR

ON MY COUCH with a glass of wine and a purring Ferdi, I reflect on the surreal night I've had. From the phone number that's burning a hole in my phone, to seeing my dad and Jessica kiss for the first time, and finally to my frank, surprising conversation with Kevin after the game.

I almost didn't talk to him. Vincent was right—Leo's team wiped the ice with the Ice Holes. Leo himself scored four goals, basically making everyone else look like schmucks in ice skates. Vincent also confided in me that his dad played horribly the first two periods, and he'd secretly worried they'd lose. Although vain, I couldn't help but wonder if his sudden change was due to knowing I was watching.

Experience told me Kevin took winning—and losing—very seriously, and I balked at the notion of making amends when he was in a crappy headspace. But the desire to get it over with won out, and after saying goodbye to Vincent and telling Jessica that Jameson would drive me home, I camped out by Kevin's car and waited.

Dr. Wilson and I ran through different scenarios of what might happen when I told Kevin the truth, from good to really bad. In reality, it was somewhere in between. He was surprised to see me, glad I was doing well, and apologized multiple times for his infidelity.

I made amends for destroying his record collection and finally told him about the baby. He wasn't angry that I kept it from him, more confused as to why I didn't want his support—financially or otherwise. I tried to explain, but eventually realized the futility of articulating something I didn't fully understand myself.

By the end of the conversation, we were laughing about the bonfire on the front lawn like two friends reliving wilder days. He waved off my offer to replace the records or give him money for them, then we laughed again when I joked that we'd both be dead by the time I paid him back, anyway. We hugged and that was that.

By the time I went looking for Jameson—and found him chatting up a blonde near the concessions stand—the parking lot was nearly empty and Leo and his family long gone.

Now, my phone sits like a lead weight in my hand. Nina Simone croons from my record player, and Ferdi is doing cat yoga to reach his belly with his tongue.

"Fuck it," I mutter and gulp the remainder of my wine.

Hi, it's Amelia. I've reconsidered your offer

His reply comes twenty minutes later, long enough for me to think myself into a hole of regret, eat two string-cheese sticks, drink another glass of wine, and seriously consider dyeing my hair blue.

> I don't think there was an offer on the table for surfing lessons

> The other offer, smartass

> Ah, good. Where do you live?

> Venice

> Leaving Marianne's. I can be there in 20. What's your address?

My heart jackknifes into my throat. *Oh, shit.* A small part of me was hoping he wouldn't reply at all. Another part was planning a rendezvous several days from now. Like after a waxing appointment and copious Kegels. Not *right now.*

Ferdi gives me a kitty grin and licks his chops.

I text Leo my address, because I'm apparently still a slave to impulse. At least this one. *Him.* And because even now, my skin feels laced with live wires and all I want is Leo to turn the voltage higher and higher until I combust. And finally, because I might still be 10 percent crazy.

Even though Dr. Wilson said I shouldn't think so much about *wrong* and *right* but instead pursue what makes me happy, I have the feeling this isn't what she meant.

Too late now, sings Vagina happily.

Heart is resoundingly silent.

EVEN THOUGH I'M waiting for it, I jump when the knock comes. I texted him the gate code a few minutes ago, got a reply that he was close, and have spent the intervening time staring at the front door and periodically sniffing my armpits to make sure my deodorant is still working.

My fingers spasm on the doorknob, but I manage to turn it and open the door. *Leo.* The sight of him steals my breath, his tall frame taking up most of my doorway, the ocean breeze flowing around him and bringing his scent to me. My mouth waters.

He's dressed down in sweats and a black tee, his hair wet from a recent shower. Our staring contest lasts until he clears his throat. "I wasn't sure you'd actually open the door."

My first attempt to speak is an unintelligible sound. I cough in embarrassment and try again. "Um, hi. Come on in."

I step back to let him pass, then close the door and lock it. Leaning against the wall to give my shaking legs a break, I watch him look around my small sanctuary. My eyes track his every movement, my brain still not convinced he's really here.

"I like this. It's very you." Turning, he smiles softly. "Colorful. Eclectic. Lovely."

"Thanks," I squeak. "Do you want something to drink? I don't have anything fancy. Just water or wine. It's like the Last Supper up in here." I snort, then throw a hand over my mouth.

Leo grins, eyes dancing. "You're nervous."

I wince. "What gave it away?"

He takes a step toward me. "To be honest, I'm nervous, too."

"You don't look nervous," I retort, then lose control of my mouth. "You look perfectly calm, like this is no big deal. Do you do this often or something?"

His smile kicks up a notch as his brows lift. "Do what? Obsess for months over a woman I can't have? Make impulsive decisions like stalking her at a party to basically beg for sex? Drive over the speed limit to get to her house like an addict in search of a fix?"

"Uhh—"

Three more steps swallow the space between us. He palms the side of my face, the contact of his hot hand ricocheting down my arm, across my chest, and settling like a shot of liquor in my belly.

Gaze on my mouth, his thumb strokes lightly across my lips. I watch his eyelashes flutter and feel the beginnings of something dangerous. So, so dangerous.

"Amelia," he whispers. His eyes lift to mine, indigo in the candlelight. "I want you so much."

Danger has never sounded so good.

35

GLOW SO BRIGHT

LEO LIFTS MY CHIN GENTLY, reverently, and grazes his lips over mine. That second—that one, perfect second—we sigh together in relief, in abject surrender. There's no going back now. The train has left the ever-loving station.

Strong hands sweep down my arms and settle on my waist, fingers stretching up to claim the space just beneath my braless breasts. My nipples tingle in anticipation, but he only teases me there with slow strokes, not moving any higher, as he takes decadent, deep kisses from my mouth. Every cell in my body is awake and screaming for *more-pleasenow*, but when I squirm in need he only whispers, "I didn't wait this long to rush."

Moving from my lips, he kisses my cheek, my jaw, then finds an incredibly sensitive spot on my neck just beneath my ear. He murmurs approval as I arch forward, seeking friction but finding none.

"Leo," I gasp, "please."

He pauses his worship of my throat and speaks against my skin. "I like the sound of you begging, Amelia. But I also like it when you take what you want."

I grab his hips and pull him against me. We groan together at the contact of hard against soft. His teeth nip at my throat before his head lifts, eyes finding mine.

"Do you feel how much I want you?"

I'm currently rubbing myself against said *feeling* like a cat in heat. Nodding mindlessly, I hook one leg around his hips for better access. His smile molds to mine.

"Where's the bedroom?"

"Over there somewhere. Who cares," I mumble.

Finding the waist of his sweatpants, I yank them down. They don't move very far, but my brain doesn't understand that my leg is in the way. I continue my futile tugging until Leo chuckles and grabs my thighs, hoisting me into his arms.

I lick and nip at his jaw, neck, and ear as he walks down the hallway, turns into the bathroom, reverses and turns, and finds my candlelit bedroom. He follows me down to the bed, putting delicious pressure between my legs. At my needy moan, some of his control unravels—enough that he finally gives my breasts the attention they crave, palming and kneading them like his mission in life is to memorize their shape. When his mouth closes over one tight peak, wetness seeping through my shirt, the animal inside me claws to the surface.

I clumsily attack his clothing, muttering nonsensically about *slow sucks* and *gimmegimmenow*, until he vibrates with laughter and finally helps in my quest. His shirt is first, whipped off with one hand, then his pants are kicked clumsily down his legs. While he's occupied I manage to get my own shirt off and wiggle out of my shorts and underwear. Another joined sigh, another surrender, as our bodies find each other with nothing between.

His hand delves between my legs. I spread eagerly for him, arching up to capture his lips. He groans into my mouth, "You're wet for me, Amelia."

"Always," I mumble, my hands seeking and finding his thick cock. "You're hard for me, Leo."

He thrusts lightly between my palms. "Always," he whispers back and dips one, then two fingers inside me. "Still have your IUD?"

"I love it when you talk dirty to me."

I feel his smile against my cheek. His thumb circles my clit, teasing around it but *not quite* where I want the pressure. Which he knows. Of course.

"Yes," I concede, "and I haven't been with anyone since you."

His head rears back, startled eyes on mine. "Really?"

I frown. "Yes, really. Random dick isn't my thing."

His nose crinkles even as his lips twitch with a smile. My heart wakes up, squeezing painfully at the adorableness of his expression. To distract myself, I give him another firm squeeze. He twitches in my hands.

A little frown puckers his brow. "I'm—I need to be inside you. Do you want more foreplay?"

Is he kidding?

"Are you kidding?"

The frown clears, swept away by savage need. In all my years, I've never seen the look in his eyes from any lover. Like I'm more than exquisite—like I'm worthy of worship.

One hand anchored behind my neck, the other disappearing between us, Leo kisses me. He kisses me until we are one taste and one breath. For all his hunger, he slides inside me slowly, breaking barriers of sensation I never knew existed.

Although he's been inside me before, this time is different. So fucking different. There's no frenzy, no overriding sense of illicitness. His hands capture my wrists over my head while his eyes stay on my face, studying every nuance of my shifting expressions. Every slow withdraw and smooth thrust breaks me open wider, pierces me deeper. I've never felt so utterly possessed or been more aware of my own femininity.

"You're beautiful, Amelia. So fucking sexy. You have no idea what you do to me."

Though his words veer dangerously close to my heart, I answer by locking my ankles behind his back. "Show me, Leo."

He releases my wrists, hauling me against him with his arms locked tightly around me. Head lowered to my shoulder, his rhythm changes. Harder, deeper. Halfway to oblivion, I don't even attempt to dampen my cries. No doubt I'll be hearing from the neighbors tomorrow, but right now I don't give a flying fuck.

"Oh, God, Leo, yes, right there, *there!*"

A cataclysmic event tingles in my fingers and toes, surges up my arms and legs, trembles in my chest, and finally coalesces where we join. I scream in bliss. Teeth clamp on my neck so hard I see stars, and the pleasure sharpens. Explodes.

He says my name and finds his own release. When he relaxes and kisses me softly, I start crying.

Sobbing, actually.

Leo rolls onto his side and holds me against his chest. He murmurs words I can't hear, but I feel his heat, and the soothing touch of his hand making ceaseless journeys up and down my spine.

I finally assemble enough sanity to say, "I don't know what's wrong with me. I'm sorry."

"Don't be sorry," he says softly. "Do you feel sad or anxious right now?"

I shake my head, hiccupping. "I feel like your monster cock annihilated me."

The hand on my back freezes. "My what?" Leaning back to see my face, Leo regards me with wide eyes and an open mouth. "Did you say *monster cock*?"

I bite my lip and nod. "Sure did."

He laughs—a deep belly laugh I've never heard before—then kisses the tears from my cheeks. "Tell me you're okay."

"Fine. Totally fine. Better than fine. I can't see straight, though. Hey, what happened to your glasses?"

Still chuckling, he says, "I got LASIK last month."

"Ah, that explains it." Yawning, I curl contently into his heat. In my last moments of consciousness, I say, "Wake me up in twenty. I want more."

A soft kiss presses to my forehead. "Sleep, Amelia."

I do.

———

WHEN I WAKE UP, the sun shines through my filmy curtains, glowing brightly on my empty bed. I hold back panic long enough to sit up and see my phone plugged in on the night-stand. Definitely not where I left it last night.

Sure enough, the first notification is for three new text messages from Leo, all sent between five thirty and six thirty this morning.

> Had every intention of waking you in twenty but fell asleep. Woke up at four with a giant cat sitting on my chest. Might have shaved a few years off my life. Warning next time?

> So you know, I wasn't trying to sneak out. You must sleep like the dead because I knocked into at least five pieces of furniture trying to find my clothes, keys, etc.

> What are you doing tonight?

I read the messages over and over, a stupid grin on my face, then text him back. His instantaneous response tells me he was waiting for it. Maybe worried I might not reply.

Silly man.

> Working until nine. After...?

Good morning :) Forgot to mention I found an interesting note on your front door from your neighbors. Turns out you have thin walls. Want to come to my place tonight?

Yes.

Yes, I do.

36

CONSEQUENCES

Work flies by in one of those dreamy streaks that happen when your mind is occupied by rainbows and unicorns—and sexy, smart men with monster cocks. I can't stop smiling. My coworkers tease me, my customers leave awesome tips, and when I leave for the day I all but sprint to my apartment.

As I'm staring at a half-full, battered backpack and wondering if Leo expects me to stay the night, my phone vibrates with a call.

"Hey, Kins," I chirp.

"Hey," she says morosely.

"What's wrong?"

"I need to confess something I did that I feel really bad about."

I bite my lips on a smile, knowing exactly what she's going to apologize for. "Oh?" I ask noncommittally.

"Yeah, um... remember how I told you not to leave the

Halloween party before midnight? Well, see, it was because—"

I can't take it anymore and laugh. "You knew Leo might show up late. It's okay."

"OhmyGod, I've been freaking out, worried that something shitty happened and it was all my fault. I saw him talking to you, but then he left by himself, and you went home alone, and—"

"I'm going over to his place tonight."

"What?" she screeches. "Spill. Now."

I fill her in on everything that's happened since Halloween, then wait for her blubbering excitement. It doesn't come; instead, she's uncharacteristically quiet.

"Kinsey?"

"I'm here." She pauses, then sighs. "Are you sure this is okay? A sex-only relationship? I mean, it is *Leo Chastain* we're talking about. You're pretty much in love with him."

I laugh uneasily. "It's just sex, Kins. I'm not in love with him. I barely know him."

Another pause. "I don't believe you. You guys have way more than just a physical connection."

I don't really believe me, either.

"I'm aware of the risk," I tell her soberly. "I know he might break my heart. But I can't... I don't want to stop. I want him. Want to be around him for however long he wants me. I can't explain it, really, but I don't feel like I used to—like he's just a means to an end, someone I can use. He's... different. I'm different."

"Shit," she groans. "Okay, Mia. I love you and support

you no matter what. Just… please be careful. I don't want you to get hurt."

"I know. Love you too. I'll check in tomorrow."

"You'd better."

Ending the call, I sit listlessly beside my backpack. Kinsey didn't say anything I don't already know, even if I've tucked the truth away in a tiny, locked box in my head. As much as I tell myself I don't have feelings for Leo, that my attachment is merely a byproduct of the pseudo-intimacy of our many sessions at Oasis, I know it's not that simple.

This time when I fall, there will be no parachute. Nothing but wind between me and the ground.

So be it.

LEO'S HOUSE isn't what I expected. When the Uber drops me off outside, I double-check my phone to make sure I have the right address.

I always imagined him in some high-rise condo or a modern masterpiece of glass, wood, and clean lines. Instead, he lives in Echo Park on a quaint street with kids bikes leaning on front porches, small but lovingly tended yards, and sidewalks shadowed by big trees.

The bones of the house in front of me give the impression they've been standing for a century or so but have the immaculate polish of an extensive remodel. Half of the yard is grass, the other half full of overflowing garden beds.

There's a picket fence, for God's sake. Not white, but still, a *picket fence.*

I walk up the path to the front porch, battling a full-blown case of *what-the-hell-am-I-doing-heres.* Two bikes rest against the vine-covered lattice beneath the porch, one man-sized and one kid-sized. A forgotten baseball bat lies in the grass, along with a worn baseball and a sun-faded nerf gun.

I make it up the steps onto the porch and pause to catch my breath. I'm winded. *Why the fuck am I winded?*

I'm only about 30 percent recovered when the front door opens, spilling light and soft music. I jerk upright and plaster on a smile I hope doesn't look like a crazy person's.

"Hi," I wheeze.

Leo smirks, crossing his arms and leaning against the doorframe. He's in business slacks and a white shirt sans tie, the sleeves rolled to his elbows. A kitchen towel drapes over one shoulder, and his hair is styled, boasting the familiar razor-sharp part. That, of all things, is what calms me down.

"Did you walk here?" he deadpans, noting my flushed face and erratic breathing.

I push a few stray hairs from my face. "Can I lie to you?"

His smile grows. "Go for it."

"Yes, I walked. Needed some exercise."

He bites his lower lip, glancing behind me. "It's a strenuous trip from the curb up to the porch, huh?"

I nod. "Basically an Iron Man competition."

A smile blooms, crinkling his eyes. "Come here, Amelia."

"Okay," I whisper, not moving.

So he comes to me, smile softening as he takes the straps of my backpack and pulls it off, then captures my hand in his.

"I still make you nervous," he says mildly as he escorts me into the house. I barely notice my surroundings other than pale walls and reclaimed wood floors. His hand is hot, like a small sun on my clammy palm.

"No. I mean, yes. I wasn't expecting…" I trail off, staring into a beautiful living room with comfy couches, a low coffee table littered with various toys and man-clutter, fireplace, and big flat-screen TV.

"You thought I lived in a sterile box, didn't you?"

My gaze jerks to his face and wry expression. "Maybe."

He chuckles, dropping my backpack inside the front door. "Are you hungry? I got home late tonight and just cooked dinner. There's enough for two."

My stomach is in knots, but I nod. "I could eat, sure."

His fingers squeeze mine then release. "I was just about to throw pasta in some water. Is meat sauce okay? I can't remember if you're a vegetarian."

Stop being so perfect, asshole. I can't handle it.

"I'm not. That sounds great. I love pasta and meat. Me and meat and pasta go way back."

Fuckitty-fuck, Mia. My eyes roll upward, hoping to manifest a lightning bolt to strike me down and end it all.

Leo's hands cupping my face jolt me into the moment. His bright blue eyes are mere inches from mine. I wonder how I ever thought they were icy. There's nothing remotely cold in them now.

"Hey," he whispers.

I release a shuddering breath. "Hi. Sorry for the freak-out."

"No need to apologize. I don't want you to pretend with me. I want to know what you're thinking and feeling. Full disclosure here, okay?"

Not gonna happen, buddy.

I nod. "Sure."

His lips touch mine lightly, coaxing them to part. I surrender and sag against him, tension unraveling from my body as his tongue finds mine. The kiss is dizzying, his touch and heat permeating my senses.

I palm him through his slacks, delighting in his grunt. "I'm turning the stove off," he growls against my mouth. "We can order food later."

This I know.

This I want.

This I can handle.

37

______

ACCELERATION

W E   M I S S the window for food delivery and end up making the pasta and reheating sauce at one in the morning. Then we stumble upstairs and embrace carb-comas until Leo's alarm goes off at the ungodly hour of 6:00 a.m.

Gently removing his arm from beneath my head, he disappears into the bathroom. The shower comes on a minute later. I wiggle into the strip of heat left by his body and drift between sleep and waking until the water shuts off. Then I haul myself from bed in the hazy dawn light to rifle through my backpack for clean clothes.

I'm sitting on the bed, a sleep-deprived zombie with bedhead, when Leo reappears. He smirks at me as he deftly buttons his charcoal dress shirt.

I scowl back. "How do you look so bright-eyed and bushy-tailed? It's not natural. I feel bulldozed."

"Practice," he drawls, dropping a kiss on my head before moving to a nearby dresser. He smells unbelievably good. Me? Not so much.

I flop back onto the bed and stretch my arms, wincing at how sore I am in places with no business being sore. Returning from the dresser, Leo sits near my hip to put on socks. I memorize his handsome, relaxed profile, the flex of muscles in his back, the thick wrists and strong, talented hands. Even the muted *swish* of his shirt as he moves is music to me.

My chest feels unaccountably warm. Domestic bliss is so real.

He pivots, finding me watching him. "I'm glad you stayed the night," he says softly.

"Me too. Your bed is topnotch."

He grins. "So that's why you stayed. I knew it."

I suppress a smile. "You make a pretty good pillow, too."

He snorts and reaches for his tie. Sensing the end of our time together nearing, I stand and try to tame the rat's nest on my head, then slip into my shoes and repack my backpack. When I'm finished, I wait awkwardly near the bed as he puts on his tie before a mirror.

"So, um…" I clear the frog from my throat. "That is…"

Dancing eyes meet mine in the mirror. "Just say it," he says.

"AmIgoingtoseeyouagain?"

Leo abandons his half-done tie and crosses to me. He's trying hard not to laugh. Reaching up, he gently tugs a rogue strand of pink hair. "You are hands down the most adorable, funny woman I've ever met."

"Pfft. Of course I am."

He kisses me hard, then steps back. Suddenly serious, he asks, "Do you *want* to see me again?"

Flippancy escapes me. "Yes."

Do I catch relief in his eyes? I'm not sure, but his smile wakes up parts of me that *really* need a day off.

"How about Friday night?" he asks, eyes back on the mirror and his tie. "We can get dinner?"

I almost choke on euphoria. "At a restaurant?"

He freezes. "I was thinking I could cook for you here."

Ah.

I shove down a surge of disappointment and smile. Thankfully, Leo doesn't look at me until I've manufactured a genuine one. "That sounds great. What time?"

Tie finished, he sweeps a suit jacket off a hanger and shrugs it on. "I'll have to get back to you. I can't remember what time my last appointment is. Are you working?"

I nod. "But only until three."

"Perfect. Are you ready? I can drop you off on my way to the office."

"Oh, that's okay, I can—"

"*Amelia.*"

I scoff. "That tone doesn't work on me anymore."

He stares at me. Patient. Expectant. So freaking handsome. I buckle with a groan.

"Fine, fine. But it's not because you used *the voice.* I do what I want."

He laughs.

———

WEDNESDAY AND THURSDAY CRAWL BY. I go through the motions. Surf. Work. Grab drinks with my coworker Trish on Wednesday night, have dinner with Dad and Jessica Thursday. Do my nightly journaling. Feed Ferdi. Take long, restless walks. I almost call Dr. Wilson to beg for an emergency appointment, but lean hard on my friends instead.

Thank God for them, otherwise I'd have no clue how to navigate what's happening between Leo and me. My newer friends are rightly mystified by my lack of so-called dating technique. I try to tell them we're not dating, but they say sex dates count as dates, at least in the context of how to avoid coming off clingy. I'm not supposed to send text messages like *I miss you* or the dreaded, *Do you miss me, too?* and I can't call him to ask about his day. Also according to them, I'm like a thirteen-year-old girl with her first crush. They have no idea how right they are.

Kinsey and Nix, on the other hand, know the ugly truth. I've never—in my entire life—been my authentic self in a relationship, and the consequence is I'm totally out of my depth. Even during the best times with Kevin, I was aware of playing a role. Acting or looking a certain way. Almost like there was a constant spotlight on me, judging my every flaw.

With Leo, it's a moot point. He *is* the spotlight. He sees through my pathetic attempts to act like someone else, someone I think he wants. He demands the raw, unfiltered me.

I don't think he understands the cost. I'm falling, and the only question is when I'll meet the ground.

Friday is an unexpected day off. Trish has a concert she wants to go to next week and asked if I'd swap. I spend most of the morning in bed. And not because I love sleeping, which I do. I woke up paralyzed with fear that Leo plans to cancel tonight.

I've only heard from him once in the last two days. A short text that said he'll be home by five tonight. When I replied that I'd see him around five thirty, his response wasn't even a word. Just a letter.

K.

I eventually make coffee and shower, hoping the routine will alleviate the fog in my head. It doesn't. By mid-afternoon, I've cleaned my apartment top to bottom and done three loads of laundry. Still nothing from Leo, but I can't shake the sense of impending doom.

I call Callum and luck out, catching him between shoots.

"Goldie!"

"I'm losing my mind."

He laughs. "Again?"

"Not funny," I gripe. "I'm seeing Leo tonight."

He whistles. "Third sleepover, huh? Has he manned up yet?"

Callum, like Kinsey, thinks Leo is an ass for refusing to officially date me. Or be seen with me in public. Or text or call between sexcapades.

"I agreed to this," I remind both Callum and myself. "He's been completely upfront."

"He knows you have feelings for him, Mia! It's fucked up. I'm disappointed in him."

"Does he?" I echo, mentally scraping my memories of the last two weeks. "I don't know. Obviously my lady parts like his man parts. We get along really well when we're not having sex, too. But what have I actually done or said to make him think I have feelings for him? Maybe he's waiting for me to make that step? Or maybe he's worried about my, uh, mental state?"

"Remind me to never date my psychiatrist," grumbles Callum.

"We're not dating! And he's not my psychiatrist! Damnit, Callum. Can't you say something that makes me feel better? That's all I want from you!"

His laughter finally dies down. "There are two options. Option one, you tell him you want a relationship and see what happens. Option two, you don't rock the boat. It's as simple—and hard—as that. But I think the bigger question is who *you* want to be. Do you want to be the old version of you? Someone who smothers their feelings and acts out in other damaging ways? Or do you want to live an honest life?"

I shouldn't have called Callum.

38

DISCOMBOBULATION

I MULL OVER the phone call as I get ready to head to Leo's house. I'm on autopilot. Not until I glance in the mirror do I realize what I'm wearing. A modest sheath dress and my only pair of heels. I even put on diamond-solitaire earrings. *What the shit?*

After a five-second existential crises, I rip off the dress and pull on cut-off jean shorts, a comfy T-shirt, and a lightweight cardigan. Battered Converse? Check. Instead of doing something with my hair, I stuff a beanie on my head. Instead of makeup, I put on chapstick and call it a day. I feel defiant. Borderline angry.

Because Callum was right. Despite my focus on the contrary, I've been blindly trapped in old habits. Obsessing over ways to get what I want from someone. A chameleon at heart who's never felt safe enough to simply *be*.

"Fuck that," I tell my reflection.

As I request an Uber and head outside to wait, I ignore

the final dilemma. Tell him I want more and drive the train off the tracks tonight, or keep my mouth shut.

An hour and fifteen minutes later—because it's Friday evening in Los Angeles—I knock on Leo's front door. My hand has barely left the wood when it swings open.

"That was fas—"

His mouth swallows the final consonant. Arms sweeping behind my thighs, he lifts me up, shuffles backward into the house, and kicks the door closed. Hanging in his arms, I lose myself in his rough, needy noises and the heat of his tongue against mine.

When we come up for air, Leo rubs his nose against mine. "It's so good to see you. Feel you. Taste you." He punctuates the words with soft kisses on my cheeks and lips.

The smile on my face might be slap-happy, but I don't care. Staring at the naked truth in his eyes, I don't care anymore whether I'm a lovesick fool. I don't care if he doesn't want to date me right now, or even weeks from now. I'll wait for him to figure out whatever's holding him back. I'll risk the possibility he never does. Because what I see on his face is a mirror of what I feel in my heart.

For now, it's enough.

Pieces of our clothing leave a trail from the entryway, up the stairs, and down the hall to his bedroom. When I expect him to veer toward the bed, he turns instead toward the bathroom.

"I have a thing with you being wet," he murmurs against my mouth, then sips from my answering smile.

We kiss as he fumbles for the shower knobs, caress and

explore as the water heats. He is smooth, supple lines and hard angles. Remains of aftershave and delicious male musk. With his hands and mouth on me, I feel soft and small and pliable. Utterly wanted and fully possessed.

We make it into the shower, moving into the thick, decadent fall of water. A finger slips inside me, then another, as our tongues continue their slow, sensual dance. I rock against his hand, then hum in protest when his body withdraws from mine. Opening my eyes, I find him on his knees before me, my body blocking the spray from his face. The intent in his bright blues makes my knees quiver and sends a surge of blood to my core.

Leo leans forward, hands spreading my thighs for his viewing pleasure. "You were made for me, Amelia," he growls, then kisses me right where I need him most.

Clutching his shoulder with one hand and the wall with the other, I gasp at the sensation, then again at the first flick of his tongue. He begins licking in earnest, diving between my folds and sweeping up to circle my clit.

My ragged moans make him ravenous. Mouth still pressed against me, he pulls one of my legs over his shoulder and braces me with strong hands on my ass. Then he draws back just enough to give me a heated glance.

"Ride my face, Amelia. Don't stop until you come."

I nod weakly. "No protest here."

A wicked grin flashes my way before he…

goes

to

town.

I come with a strained cry, bucking against him, his

name on my lips. There's barely a second in which to reacquaint myself with gravity before I'm hoisted against the wall of the shower and impaled with every last inch of him. The invasion is exquisite, the burn only adding to my pleasure.

My legs lock instinctively around his waist, my arms around his neck. I find his mouth and feed on the taste of him, the taste of me, until we both gasp for breath.

"Has it ever been like this?" he whispers in my ear.

I'm past speech at this point, so I shake my head. With a low growl of approval, he lets loose. The wet slap of our bodies joins the billowing steam. My sense of time and place shivers and blows apart as he drives again and again to that place of deep, brutal pleasure.

"Fuck, Leo, I'm—" The rest is lost in a cry of surrender.

He stiffens, pressed tight inside me, and comes with a roar. Aftershocks rock my womb like little firecrackers. I twitch in his arms and relearn to breathe.

"Holy shit," he pants. "I can't feel my legs."

I gasp a laugh. "Don't drop me!"

His eyes, full of wonder and tenderness, find mine.

"Never."

———

TAKEOUT CHINESE FOOD boxes litter the coffee table. There's a movie on but neither of us is watching. My head in Leo's lap, I flip through an architectural magazine while he scrolls through emails on his phone.

Staring at an ad for a tropical resort with a tagline of

Find Your New Oasis, a question pops into my head. "Hey, do you know if Preston is okay?"

Leo freezes for a moment, then looks down at me. Sensing his discomfort, I sit up quickly. "It's okay. Sorry I asked. I just, uh, never got his number and was thinking about him."

His expression softens. "He's fine. Doing really well, actually."

I sigh. "Good. Great, thanks."

For the rest of the night, we ignore how close we came to acknowledging the elephant in the room.

39

THE ELEPHANT

Leo and I lie entwined on his bed, which has fast become one of my favorite places in the world. The sheets and pillows are on the floor, victims of our recent passion. His head rests on my chest, facing away, and for the last few minutes his fingers have been playing on my abdomen. I know what has his focus—the three small moles just beneath my belly button.

"It's Orion's belt," I murmur, stroking the hair at his temple. "Jameson has the rest of the constellation—minus the belt—on his right shoulder."

Leo turns over and looks up at me. "Really?"

"Yep. My mom first noticed it. She was obsessed with the idea that we carried missing pieces of the other. When we fought, she often told us that no matter how far apart we felt, we would always complete each other, that it was a code written on our bodies. I remember one day she came home super excited from the craft store. She was always getting weird, artsy ideas, most of which ended up in the garbage. But this one came out pretty cool. She used tracing paper to mark our moles, then showed us how our combined constellation compared to the actual one."

"And?"

I smile with the memory. "It was pretty darn close. Kinda freaky, really. For our seventh birthday, she presented each of us with framed copies of the constellation as it appears on our bodies. She did it so it looks like an actual map of stars."

Soft lips press against my breastbone. "Do you still have it?"

I nod. "It's in my bedroom."

"I want to see it next time I'm there."

My fingers pause in his hair, my gaze on the vaulted ceiling of his bedroom. "Okay," I force out.

"Hey," he says softly. "Come back."

I meet his eyes with effort. "I'm here."

He sits up and I follow, scooting back against the pillows and pulling the sheet over my breasts.

"What's wrong?" Leo asks gently.

I shake my head. "Nothing. I'm good. Memory lane, you know. It's a trip."

"Amelia."

I smirk. "Yeah, Doc?"

As soon as the nickname trips from my mouth, my stomach sinks. *Stupid, Mia.* Sure enough, Leo stiffens.

"I wondered how long we'd avoid the issue. Does it bother you a lot, that I was your therapist?"

I disguise panic with a laugh. "Shouldn't that be my question?"

Leo sighs, turning away and dropping his legs off the bed. It's late—sometime after midnight. We're both tired, but for some reason we haven't tried to sleep. Sex before dinner, sex after dinner, and sex for dessert. We're insatiable, each time somehow better than the last. More intimate. More profound. There were moments tonight I forgot we weren't together, that we hadn't *always been together.* That we're a landmine waiting for a single misstep.

My slip of the tongue is the misstep.

"Yes," he says finally. "It bothers me."

Pain rings a discordant note in my heart. "Okay. I mean, I get it. Obviously. And I don't want you to risk—"

"It's not about my career, at least not in that way. Sure, if someone dug deep enough, they'd find out we were at Oasis at the same time, but the place is basically wallpapered in nondisclosures. Nothing would come of it. And I only treated you peripherally after your accident in 2016."

"Then I don't understand," I say helplessly. To my horror, tears fill my eyes. "Am I not good enough for you?"

He swivels toward me, features etched in horror. "What? No! Jesus, why would you even say that?"

I laugh shrilly. "Because you don't want to date me, maybe? Is it the pink hair? The eight-year age difference? The fact I'm a waitress with a useless art history degree? That I'm not long-term material? That I was at Oasis in the first plac—"

Leo grabs my shoulders. "Sweetheart, stop. Please stop."

I suck in breath, my chest tight, my heart stampeding against my ribs. Leo's face comes into focus as I blink away tears. My face burns with embarrassment. "I'm sorry," I choke.

"Never apologize for telling me how you feel," he says sharply. "I'm the one who should apologize, for not realizing you might feel rejected. None of what you said is true, Amelia. I don't care what job you work or about your education or anything like that."

"Then why?" I whisper.

His eyes shutter and he looks away, but not before I see it. Guilt.

And I know.

"It's because of what happened between us at Oasis, isn't it? *That's* what bothers you, what you can't deal with. That you were technically my doctor when we slept together."

His hands fall from my shoulders. "Yes," he admits mutedly. "I've tried, Amelia. There are moments I even forget about it."

"But it was consensual," I say, even though I know that's not the issue for him. His conflict is deep and personal, and one I can do nothing about.

Turning distraught eyes on me, he murmurs, "Do you remember the conversation we had about power? I knew how hard it would be for you to open fully to me, and I asked you to trust me not to abuse my power."

I shake my head numbly, totally helpless. I can't make a valid argument against his point. There's no use. So I tell him the truth.

"It was my fault, Leo. *Mine.* I've been breaking people for twenty years. You were by far the hardest, but you still broke. I got what I wanted and this is my punishment. You'll never forgive yourself, will you?"

"You're still looking at yourself through the wrong lens," he says softly, eyes tender on mine. "You aren't—have never been—the destructive person you think you are. You're… a force of nature. A perfect wave. Everyone who has tried to ride that wave has wiped out, but mark my words, every one of them would give anything to ride it again. Even for a few seconds."

I want to bask in his words like a cat in sunshine, but I can't. Not when our train's wheels are throwing sparks. Not when the conductor is screaming for everyone to jump off. Not when my brain can only think in stupid fucking metaphors.

"What the hell does that *mean*?"

He drags a hand through his hair—once upon a time he would have removed his glasses.

"Can you blame a wave for crashing to shore?"

I throw my hands up. "For the love of everything good in the world, will you stop with the metaphor?"

He cracks a tiny smile, but it only lasts a second. "I don't blame you for what happened, Amelia. I *can't* blame you. I was responsible. I could have said no. Should have said no. But when you stood up, the way the moonlight… I lost my fucking mind."

I recoil physically and mentally. "So that's it, then? It was a mistake, you blame yourself, you'll never get over it, the end? Having sex with me now is what, some sort of self-flagellation for your sin?"

He rubs his face roughly, muttering, "I don't want this."

For once, the truth is easy to speak.

"Neither do I."

We dress. He drives me home.

40

ISLAND ESCAPE

JAMESON IS the only reason I make it to Sunday breakfast. Last night I told him I wasn't going because I didn't have money for an Uber. It was kinda true—I've been spending way more than usual—but still a bullshit excuse in his estimation. To avoid a lecture about money management, I thanked him for the offer to pick me up, promised to be ready at nine, and hung up on him.

The main reason I *didn't* want to come this morning is currently staring at me with concerned eyes.

"Quit hovering, Dad, I'm just tired."

"You've been sitting on this couch watching football for an hour. You don't even like football. Are you sure you're okay?"

"Yep. Totally good. Is there any more salsa?"

Dad nods, and with a final, worried glance, heads for the kitchen where Jessica is making sandwiches. A gummy bear hits the side of my face. I glare at Jameson, sprawled on the other end of the couch.

"What?" I bark.

"You're doing that thing."

"What thing?"

"The fake-person-who-doesn't-feel-anything thing."

"Suck it, Jaybird. I'm not repressing anything. Like I told you on the drive over, I simply don't want to talk about it. Why do you want to know anything about my sex life, anyway? Freak."

Another gummy bear bounces off my shoulder. It joins the first in my mouth.

"You're right. The thought of you having sex makes me want to hurl. I'm still not over you growing boobs."

"Wow. So mature."

"I know you don't want us to treat you like glass, Meerkat." His serious tone pulls my gaze begrudgingly to his face. "But I think we're entitled to worry a little when you look like that."

I frown. "Like what?"

Jameson cocks a brow and points at different parts of me. "Your hair looks like it hasn't been brushed in days. You're wearing a bright-red shirt, yellow shorts, and socks with sandals. You're a retirement home in Florida."

Candy goes down the wrong pipe. I bend in half with a coughing fit, but I'm also laughing so hard I can't breathe even if I wanted to. Jameson pounds on my back. Dad and Jessica run from the kitchen asking what's wrong. It's a shitshow.

When Jessica steps forward with her Nurse Face on, I hold up both hands. "I'm okay," I say hoarsely, wiping tears from my eyes and swallowing past a sore throat.

Looking up at the three people watching me like they don't know whether to call an ambulance or find a straight-jacket, I pull myself together.

"I'm sorry I look like a retirement home," I tell them.

"Say what now?" asks my dad, while Jessica tilts her head, eyeing my attire and nodding thoughtfully.

Jameson ruffles my gross hair. "She's okay. You're okay, aren't you?"

I nod, sighing. "I was seeing someone for a laughably short period of time, but I really liked him. It ended last night. I'm just sad. It was my first mostly sane effort at a relationship."

Jameson and Dad exchange a glance of abject terror. Jessica rolls her eyes at them, then perches beside me. "Oh, honey," she coos, "I know just what you need."

"What?" snaps my dad. "What does she need?"

Jessica gives me a conspiratorial grin. "An afternoon at the spa."

I knew I liked her.

WHEN JESSICA and I arrive at an upscale day spa in Malibu, I'm expecting a Swedish massage. What she signs us up for instead is called Island Escape, which includes a tropical bath soak, massage, custom facial, and a mani-pedi.

As Jessica hands over my dad's credit card, I whisper-hiss, "Are you sure he's okay with this?"

She gives me a surprised look. "Yes, Mia. Your father would hand you the moon if you'd let him."

I search her face for signs of ulterior motives. "Does he give you his credit card a lot?"

Jessica laughs, unoffended, and takes my arm in hers. "All the damn time. I haven't used it until now, though. But I really can't stand football, so let's pretend I'm only doing this for you."

I release a short laugh. "I like you, Jessica."

She winks. "I like you too, Mia."

Three decadent, blissful hours later, I wobble-walk into the ladies' locker room to change into my street clothes. I feel like I've been through a blender. In a good way. Like Klaus the Humongous Russian massaged all my mismatched pieces back together.

Drunk on endorphins, it takes me three tries to clasp my bra. "Motherfu—"

"Amelia, right?" asks an unfamiliar voice.

I glance over my shoulder, expecting a spa employee. Instead, I find a beautiful woman in her mid-thirties with long, wavy dark hair and a big smile. Her eyes are dark but expressive, currently radiating excitement, and she's wearing the spa's white robe.

"Uh, yes? Have we met?"

Do I owe you money?

Did you have my brother's secret love child?

It's worse.

"I'm Marianne." A trim, feminine hand extends toward me. "Vincent's mom."

My heart slams into my spine. "Oh! Oh, wow. Okay. Hold on." I quickly pull on my shirt, internally grimacing at the garish display of color. The red shirt and yellow shorts aren't even on the same style planet, the shirt primary red and the shorts halfway between lemon and orange. Jameson was right. I look like a blind retiree.

Smiling like I'm not dying inside, I shake Marianne's hand. "It's nice to meet you. I'm sorry I didn't introduce myself at the hockey game. You were probably wondering who the random chick talking to your son was."

She laughs, an airy, addictive sound. "Oh, I knew who you were the second I saw you. Vincent told us all about the nice, pretty lady with pastel pink hair. Any luck with the surfing lessons?"

I don't miss the knowing gleam in her eye. "Nope. I guess Leo thought cold-calling him for a business proposition was a little presumptuous."

Marianne looks crestfallen. "Darn. I was really hoping to hear you were dating."

I'm not sure how many more shocks my heart can take. "What? No. That's crazy. We're, uh… not even—"

What the fuck happened to my ability to lie?

"I know he drove to your place after the hockey game last week."

Full. Stop.

My knees decide to take a break, depositing me ungently on a wooden bench. "Jesus," I mutter. "I don't know what to say."

Marianne sits beside me. Up close, she's even more lovely. I can definitely see a young Leo trailing after her. They would have been beautiful together—the proof of it lives in their son.

"I'm not here to interfere or offer advice," she says

softly, "and as much as I may want to, I won't make excuses for what a complicated man Leo is. I think you know."

I sigh. "I don't think he's complicated. Just burdened by excess morality."

Marianne laughs delightedly. "You do know him well. I take it you were once in a *different* kind of relationship? I'm not judging."

Oddly, I can tell she isn't. I give a short nod. "We were."

"Well." She pouts. "Shit."

I shrug, ignoring the pang in my chest. "It is what it is. Can't change the past, unfortunately. Or Leo's mind."

Marianne gives me a long, searching look, then smiles softly. "It was really great to meet you, Amelia. I hope I see you again soon."

She gives my shoulder a squeeze, then stands and heads for the exit. Pausing in the locker room doorway, she looks back.

"I do have one bit of advice. Take it or leave it. I've known Leo a long time. He's many things—bullheaded being one of them—but he's also brave. If you mean to him what I think you do, give him a little time to come around."

"Thanks, Marianne," I say politely.

But I'm lying.

41

EMBRACE THE WIND

MY DAYS off this week are back-to-back. I take it as a sign and fill my calendar with activities that used to make me happy. On Wednesday I go skydiving in the morning and paragliding in the afternoon. On Thursday I take the first boat to Catalina Island and spend the day scuba diving. By the time I arrive home, my credit card hates me, but I feel good. Proud of the fact I didn't spend my time off wallowing. I crawl into bed that night and pass out without thinking of Leo once.

I dream about him instead. It's an old dream, the one where I'm surfing on sand dunes. Only this time the dunes are moving like real waves, a fierce wind driving coarse sand into my eyes. Leo is waving from the top of a nearby dune, flickering in and out of sight like a mirage. No matter how hard I try to reach him, the sand waves push me back, back...

I wake up covered in sweat, with just enough light in the sky to give me an excuse to get up. Grateful I'm working the breakfast shift today—I'm in no mood to go surfing—I take an extra-long shower and nurse two cups of coffee. At seven thirty, I grab a granola bar and head out. Ferdi slips outside with me, embarking on whatever adventures his day holds.

Even though November is in full swing, there's a wicked heat wave in town. And heat wave means thousands of people flock to the coast. The café is slammed for breakfast, barely slows midmorning, and ramps up again at lunch. Outside, the boardwalk and beach are packed with the usual circus of tourists and locals.

"Dying," gasps Trish, sagging against the hostess podium in a rare lull. Her dark skin glistens with a sheen of sweat, her cheeks deeply rose. The air conditioner stopped working an hour ago. Ceiling fans whir overhead, but without a breeze they're just stirring hot air.

Fanning myself with a menu, I nod. "Shouldn't have bothered showering this morning, that's for sure."

I glance back to check on my tables, and when I turn back around, a familiar figure stands in the doorway.

Déjà vu.

Vincent waves at me and steps inside. "Hi, Amelia! It's hot today, huh? Bet you wish you were surfing."

"Hi," I say weakly, my gaze darting past him but not finding an adult. "Shouldn't you be in school?"

"Half-day today. Dad picked me up. He forgot something in the car, but he'll be here in a sec. Oh, I'm supposed to give you this."

I accept a folded square of lined paper, aware of Trish's

avid focus and my own pounding heart. This can't possibly mean what I think it means.

"Open it!" says Vincent brightly.

"Yeah, open it," hisses Trish from the corner of her mouth.

The paper is smooth, almost cool. I unfold it to find a square of writing in the center.

Amelia,

Will you go on a date
with my dad?

YES   NO

(circle one please)

Trish leans over my shoulder. "Here's a pen," she whispers, pulling it from behind her ear and all but shoving it into my fingers.

"Hi, Dad!"

My head whips up. The first thing I see is a bouquet of wildflowers. The second thing is a set of hopeful, crystal-blue eyes. I blink hard, but he's still there. So is Vincent, who grabs the flowers and pushes them into my arms.

Behind me, I hear several "Ahhs" and "Ohhs" from customers and coworkers.

"She hasn't circled one yet, Dad," whispers Vincent.

Leo glances at the paper, currently crumpled against the stalks of flowers. I can't feel my face, but I must be smiling or crying or shaking or something, because Leo grins.

"Are you busy tonight?" he asks.

I shake my head.

"Can I pick you up at six?"

I nod.

HE TAKES me to a popular sushi joint in Santa Monica. The place is wall-to-wall people, and the servers must be part-time acrobats for how fast and skillfully they move in the narrow aisles between tables.

Up until we were seated, I was nervous Leo was nervous, and constantly scanned him for signs of distress. Though I didn't find any, I wasn't convinced of his shift in attitude until we sat and he reached across the table to link his fingers with mine. Since that moment, I've been in heaven.

The restaurant is so loud we don't talk much, but communicate in subtle touch. He barely looks away from me throughout our meal, following the path of every morsel to my mouth with hungry eyes. The air between us grows painfully electrified.

I never knew eating could be foreplay.

When I lick a drop of soy sauce off my lip, Leo's expression turns pained. He lifts a hand. "Check please."

Giggling like teenagers, we hightail it back to his car. In unspoken agreement, he drives to my place. It's closer. By the time we get inside, my hand is down his pants and my bra dangles at my waist. Undressing the rest of the way isn't graceful, but it's fucking perfect.

"God, Amelia," he groans, peppering kisses across my breasts as he carries me to the bedroom.

I'm unhinged. Dying to have him inside me. But I'm also drunk on his response to me. It makes me bold. It makes me *free*.

Before Leo can lay me on the bed, I wiggle from his arms, jerk him around by the shoulders, and shove his chest. He lands on his back, eyes wide with surprise, miles of beautiful, aroused male for my viewing pleasure.

Dipping my fingers between my legs, I cup a breast with my other hand. "Do you want this?"

He hisses, his cock twitching in anticipation. "You have no idea how much. Come here, please."

I drag wet fingers to my clit and play with myself, delighting in his agonized groan. It doesn't take long for me to be perilously close to orgasm. "I like it when you beg, Leo, but I also like it when you take what you want."

In two seconds flat, I'm facedown on the mattress. Leo's hot body descends on my back, his teeth finding purchase on my shoulder. I'm still reeling from sensory overload when he drags me to my knees and slams inside me.

"Fuck! *Yes!*"

I don't know which of us the words come from, if they're spoken or in my mind. But his next words ring loud and clear, punctuated by deep, possessive thrusts.

"I'm keeping you," he murmurs darkly. "This pussy belongs to me. It's been mine for years, but I was too much of a chickenshit to take it. I'm not making the same mistake twice. Do you understand?"

My filthy unicorn.

"Yes, yes, yes," I gasp with every breath.

"Tell me you're mine."

"I'm yours!"

"Nothing is going to come between us," he growls. "I won't allow it. You. Are. *Mine.*"

"Oh… God…"

I come so hard I see white. Leo is seconds behind me— hot breath on my neck and a low grunt in my ear. He collapses atop me. The weight of him is so epic I don't care that I can barely breathe, and I even murmur a protest when he flips us over so I'm sprawled on his chest. Stroking the sweaty hair at my temples, he gently lifts my head.

"I love the look on your face right now."

"Derrrf?"

His smile is smug. "Exactly. Freshly fucked. No guards up, no thoughts, just feeling."

I smile and kiss his chest. "Shut up, Leo. I'm not thinking. Talking requires thinking."

He chuckles and wraps strong arms around me, shifting us once more onto our sides. I bask in the afterglow, my limbs loose and warm, my face tucked against his neck.

"Amelia?"

"Hmm?"

"I meant what I said."

"I know. My pussy belongs to you."

He pinches my hip. "That, too, but I meant the other part."

"Too much thinking," I moan.

"I'm keeping you," he whispers.

My heart swells, so full, so hot. "Okay," I whisper back. "Can I keep you, too?"

"I'm already yours."

A smile on my face and peace in my heart, I drift to sleep.

42

SPARKLE

Leo is horrible on a surfboard.

Really, really horrible.

Some people get on a board for the first time and take to it like it's in their blood. Some cellular coding allows them to harmonize their bodies with the water and the board beneath them. There's a learning curve, obviously, but it's worlds easier for them to expand the new skill. I'm not an extraordinary surfer by any means, but I'm still one of the lucky ones. It's in my blood.

The longest Leo has stood up is five seconds, timing courtesy of a hysterically laughing Vincent. He, on the other hand, is a natural. Up on his first try, even managing a few short trips on waves.

After his umpteenth wipeout, Leo paddles to where Vincent and I stand in thigh-deep water, our boards floating nearby. The sun is warm overhead, though we're in full wetsuits because the water's bloody cold in December.

Leo is understandably disgruntled by his performance,

but he's mature enough to laugh at himself. "So much for impressing you," he says, hopping off the board and wiping water from his eyes.

"You suck, Dad!" exclaims Vincent. Leo sends a funnel of water into his face. "Hey!"

"Don't embarrass me in front of the lady, bud!"

Vincent chortles. "You don't need *me* for that."

Cue water fight.

Watching them hollering and laughing, I'm high on happiness. The last five weeks with Leo have been frighteningly perfect. During the week, we juggle schedules to see each other at least every other day. He has a toothbrush in my bathroom; I have one in his. When my work schedule allows a weekend day together, we take advantage. We've already been hiking, kayaking, and cycling. Once, we spent an entire day making love.

Despite Leo's insistence that it's okay, I haven't stayed over yet on the nights Vincent does, mainly out of respect for their bonding time. But they're both working on me—Vincent's fond of telling me how dumb it is when I'm not there for breakfast.

Vincent... God, I adore that kid. He's witty, smart, and kind, just like his father. We've taken him to a Kings game, the arcade, and had several pizza-and-movie nights. But my favorite moment of all was when I dropped him off at a friend's house for a sleepover one night because Leo was tied up on an emergency call from a client. Driving Leo's car—and Leo's human—and knowing that both father and son felt safe having me do so was a defining moment of my new life. I floated on a pink cloud for days.

Our Thanksgivings were separate, but Marianne extended an invitation for me to join them for dessert. After being assured multiple times by Leo that the offer was genuine, I bit the bullet and showed up. Of course I was worried for nothing. She and Celia are some of the most good-natured, humble people I've ever met. Both of them were beyond tickled by Leo's casual signs of affection—a hand on my back, a kiss on my cheek, a whisper in my ear.

I'm in love with him.

So hopelessly in love.

Back at Oasis, when Callum asked me what romantic love felt like, I didn't know how to answer him. I could only relate via my unhealthy patterns of my past. Turns out I had no fucking idea what love felt like because I'd never been *in it* before.

My answer would be different today. Love is waking up in the middle of the night and feeling someone's hand in yours. Love is squabbling over the remote and playing footsie during dinner and peeing with the door open and planning for birthdays and holidays. Love is the firmest ground in the world and a never-ending fall.

"What are you smiling about?" asks Vincent, poking me in the arm.

I grin down at him. "I'm happy."

"Me too! You know what else?"

"What?"

He splashes me in the face. Leo thinks it's hysterical—until Vincent and I attack.

AFTER DROPPING Vincent off at Marianne and Celia's, Leo and I grab burritos to-go and take them back to his place. We eat in the living room by the light of the fireplace and an enormous Christmas tree the three of us decorated last weekend.

We inhale our food, then clean up and return to our spot before the glowing fireplace with glasses of wine. It's not really cold enough for a fire, but Leo knows I'm a sucker for ambiance.

"So what'd you get me for Christmas?"

Leo smirks at me, the firelight playing over his features. Lounging on an elbow with his bare feet near the heat, he looks cozy, content, and ridiculously sexy.

"Nunya business."

"Come on," I whine. Switching tactics, I run a hand up his thigh to his crotch. "I'll give you a handy if you tell me."

He chuckles, lifting his hips to give me better access to his zipper. "You'll do that anyway."

I swat his hard stomach, then tilt my head. "You're right. But I still want to know. Or open a present."

He gapes. "What's wrong with you?"

"My mom was like a little kid at Christmas. It was her favorite holiday, but she couldn't stand waiting for the actual day. Starting on the twenty-second, she'd let us open one small gift after dinner. Basically you're disrespecting Sloan tradition if you don't let me open something."

Leo laughs. "That's low."

I offer my sweetest smile.

Grumbling good-naturedly, he rolls toward the tree and

snatches a small, flat box from a branch, then tosses it in my lap. "There you go, master manipulator."

I squeal and clap excitedly, then lift the box. It's light in my hands, wrapped haphazardly in newspaper with a generic red bow stuck to the top. Since Vincent's wrapping is borderline Pinterest-worthy, I know this disaster is Leo's doing.

"You really missed your calling as a backup Santa Claus."

He chuckles. "Hey, it's not the wrapping that counts. And I did put some thought into it—I used the Sunday Funnies. Come on, quit staring at it and open it. The suspense is killing me."

I tear the paper, exposing cardboard, and pull off the top of the box. Under a small piece of tissue paper is a delicate gold chain. My breath stalling, I lift the necklace to see the circular pendant.

It's a wave.

"Read the inscription."

I turn the pendant over. Etched on the back of the delicate central icon are words that bring instant tears to my eyes.

My perfect wave.

I look up at Leo. At his soft smile and eyes that dance with hope and hesitance.

"Do you like it?"

I launch myself into his waiting arms.

43

A PERFECT WAVE

THE AFTERNOON BEFORE CHRISTMAS EVE, Kinsey, Nix, and I head to the Santa Monica's Third Street Promenade for shopping and to sit on Santa's lap—because we're only pretending to be well-adjusted adults. After twenty minutes in line, however, I'm as miserable as the screaming kids who don't want to sit on a strange, bearded man's lap.

"Whose idea was this?" I grumble, wincing at a particularly shrill scream.

"Come on," Nix cajoles, "don't give up! We're starting new traditions."

Kinsey looks between us, weighing Nix's excitement with my angst. She gives Nix a kiss and takes my arm. "Mia and I are going to grab some hot chocolate. We'll be right back. Text me if you get near the front of the line."

"Okay, babe." He points a finger at me. "No bailing."

I laugh. "Fine, fine."

Escaping the press of stressed parents and traumatized toddlers, we beeline for the nearby Starbucks. I can already taste a peppermint hot chocolate, and from Kinsey's eager steps, her sweet tooth rivals mine. The atmosphere is festive, the air cool and sun mellow, and despite an undercurrent of holiday anxiety, the mood of the crowd is celebratory. It reminds me powerfully of my childhood, of holding my mom's hand as we munched on candy canes and shopped for last-minute gifts for Dad and Jameson.

Thinking about her, I feel something I haven't in decades—the insulation and safety of her presence, the cocoon of her unconditional love. Hot, heavy emotion fills my chest and prickles behind my eyes.

Hi, Mom. I miss you.

Lost in my private communion with the memory of my mother, I don't immediately notice when Kinsey stops. Only when her grip on my arm yanks me back does my awareness snap into the present.

"What the hell, Kins?" I glance swiftly around, then at her face. Her expression is pinched, the color gone from her cheeks. "What's wrong?"

"Ten o'clock," she says stiffly.

I follow the path of her gaze to the small patio outside Starbucks. People pass across my line of vision, giving me brief, startlingly clear glimpses of three men occupying a corner table. One man laughs, the other two grimace. All three gesture, conversing in a light, familiar way. Like they've known each other for years.

It doesn't make sense.

None of it makes sense.

Everything slows and dims—the crowds, the noise, the

music from a nearby busker. Even the twinkling of Christmas lights on stores and lamp poles fade away.

Kinsey's face floats before mine, her eyes wide and concerned. "Mia? What do you want me to do?"

My fingers curl, the woven strap of a shopping bag digging into my palm. In the bag is a last-minute gag gift for Jameson and goodies for Leo's and Vincent's stockings.

I swallow. Focus on Kinsey's face. "Leo," I rasp, my eyes jerking back to him.

As though speaking his name ignites dark magic, Leo's eyes suddenly find me amidst the crowd. They widen. His olive skin goes ashen. Despite the chaos of sound around us, I hear the metal-on-cement scrape of his chair as he stands fast. The chair falls, clashing against iron railings. The other two men jerk, half-rising, both of them talking at once.

"Why is your brother having coffee with Leo?" growls Kinsey. "And more importantly, what the *actual fuck* is your ex-fiancé doing with them?"

My lips are cold. "I-I don't know."

Leo scrambles around tables, angling for the exit of the patio and, presumably, me. Jameson looks around wildly and finally sees me. My twin's lips shape my name, his features collapsing into lines of misery.

"Amelia!" shouts Leo.

Eyes blazing, Kinsey snaps, "Go back to Nix and tell him we're leaving. I'll meet you at the car. Go, Mia!"

Grateful beyond words for the direction, I go, running on numb feet back toward the line for Santa. Nix sees me coming, his welcoming smile instantly falling. Wheezing for air, I stumble into his arms.

"Nine-one-one. We have to go," I pant. "Kinsey will meet us at the car."

He's instantly alert and ready for violence. "Is she safe?" he snaps.

I nod. "Completely. She'll be right behind us."

"All right." He scans my face. "Do we need to run?"

I think of Leo as I last saw him, distraught and pushing toward me.

"Yes," I say shrilly. "Yes, please."

So we run.

⁂

Hindsight is everything, isn't it?

Late that night, as I lie sleepless in Kinsey's guest bed with puffy eyes, I think about Oasis. About Leo, my brother, and Kevin. It's like fitting together pieces of a puzzle I didn't know existed, and the picture it creates is as mystifying as it is crippling.

"I can hold my breath for two minutes and twenty-three seconds."

"Yes, I know."

My eyes narrow. "Fucking Jameson. Did he tell you my favorite food, too?"

"Ceviche," he says with a twitch of lips.

I feel my own mouth curve. "Favorite movie?"

He grimaces. "Reservoir Dogs."

All the personal details, large and small, that Leo knew about me. How many times I've gone skydiving, the details of my sealed record, my most embarrassing moment, high school boyfriend, stunts and pranks spanning years... On and on.

Never once did it occur to me that there was something suspicious about the level of his knowledge. How he seemed to have it all memorized, reciting it with no hesitation or reference to notes. I always thought he was just that good. And that Jameson was a weirdo and had secretly compiled a dossier on my life.

Even from the minimal interaction I witnessed today, it's obvious Jameson and Leo have known each other for a long time.

How? How did I miss it?

Sadly, the answer is *Easily*.

I was a shitty sister and friend to my brother for the bulk of our twenties. Our social lives never overlapped, and I was largely apathetic about what was going on in his life.

While he was going to law school, I was doing shots in Cabo on a stranger's yacht, backpacking Machu Picchu, and heli-skiing in Canada with some people I met surfing. While he was getting a Big Boy job and starting a 401K, I was making ends meet waitressing and picking up odd jobs like working on pot farms during harvest months.

"It was a fucking nightmare getting you into this place, Mia. You have no idea the convincing I had to—"

*"So, uh, you looked pretty cozy with your therapist in the car.
You guys were all whispers and cuddles most of the drive."*

What I don't understand—can't understand—is why neither of them simply told me. Did Leo think my treatment would suffer if I knew he was friends with my brother? *Would it have suffered?*

Probably.

But why keep it from me after the fact? Does Jameson know I've been dating and sleeping with Leo for almost two months? Does *Kevin* know? And where the fuck does Kevin come into this scenario?

My phone started blowing up as soon as Nix and I reached the car. After reading the first few desperate, pleading texts from Leo, I turned the device off and gave it to Nix. It was either that or put it under the back tire to be destroyed. When Kinsey slipped into the passenger seat minutes later, she didn't speak, just nodded at Nix, who put the car in gear and got us out of there.

I don't know what Leo told her. She brought it up when we got back to her place, but I shook my head and walked from the room. Though a part of me wants to devour whatever explanations might be waiting, the rest of me is too angry to listen.

"Tell me a secret."

"What kind of secret?"

"Your biggest one."

"I don't think so."

Of course, what hurts the most is the proof that Leo isn't who I thought he was—someone I trusted implicitly, someone I believed in with all my heart. The last weeks weren't perfect like I thought. They were built on a cracked foundation. As I embraced and reveled in the transparency of our intimacy, he was the one wearing a mask.

"You're a very good liar, but you'd do well to remember I'm a better one."

He *is* a better liar.
The best.

44

BIRD'S-EYE VIEW

I WANT to quit my job and move far, far away.

God, how I want to run.

But it's Christmas Eve. My dad and Jessica will be crushed if I no-show for dinner.

Kinsey and Nix are still sleeping when I find my phone attached to a charger in the kitchen. Ignoring the notifications, I order an Uber. Ten minutes later, I head outside, my phone remaining on the counter next to a note telling them I'll check in later.

At home, I find Ferdi curled on my comforter. I lie beside him and stroke his ears, his purrs vibrating through my fingers. Tears slip from my eyes as I realize how much I love the little beast.

"I'm getting you a collar for Christmas," I whisper into his fur. "Don't leave me, Ferdi."

He mewls and begins sandpapering my chin with his tongue. His breath is horrendous, but his spontaneous affection makes up for it. Cat therapy for the win.

I shower. Get dressed. Drink tea and manage to stomach a piece of toast. I finish wrapping Dad's and Jessica's presents. I even wrap the gift I picked up for Jameson yesterday. Right now I may want to cover him in honey and throw a beehive at him, but he's still my brother.

Packing everything in mismatched shopping bags, I kiss Ferdi goodbye and grab my coat and keys. Then I realize I don't have a phone. Hailing a cab in L.A. doesn't really happen unless you're outside a nightclub at closing time.

Thankfully, the third neighbor whose front door I accost is home. Twenty minutes later, I'm in the back of a cab that smells like day-old Chinese food. I really need to get a car.

Or move to New York City. Or maybe Paris or Amsterdam.

By the time I'm dropped off at Dad's, the sun is setting. The house sparkles with hundreds of professionally strung lights. Palm trees boast alternating red and white strands and a massive, blow-up Santa wavers on the front lawn.

I haven't seen a display like this since my mom was alive, and for a few minutes I stand in the driveway, taking it all in. How grateful I am to Jessica. How lucky I am to have a relationship with my father.

"Mom would have loved this, huh?" asks Jameson, walking up beside me.

I nod.

"Can we talk, Meerkat?"

The front door opens on Dad and Jessica. They're wearing matching Christmas sweaters and Santa hats and grinning from ear to ear.

Sighing, I look at Jameson. "Not now. Maybe later. *Maybe.*"

He nods. "Whenever you're ready. Want me to take those bags?"

I hesitate, then hand them over. They're heavy. "Thanks."

He peeks into one of the bags. "Is there anything here for me, or did you burn my presents?"

My smile is tiny, but it's real. "Burned them."

He grins. "I figured."

"Come on, you two!" shouts our dad. "We have the karaoke machine up and running!"

"Is he kidding?" whispers Jameson as we walk toward the front door. "Tell me he's kidding."

I shake my head, grinning in spite of myself. "I think he's making up for lost time, Jaybird. I see rivers of eggnog and black-and-white movies in our immediate future."

My guess is right on the money.

———

IT'S LATE. Dad and Jessica are in bed. Jameson and I cleaned the kitchen and are presently on the living room couch. Since we're staying the night, we've decided to relive a preteen catastrophe and get drunk on pilfered Peppermint Schnapps. So far I've managed to avoid being sucked into sad-drunk territory, but the risk rises with every sip.

Eventually we run out of small talk. Quiet lasts less than a minute before Jameson says, "Ready?"

Am I?

"I don't know. I might be too drunk for this."

"I can tell you again tomorrow."

I straighten from my slump, rubbing my face roughly. "Fuck, fine. Tell me."

Jameson mirrors my position, sitting up and facing me. "I'm not going to speak for Leo or Kevin, just myself." When I nod, he continues mutedly, "When you had the accident earlier this year, I thought I was going to lose you. Not necessarily physically, but in every other way that counts. You'd been slipping away for years, and all I could do was watch it happen. I never knew how to help you. Are you with me?"

I nod, resisting the urge to grab his hand.

"Leo was one of the founding players in our hockey league. He started the Ice Holes a few years before I joined. About five years ago, we went for drinks after a game. It was right after you called from a shoddy phone-line in Mexico and told me about your parachute not opening in the Cave of Swallows. I was upset, to say the least. Before I knew it, I'd dumped everything on Leo. I didn't know then what his line of work was, just that he was a really good listener. He has a way of simplifying things, of bringing them into perspective."

"What did he tell you?" I whisper.

Jameson cracks a smile. "That you could benefit from therapy."

Even though I don't want to, I laugh. "Figures."

"Anyway, fast-forward another year and you showed up at a game. At this point Leo and I had a running joke that I owed him money for all our casual therapy sessions.

Most of them were just while hanging out. We talked a lot about you, about how I could maintain healthy boundaries and not get caught up in worry or fear."

I pinch the bridge of my nose. "Jesus. I'm suddenly grateful I'm three sheets to the wind."

"Ditto." Jameson sighs. "This isn't easy. There are certain things I conveniently ignored, like the look on Leo's face when I pointed you out in the crowd."

"Do you mean…" I can't get the words out.

He nods. "Dude was smitten."

I shake my head helplessly. "I never even saw him. Didn't meet him after the game."

Jameson shrugs. "Yeah, he split right after. I don't know why. You and Kevin started dating and I forgot about it. Things started looking up for you. You seemed happy."

"Then *ka-boom*," I say, raising my glass and downing the dregs.

He nods shortly. "I didn't know who else to turn to but Leo. We hadn't talked about you in a while. He'd left the team and started a new one by this point. When you came home from the hospital and… and took those pills"—he clears his throat—"I called Leo and he diverted the ambulance to UCLA, where he was an attending."

"And he diagnosed me," I conclude.

"Yeah, with confabu-something or other."

"Confabulation," I answer mutedly. "I fabricated memories to replace missing ones. In my case, the trauma of the accident caused me to cut out all memory of being pregnant and everything after."

Jameson reaches for my hand, grabbing it before I can

retract my arm. I tense for a moment, then give in and let his fingers wrap firmly through mine.

"Dad and I waited, Mia. We let you have space. Didn't bring up the accident at all. Leo said it would take time."

"But then I had another accident, and you thought I'd tried to kill myself."

"I didn't know, honestly. But whatever happened, you weren't getting better like we'd hoped. So I called Leo again. He finally told me about an intensive, ultra-private treatment facility he'd been working at for a couple months out of the year."

"You had to convince him?"

Jameson smirks at the affront in my voice. "I had to convince him to admit you when *he* was there. He didn't want to treat you. He said—"

"It was a conflict of interest."

"Something like that, yes. I'm sorry I didn't tell you, Mia. When Leo and I drove out to Oasis to pick you up, we agreed it wasn't the time. Not with Dad in the hospital and all the chaos. On my end, it was purely selfish. I'd just gotten my sister back and didn't want you to hate me."

I stare at the Christmas tree until the lights blur.

"Mia? I'm sorry."

"Did you know we were seeing each other?" I ask at length.

He sighs. "Yes."

"And you still kept the truth from me?"

"Yes. I was scared you—"

"Thank you for telling me," I interject, then use the

coffee table as leverage to stand. My hand slips from Jameson's grip. "I'm going to bed. You get the couch."

I only stumble twice on the way to the guest room. Crawling beneath the covers fully clothed, I curl around a pillow and wait for the tears to come. They do, slow and thick. Silent.

I wish I could turn off my heart again. Undo all the work of the last months. Erase Leo's mark on me. Reject this fragility. This love.

But I don't know how.

45

FIND THE STARS

CHRISTMAS DAY IS BITTERSWEET. Though I do my best to hide it, a pall of melancholy hangs over me. I wish I had my phone. I wish I were watching Vincent open presents.

I wish…

I'd never met Dr. Leo Chastain.

Jameson's revelations added more pieces to the puzzle, which although clearer is still incomplete. I understand now where my brother was coming from. And seeing Leo, Jameson, and Kevin sharing a cup of coffee and catching up isn't so shocking anymore. They played hockey on the same team for years.

I wish I didn't have so many unanswered questions. I wish the heaviness in my chest would go away. I wish I weren't so angry, because I miss him. I want to understand, to forgive, to fall back into the safe space we were making in the world.

I don't know if I can.

"Want to talk about it?" asks Jessica, perching on the patio chair next to mine.

I close my eyes. Focus on the warmth of the sun on my face. Listen to the wind rustling through trees in the backyard, dogs barking, distant cars, and muted Christmas music from inside the house.

In the back of my mind, I hear Dr. Wilson's voice.

"What if instead of focusing so much on what you should and shouldn't do or what is or isn't healthy, you try focusing on what makes you happy?"

"You still don't get it. I don't trust the things that make me happy."

And therein lies the problem. As much as I don't want it to be true, Leo proved me right. I shouldn't have trusted him.

"I don't know how to forgive someone who lied to me," I tell Jessica, turning my head to look at her.

She studies my face. "How bad was the lie?"

"On a scale of one to ten? Maybe a six." Sitting up, I swing my feet to the ground facing her. "Did Dad tell you where I was right before his heart attack?"

She nods. "A treatment program of some kind. He said you had some lasting trauma from an accident and miscarriage. I'm so sorry, honey."

I smile tightly. "It's okay. I'm glad you know. Saves us an awkward conversation. Anyway, I fell in love with my therapist there. We ran into each other at my work a few months ago and have since started seeing each other."

Her eyes widen comically. "Oh. Yikes."

I snort. "To put it mildly."

"Do you mind me asking what he lied about?"

I have no idea how to explain, but I try. "He's, um, known me—about me—for years, but I didn't meet him until going to rehab. He and Jameson are friends, but neither of them told me."

Her head tilts. "Has he explained why?"

I look up to see a hawk soaring high above. "That's the problem. I'm so fucking angry about the fact he lied, I can't listen to him. I *want* to, but feel… all fucked up inside about it. I can honestly say I never trusted a partner before him. I've never been so blindly, stupidly in love. I *knew* it was going to implode, but I got involved with him anyway."

"Sounds like you're more angry at yourself than him," murmurs Jessica.

My gaze jerks to her. "Ew."

She smiles gently. "For me, when I'm struggling with someone else's behavior, it's always a good idea to look at my own first. Maybe it's so hard to forgive him because you still haven't forgiven yourself for something. I don't know everything this family has gone through over the years, but I know you've had your share of troubles. Have you forgiven yourself, Mia?"

I glare at her. "I don't like you anymore."

She laughs, then stands and drops a kiss on my head. "I still like you. When you're ready, you can borrow my car if you'd like."

She walks back into the house. I hug my knees to my chest and watch the sky slowly darken.

Have I forgiven myself?

For lying, stealing, and manipulating? For causing so much worry, then dismissing or minimizing that worry? For ignoring and resenting my brother and dad? For finding weaknesses in others and exploiting them? For taking risks, pushing boundaries, putting people on edge... For breaking them?

I think back to the amends list I made at Oasis with Dr. Reynolds—*may she suffer an incurable yeast infection*—and my progress. The list itself was shockingly short. Seven names. It would have been eight, but I'd already apologized to Declan for ghosting him.

Amends to my father and brother are done, at least in the sense of formal apologies. I'm still making up for a lifetime of assholery, rebuilding trust, et cetera. Kevin is also handled. I even called Jill, my dad's ex-wife; she was stunned to hear from me, initially suspicious, but in the end surprisingly receptive.

The next two were more random—I owed an old friend two hundred dollars that I borrowed years ago and never paid back, and I unknowingly slept with my college roommate's boyfriend in a drunken blackout. She caught us in the act and was devastated. That one was by far the hardest, the shame deepest. After sending her a message on Facebook asking if she'd like to meet for coffee, she responded she'd rather light herself on fire. I finally typed out the amends and sent them, but never heard back.

Only one name is left on the list. One I've ignored until now.

Amelia Sloan.

Mine.

———

I DON'T END up borrowing Jessica's car, though I do fantasize overlong about showing up at Leo's in a blaze of Christmas presents and glory. He'd atone, tell me he loves me, and beg convincingly for me to forgive him. Because I'm such an awesome person, I'd accept. But not before giving him a piece of my mind—as long as Vince wasn't around, of course.

Instead, Jameson drops me off at home late that evening. I work early in the morning but more importantly, I need to feed Ferdi. Leo or no Leo, life goes on.

Kinsey and Nix come over for a while to exchange gifts and drop off my phone. Their effort to act like nothing's wrong is more appreciated than irritating. They go apeshit over the gift certificate I got them to go skydiving together, and I almost faint when they give me a brand-new wetsuit I can only afford in my dreams.

When they finally leave, it's past eleven. I get ready for bed, then curl up under the comforter with a purring Ferdi. And finally, I power up my phone.

Thirteen text messages.

Six calls.

Three voicemails.

Some of the texts are from friends wishing me a merry Christmas. Most of the calls and voicemails are from Jameson. There's only one missed call from Leo and no voicemails. My heart beating a staccato rhythm in my chest, I open Leo's texts. After the initial burst of *It's not what you think* and *Please, let me explain* lines, he sent one more.

When you're ready to talk, I'll be here.

46

ONE STEP FORWARD

Eight days later, the plan for my amends to myself comes —as arguably all good ideas do—in the shower. The prior moments aren't a high point in my life, comprised of me sitting with my knees to my chest, sobbing my guts out, while the hot water slowly turns cold. Only after the picturesque experience of nearly choking on snot do I take a breather and drag myself to my feet.

Leaning on the wall, I stare sightlessly at the frosted-glass shower doors. I'm not thinking of anything in particular, my brain and body exhausted from running in ceaseless circles since Christmas. I've done everything in my power to keep busy, working as much overtime as possible and spending downtime with friends and family.

As I told Dr. Wilson yesterday, I'm not avoiding the unfinished business between Leo and me so much as waiting for a sign. Some internal *ah-ha!* moment that means I'm ready to face him. To face the truth. Even though each day is glazed with the ache of missing Leo and Vince, the last thing I want is to act impulsively. There's a child in the mix, and things are no doubt already confusing for him.

Whatever move I make next, I want to be sure. I want to be free of the last emotional baggage I have—the final chains linking me to my past. Until that happens, no matter what Leo tells me, I won't be in the right mind frame to hear it. Forgiving myself has to come before forgiving him.

That's when the idea comes. An idea so random, so totally unlike me, that I know it's the real deal. The key to letting go of who I was once and for all and embracing who I want to be.

With a surge of newfound energy, I scramble from the shower and throw on clothes. I'm out the door twenty minutes later, a beanie on my wet hair and an oversized hoodie over jeans. I hop into Jessica's black Mini Cooper and start the engine. I have yet to think of the car as mine, even though it is.

Dad bought Jessica a new Lexus for Christmas. He did the whole deal—shiny sedan in the driveway Christmas morning with a big red bow on top. Poor woman almost had her own heart attack and nearly abandoned the Sloan-ship. Only after Jameson and I assured her we'd *never* seen our dad so bonkers for a woman since our mom did she accept the gift. And a few days later, after she assured me she'd never been so bonkers for a man, I accepted the keys to her old car.

Win-win.

I drive straight to my dad's, surprising him and Jessica in the middle of dinner. Waving off an invitation to grab a plate, I take an empty seat at the kitchen table and spill the beans.

My dad is ecstatic.

"That sounds perfect, Mia. Absolutely perfect for you." He and Jessica share a grin.

My idea is small, a tender-skinned infant I'm not quite sure what to do with, how to feed or care for. "I might need some help," I say haltingly. "I don't mean with money—I've wasted too much of yours already. With other stuff. Shit, I don't even know what I'm saying. Just…"

"Moral support?" offers Jessica.

I sink in relief. "Yes."

"Whatever you need," my dad replies eagerly. "We'll be your number one cheerleaders. Right, Jess?"

She nods. "Absolutely. I have some time in the morning if you want me to sit down with you. We can do some research, figure out your next steps. I'd be happy to come down to Venice."

Filled with gratitude, I smile. "That sounds great. Want to grab breakfast, too?"

"Definitely."

"Can I come?" asks my dad.

Jessica and I exchange a glance. We shake our heads in unison. Dad sighs in exaggerated disappointment, but there's a twinkle in his eye.

"A MASTER'S degree in education psychology?" echoes Jameson, eyes wide as he lowers the mug of coffee from his mouth. "That's for what, being a school counselor?"

"Yep," I confirm. "A middle school guidance counselor to be exact. Jessica helped me look at some local programs. With loans and working full-time, I think I can do it in two or three years."

He blinks. "Holy shit, Meerkat. I can honestly say that sounds perfect for you."

"You think so? That's what Dad and Jessica said, too." I chew my lip, scratching Ferdi absently while staring out a nearby window. "I feel a little bit like I'm making a huge leap in a potentially wrong direction. Twenty-eight is a little old to completely shift directions. What if I can't do it?"

Jameson leans forward, catching my gaze with his. He wears a dead-serious expression I've secretly dubbed the Sloan Lawyer Face. Dad has the same one.

"It's never too late, and we are not old. Mia, you have *always* done exactly what you wanted to, no matter how far-fetched or impossible-sounding it was. Remember senior year when those dumb girls dared you to try and win the prom queen nomination? What did you do?"

I roll my eyes. "I hardly think that's an equal comparison."

Jameson ignores me. "You won! The wild surfer girl who preferred graffitiing the vice principal's car over going to class."

"Hey, I was never caught for that! And anyway, I always did my homework and got good grades."

Jameson chuckles. "My point, thank you. You didn't

even *want* to be prom queen, but you won because you set your mind to it. You hated school, but you excelled because you loved learning." He sits back, smug and triumphant. "Look at everything you've been through, how far you've come. You're ideal guidance counselor material. Besides, kids love you."

Another bit of my worry falls away. "Thanks, Jaybird. For being here. Letting me lean on you. I feel like I'm starting over again—or starting for the first time. It's a little scary."

He nods. "I'm always here for you, sis. You know who else would really like to—"

"Not yet."

He sighs.

GREEN FLASH

I'M READY.

A total of sixteen days have passed since I last saw or heard from Leo. Sixteen excruciating, transforming, scary-as-fuck days. My phone weighs a thousand pounds as I dial his number. Despite timing my call for when I know he's working and won't be able to answer, I'm so nervous I'm breathless.

His recorded voice, though sterile and professional, still fills me with anticipation. *God, I miss him.* Using the script Dr. Wilson helped me with, I leave my carefully worded voicemail. Then I wait.

And wait.

At six o'clock in the evening, he responds.

I'll be there.

I barely sleep that night out of excitement and fear. I know there's a chance this will go horribly wrong. That my abrupt withdrawal caused him to reevaluate his feelings and whether or not he wants a relationship with me. But it's a risk I'm willing to take. A risk I *have* to take.

The drive to Pasadena is fairly smooth, not much traffic so early on a Saturday. I arrive at Arlington Garden twenty minutes before our nine o'clock meeting time and follow Kinsey's directions to the right spot. The gardens are beautiful in the dewy morning, sunlight falling in majestic beams through trees. I turn a corner and there it is—the labyrinth.

Standing just outside the rock-built design is Leo, his back to me, hands tucked in the pockets of his lightweight jacket. As my footsteps approach, his head lifts and his soft voice reaches my ears.

"This seven-circuit design is considered one of the most sacred in the world, its first appearance more than five thousand years ago."

I near where he stands. My hands tremble to touch him. "I know. It's the one you modeled Oasis' labyrinth after, isn't it?"

He nods, finally turning, gaze absorbing my features like he never thought to see me again. "Happy New Year, Amelia."

I smile weakly. "You too. I'd like to talk first, then, if you still want to, we can walk the labyrinth?"

"Of course."

We head to a nearby bench and sit a foot apart. It feels wrong but also right, the space necessary for this conversation. As I promised myself, I don't hesitate but jump right into free fall.

"Jameson already told me how you two met and how I was the favorite topic of conversation for a few years."

Elbows on his knees, Leo stares at the ground. "Okay." There's no surprise in his voice, only resignation. "Whatever questions you have, I'll tell you the absolute truth."

I gaze across the intricate, spiraling design. When I'm sure there's no anger in my voice, I finally speak. "I want to know why you lied to me for months. Why you asked me to trust you but wouldn't trust me back."

"Of course I trust you, Amelia. It wasn't about trust." He straightens, pivoting to face me. "I can remember the exact moment I started feeling something other than professional concern for my friend's sister. After months of hearing about you, I asked if Jameson had a picture. He showed me a shot of you on the beach before heading into the water. You were putting your hair up, your board on the sand beside you, your wetsuit already on."

I remember the moment and the photo. It was one of the rare occasions Jameson put on sunblock and came to the beach with me.

"I don't know what I was expecting," Leo murmurs. "Maybe the female version of Jameson. But there you were, blond and brown-eyed and tan, with a grin that was as wicked as it was joyful. All of a sudden, everything I'd learned about you came together in a new way. I realized how utterly captivated I was by you."

"With everything you knew about me, you were *captivated*? I was a loose cannon."

"You were wild and uninhibited."

"I was a wrecking ball."

"You were a perfect wave."

I sigh, my chin dropping to my chest. "It still doesn't sound healthy."

From the corner of my eye I see his wry smile. "Obsessions rarely are. But it's the truth. Even then, I had feelings for you. When you showed up at our game that night, I had every intention of talking to you."

"Why didn't you?" I whisper.

"The short answer is I had several missed calls from Marianne and a message that Vince had chickenpox. The long answer..." He sighs. "When I came out of the locker room, I saw you talking to Kevin. Your focus—your smile—was aimed at him. I was insanely jealous, then angry at myself for having these impossible feelings for a woman I'd never even met. Believe me, there were a million times over the next two years that I regretted not approaching you."

My eyes sting with tears. "Thank God you didn't," I tell him seriously. "I wasn't ready for you, Leo. I would have found a way to fuck everything up."

He laughs without mirth. "And instead, I found a way to do it. I'm sorry I wasn't honest with you. I knew treating you at Oasis was a bad idea. The worst, in fact. But I weighed it against the possibility of helping you and decided the risk was worth it."

The words fill me up, lift me. I'm buoyant and free. *You never needed fear, Amelia. You just needed to feel safe.* Dr. Wilson was right. Leo was right. I deserve this.

I deserve to be happy.

"I'm glad you took the risk," I tell him. "For what it's

worth, I don't regret anything. Not our sessions, not the hot springs, not everything that's happened since."

"Neither do I. You have to know, Amelia, that even when I struggled with what happened at Oasis, it wasn't because of you. You have *never* been a mistake."

Closing my eyes, I immerse myself in the moment. The peace and rightness. Then I look at him, at his beautiful, sad face. And like he taught me, I speak the truth.

"I love you, Leo. I forgive you. Can you forgive me for disappearing the last few—"

His lips meet mine in a soft, sweet caress. One hand moves through my hair, cupping my head gently as he kisses my cheeks, my eyes, my temples.

"There's nothing to forgive," he murmurs. "I love you so fucking much. Have probably loved you for years, though how I felt then is nothing to what I feel now. You walking into my office for the first time was the best and worst moment of my life."

I giggle, drawing back to see his smile. "Why the best *and* worst?"

His thumb grazes my cheek tenderly. "It was the worst because you looked at me like you wanted to tear me to pieces, and because I wasn't sure I could—or wanted—to stop you."

"And the best?" I whisper.

"It was the best because I knew I was going to help you. That you were mine, had always been mine, and I was just as much yours. You didn't bring me back to life, Amelia. You *gave* me life."

I don't know whether to sob or laugh, so I kiss him

instead. I kiss him until the darkness of the last sixteen days dissolves completely. Eventually we become aware of our surroundings, the presence of children and adults in the garden.

"Can we take this somewhere private?" he whispers in my ear.

I laugh and stand, pulling him up with me. "Yes, but there's something we have to do first."

He frowns, disgruntled. "You really want to walk the labyrinth?"

"Nope." I check my watch. "We're going skydiving with Kinsey and Nix in exactly one hour, so we'd better get moving."

The shock on Leo's face is everything.

EPILOGUE

Leo

Dropping my briefcase inside the front door, I follow the sound of voices to the kitchen. Unnoticed on the threshold, I take in the scene before me. The space is absolutely trashed. Eggshells leaking onto the counter, empty boxes of baking mix on the floor, flour all over the stove. Ferdi's sitting on the kitchen table, tail twitching as he surveys his kingdom.

It's absolutely perfect.

Amelia and Vince have their backs to me, chatting as they layer icing onto a hundred cupcakes for a school fundraiser. Vince hangs on his stepmother's every word, staring at her with blind adoration. *Like father like son.*

I gaze at my wife, her blond hair in a messy bun, her oversized T-shirt and leggings liberally sprinkled with batter and chocolate icing. I'm torn between the desire to bask in appreciation for my family and the need to drag her into our shower for a quickie.

"Do you think your friends will tease you?" asks Amelia, her concerned tone diverting my attention from the tantalizing outline of her ass.

Vince is quick to respond. "No way! They think you're awesome. They're already jealous I have three moms and that none of theirs are as cool as mine. They'll just be more jealous that I get to see you whenever I want."

Amelia ruffles his hair. "Aw, thanks, buddy. I'm so glad I get to be one of your moms."

I frown, trying fruitlessly to figure out what they're talking about.

"Besides," continues Vince, "I won't be in middle school for another year. Dad says there's no point worrying about things that haven't happened yet."

Now I understand. Amelia recently landed her dream job working as a guidance counselor. The middle school just so happens to be in Vince's school district, a huge blessing since it's close to home and means less hours apart.

"Your dad *is* pretty smart."

"Yeah, for an old guy."

I clear my throat loudly. They jump, spinning with guilty smiles.

"Hi, honey! How was work?"

"Dad! Look at all the cupcakes!"

I can't hold my frown. "Work was fine. Cupcakes look great. What do you two feel like for dinner?"

Vince grins. "Amelia said I could go to Theo's house for

dinner. They're having pizza and then we're going to play the new video game he got for his birthday."

My smile grows as I behold my wife's mischievous grin. "Sounds good, bud. When are you heading out?"

Vince looks expectantly at Amelia, who waves a hand. "Go, go. I'll finish up here. Don't forget to thank Theo's parents! We'll pick you up at eight."

"It's only a block away!"

"I don't want you walking home in the dark."

"But I'm almost eleven!"

Amelia batts her eyelashes, and it's game over.

Vince mutters, "Fine," and stomps from the room.

I take advantage of the moment, crossing the kitchen to pull her into my arms. "You have us wrapped around your little finger, don't you?"

She grins up at me. "You like it."

I nuzzle the warm, soft skin under her jaw, breathing her scent like it's my first taste of oxygen. After a long day, it might as well be. I already feel revitalized.

"You know what else I like?" I murmur, kissing beneath her ear where I know she's extra sensitive. She rewards me with a breathy little moan.

"Ew, you guys!" exclaims Vince. "Can you at least wait till I leave?"

"Bye, Vince. Love you!" chirps Amelia.

"Have fun at Theo's," I add.

A few seconds later, the front door slams. I chuckle into her hair. "Do you think we're scarring him for life?"

She laughs, leaning back in my arms. "You're the psychiatrist."

I grin. "Then the answer is no. Definitely not. Besides, it's my job to show him how to treat a partner he loves."

"Mmhmm," she says, eyes dancing.

I wipe a spot of frosting off her cheek and she grabs my finger, sucking it into her mouth. My cock twitches in interest. Wrapping an arm around her waist, I walk backward, bringing her with me. Halfway up the stairs, I almost trip when she sucks a second finger into her warm mouth.

With a sultry laugh, she rubs against me. "Well, hello there."

In reply, I sweep her off her feet and carry her the rest of the way to our bedroom. By the time my knees hit the bed, I've lost any and all patience. Luckily, so has she. As I tackle my tie and belt, she whips off her shirt and kicks off her leggings, then falls back to the comforter. Perched on my knees, I watch my goddess spread her legs and touch herself.

"You're wet for me, Amelia." My voice is low, harsh. I'm hard as a fucking rock and haven't even touched her yet.

She arches her back. "Always."

I don't bother with my shoes or socks, or even removal of my pants. They dangle from my hips as I crawl over her and circle my tongue around one pretty, pert nipple.

"Forget the foreplay," she moans, her small hands finding me and guiding me to her entrance. "I need you."

I capture her mouth, sweeping my tongue against hers, then rise up to watch her face as I sink inside her. The flush on her cheeks, her panting breath, the love and desire in her eyes… Nothing on this earth is more beautiful. Or fierce. Courageous. Rare.

Her legs come around my hips, nails digging into my waist. I give myself over to my need and hers, finding a rhythm that elevates her to a writhing, sweaty, gorgeous mess. She climaxes fast and hard, pulsing and squeezing me like a vise, and I follow her greedily off the edge.

"Fuuuck," I groan into her mouth.

"We just did," she whispers back.

Chuckling, I roll us over so she lies replete on my chest. We're a wet, sticky mess—just the way I like us. Amelia stays still for less than a minute before propping her arms and chin on my chest.

She grins. Wicked—joyful. "Guess what?"

I tuck an errant hair behind her ear. "What?"

"Vince is going to be a big brother."

It takes a few seconds for her words to filter past my pleasure-soaked mind. Then they register. Happiness pours through me like sunshine, building into a grin and misting my eyes with tears.

"Really? You took a test?"

She nods, smiling ecstatically. "Eight of them. You know, just in case. Aw, are you crying?"

I tug her to me, kissing her hard. "I love you. I'm so happy. Are you happy?"

Her laughter rings in the quiet room. "So happy I'm flying. I do have a favor to ask, though."

Nuzzling her nose with mine, I answer her unasked question. "Julia for a girl, Jackson for a boy."

She sighs contentedly. "Oh, and—"

"Pistacchio gelato in the freezer."

Her eyes soften with emotion—gratitude and love and

the barest shadow of the old lie she told herself. That she doesn't deserve happiness. That she isn't worthy of it.

I kiss her until she remembers she is.

THE END

I hope you enjoyed Amelia and Leo's unconventional love story! If you have a minute, please consider leaving a brief review.

xo,

L

ACKNOWLEDGMENTS

To my readers—I can't do this without you. You have my unending gratitude for sticking with me on this wild ride. And in no particular order, for their support, encouragement, honesty, and general awesomeness:

Danielle Rairigh, Katy Ames, Monica Robinson, Rachel Childers, Saffron A. Kent, Nicole French, Jenny Aspinall, and Gitte Doherty.

Emily Lawrence and Judy Zweifel, for immaculate editing and proofing. Any remaining errors are my own (because I just had to tweak that *one little thing*).

My alpha and beta goddesses: Steph Poe, Dawn Walsh, Anna Fay, Sarah Leal, Brianne St. Germain, Haley McGraw Smith, Amy Lutz, Lee Allen, Chery-ann Townsend, Lisa Curro, and Sheila Marie.

And to my husband—thank you for being my partner, my cheerleader, my sounding board and port in life's storm. I choose you, always.

ALSO BY L.M. HALLORAN

ABOUT THE AUTHOR

When not writing or reading, the author can be found chasing her daughter. Some of her favorite things are puzzles, podcasts, and small dogs that resemble Ewoks.

Home is Portland, Oregon.

lmhalloran.com